Quarry's Greatest Hits

Quarry's Greatest Hits

Max Allan Collins

Five Star • Waterville, Maine

First Edition
First Printing: September 2003

Published in 2003 in conjunction with Tekno Books and Ed Gorman.

Set in 11 pt. Plantin

Printed in the United States on permanent paper.

Library of Congress Cataloging-in-Publication Data

Collins, Max Allan.
    Quarry's greatest hits / by Max Allan Collins.—1st ed.
      p. cm.
    ISBN 1-59414-061-8 (hc : alk. paper)
    1. Murder for hire—Fiction.   2. Detective and mystery
stories, American.   I. Title.
PS3553.O4753Q37 2003
    813'.54—dc21   2003053924

Quarry's
Greatest
Hits

Table of Contents

Introduction

by Ed Gorman

I've always tried to imagine how the pitch went when Max (Al) Allan Collins called his agent and told him that he'd like to write a series about a guy named Quarry.

Al: Well, see, he's a killer.

Agent: Ah, yes, an avenger. Like *The Executioner.* He's a man on a moral mission.

Al: Well, not exactly. He's just trying to turn a buck.

Agent: He kills people for money?

Al: Uh-huh.

Agent: People he doesn't know? Doesn't have anything against personally?

Al: Uh-huh. A paid assassin.

Agent: But he probably feels pretty bad about it, right? Guilt eating him alive?

Al: No. No guilt. It's just a job to him.

Agent: So let me get this straight. He kills people for money and doesn't feel bad about it.

Al: Right.

Agent: And you want to want him to be the lead character in this series?

Al: Right.

Agent: But it's never been done before.

Al: I know. That's why it's going to be so much fun.

The Quarry series sold quickly. This was back in the seventies when Vietnam had skewed a whole lot of things in the United States, especially our sense of right and wrong. An ex-Vietnam vet who was a contract killer for various criminal kingpins? Yeah, why not? It was a very nihilistic time.

Quarry never went out of fashion. Not even in the eighties and nineties when some of the worst crimes were being committed on Wall Street. Quarry hung in there, a quirky, dark figure who had an engagingly wry take on how he earned his money. Many editions of his adventures were published worldwide.

Max Collins, of course, went on to write the Nathan Heller series of historical mysteries—one of the most unique and important detective series of this era—as well as the gangster masterpiece, *Road To Perdition*.

But despite attending parties with Steven Spielberg and Tom Hanks, despite hearing critics suddenly start shining their light on several of his previously neglected books and thus bringing them back into print . . . despite his sudden fame . . . Al has never forgotten his hit man.

This is the first collection of Quarry pieces, if you will. You'll like them for the same reasons that readers have liked them for more than thirty years. They're a lot of fun, Al is a past master at creating characters and plot twists that stun you, and Quarry was not only the first professional killer to head his own series . . . he's still the most indelible.

Quarry's Midwest isn't any you'll find in the travel books. It's a *noir* hell well worthy of Spillane, Ellroy, and Tarantino.

Author's Note

This is an unusual collection in that it contains three stories and one novel; further, the novel—in a rather ungainly fashion—appears in the middle of the collection, whereas it might be expected to have the final slot.

But these stories—the novel, too—have a chronology, and are better read in this order.

It had been my intention to do a Quarry collection one day, but somehow I never got around to writing enough short stories about him to do so. Ed Gorman suggested I collect the stories, anyway, and include the little-seen fifth Quarry novel, *Primary Target*, to round it out.

Quarry remains my favorite of all my characters—or anyway, it's a close call between him and Nate Heller. I've had lots of mail about him over the years, and a few people have been nice enough to notice that he pre-dates similar characters from numerous movies and book series (some by such heavyweights as Lawrence Block and Loren Estleman).

Recently a young filmmaker in California, Jeffrey Goodman, made an award-winning film from the lead story in this collection, "A Matter of Principal." I wrote the screenplay and executive-produced it. At press time, it has won one festival for "Best Dramatic Short" (the DIY competition in Los Angeles) and been accepted into another major one (Cinequest in San Jose). So Quarry seems to still have some life in him. And death.

Part of what (I hope) sets Quarry apart is the first-person

narration. The "crook" books of Richard Stark and W. R. Burnett that had inspired my earlier Nolan and Jon series (professional thieves) were third-person yarns that gave the reader distance. I wanted to ratchet up the anti-hero experience—make Quarry not just a thief, but a killer; and force you inside his head.

I wanted readers to take the ride—and have a good time, but . . . when the story was over . . . be unsettled, not quite sure why it was so easy to identify with such a bad man. Thrilled, and a little ashamed . . .

I hope these three short rides (and one long one) with Quarry will entertain—and unsettle you.

—Max Allan Collins

A Matter of Principal

It had been a long time since I'd had any trouble sleeping. Probably Vietnam, and that was gunfire that kept me awake. I've never been an insomniac. You might think killing people for a living would give you restless nights. Truth is, those that go into that business simply aren't the kind who are bothered by it much.

I was no exception. I hadn't gone into retirement because my conscience was bothering me. I retired because the man I got my contracts through got killed—well, actually I killed him, but that's another story—and I had enough money put away to live comfortably without working, so I did.

The A-frame cottage on Paradise Lake was secluded enough for privacy, but close enough to nearby Lake Geneva to put me in contact with human beings, if I was so inclined, which I rarely was, with the exception of getting laid now and then. I'm human.

There was also a restaurant nearby, called Wilma's Welcome Inn, a rambling two-story affair that included a gas station, modest hotel accommodations and a convenience store. I'd been toying with the idea of buying the place, which had been slipping since the death of Wilma; I'd been getting a little bored lately and needed something to do. Before I started putting people to sleep, I worked in a garage as a mechanic, so the gas station angle appealed to me.

Anyway, boredom had started to itch at me, and for the past few nights I'd had trouble sleeping. I sat up all night

13

watching satellite TV and reading paperback westerns; then I'd drag around the next day, maybe drifting to sleep in the afternoon just long enough to fuck up my sleep cycle again that night.

It was getting irritating.

At about three-thirty in the morning on the fourth night of this shit, I decided eating might do the trick. Fill my gut with junk food and the blood could rush down from my head and warm my belly and I'd get the fuck sleepy, finally. I hadn't tried this before because I'd been getting a trifle paunchy, since I quit working, and since winter kicked in.

In the summer I'd swim in the lake everyday and get exercise and keep the spare tire off. But in the winter I'd just let my beard go and belt-size, too. Winters made me fat and lazy and, now, fucking sleepless.

The cupboard was bare so I threw on my thermal jacket and headed over to the Welcome Inn. At this time of night the convenience store was the only thing open, that and one self-serve gas pump.

The clerk was a heavy-set brunette named Cindy from nearby Twin Lakes. She was maybe twenty years old and a little surly, but she worked all night, so who could blame her.

"Mr. Ryan," she said, flatly, as I came in, the bell over the door jingling.

"Cindy," I said, with a nod, and began prowling the place, three narrow aisles parallel to the front of the building. None of the snacks appealed to me—chips and crackers and Twinkies and other preservative-packed delights—and the frozen food case ran mostly to ice-cream sandwiches and Popsicles. In this weather, that was a joke.

I was giving a box of Chef Boyardee lasagna an intent once-over, like it was a car I was considering buying, when the bell over the door jingled again. I glanced up and saw a heavy-set man—heavy-set enough to make Cindy look svelte—with a pockmarked face and black-rimmed glasses that fogged up as he stepped in.

He wore an expensive topcoat—tan, a camel's hair number you could make payments on for a year and still owe—and his shoes had a bright black city shine, barely flecked with ice and snow. His name was Harry something, and he was from Chicago. I knew him, in another life.

I turned my back. If he saw me, I'd have to kill him, and I was bored, but not that bored.

Predictably, Harry Something went straight for the potato chips; he also rustled around the area where cookies were shelved. I risked a glimpse and saw him, not two minutes after he entered, with his arms full of junk food, heading for the front counter.

"Excuse me, miss," Harry Something said, depositing his groceries before Cindy. His voice was nasal and high-pitched; a funny, childish voice for a man his size. "Could you direct me to the sanitary napkins?"

"You mean Kotex?"

"Whatever."

"The toiletries is just over there."

Now this was curious, and I'll tell you why. I had met Harry Something around ten years before, when I was doing a job for the Outfit boys. I was never a mob guy, mind you, strictly a freelancer, but their money was as good as anybody's. What that job was isn't important, but Harry and his partner Louis were the locals who had fucked up, making my outsider's presence necessary. Harry and Louis had not been friendly toward me. They had threatened me, in fact. They had beaten the hell out of me in my hotel room, when the job was over, for making them look bad.

I had never taken any sort of revenge out on them. I occasionally do take revenge, but at my convenience, and when a score strikes me as worth settling. Harry and Louis had really just pushed me around a little, bloodied my nose, tried to earn back a little self-respect. So I didn't hold a grudge. Not a major grudge. Fuck it.

As to why Harry Something purchasing Kotex in the middle of the night at some backwoods convenience store was curious, well, Harry and Louis were gay. They were queens of crime. Mob muscle who worked as a pair, and played as a pair.

I don't mean to be critical. To each his own. I'd rather cut off my dick than insert it in any orifice of a repulsive fat slob like Harry Something. But that's just me. And me, I'm naturally curious. I'm not nosy, not even inquisitive. But when a faggot buys Kotex, I have to wonder why.

"Excuse me," Harry Something said, brushing by me.

He hadn't seen my face—he might not recognize me, in any case. Ten years and a beard and twenty pounds later, I wasn't as easy to peg as Harry was, who had changed goddamn little.

Harry, having stocked up on cookies and chips and Kotex, was now buying milk and packaged macaroni and cheese and provisions in general. He was shopping. Stocking up.

And now I knew what he was up to.

I nodded to surly Cindy, who bid me goodbye by flickering her eyelids in casual contempt, and went out to my car, a blue sporty Mazda I'd purchased recently. I wished I'd had the four-wheel drive, or anything less conspicuous, but I didn't. I sat in the car, scooched down low; I did not turn on the engine. I just sat in the cold car in the cold night and waited.

Harry Something came out with two armloads of groceries—Kotex included, I presumed—and he put them in the front seat of a brown rental Ford. Louis was not waiting for him. Harry was alone.

Which further confirmed my suspicions.

I waited for him to pull out onto the road, waited for him to take the road's curve, then started up my Mazda and glided out after him. He had turned left, toward Twin Lakes and Lake Geneva. That made sense, only I figured he wouldn't wind up either place. I figured he'd be out in the boonies somewhere.

I knew what Harry was up to. I knew he wasn't exactly here to ski. That lardass couldn't stand up on a pair of skis. And he wasn't here to go ice fishing, either. A city boy like Harry Something had no business in a touristy area like this, in the off-season—unless Harry was hiding out, holing up somewhere.

This would be the perfect area for that.

Only Harry didn't use Kotex.

He turned off on a side road, into a heavily wooded area that wound back toward Paradise Lake. Good. That was very good.

I went on by. I drove a mile, turned into a farmhouse gravel drive and headed back without lights. I slowed as I reached the mouth of the side road, and could see Harry's taillights wink off.

I knew the cabin at the end of that road. There was only one, and its owner only used it during the summer; Harry was either a renter, or a squatter.

I glided on by and went back home. I left the Mazda next to the deck and walked up the steps and into my A-frame. The nine-millimeter was in the nightstand drawer. The gun hadn't been shot in months—Christ, maybe over a year. But I cleaned and oiled it regularly. It would do fine.

So would my black turtleneck, black jeans, black leather bomber jacket, and this black moonless night. I slipped a .38 revolver in the bomber jacket right side pocket, and clipped a hunting knife to my belt. The knife was razor sharp with a sword point; I sent for it out of the back of one of those dumb-ass ninja magazines—which are worthless except for mail-ordering weapons.

I walked along the edge of the lake, my running shoes crunching the brittle ground, layered as it was with snow and ice and leaves. The only light came from a gentle scattering of stars, a handful of diamonds flung on black velvet; the frozen lake was a dark presence that you could sense but not really see. The surrounding trees were even darker. The occasional cabin or cottage or house I passed was empty. I was one of only a handful of residents on Paradise Lake who lived year-round.

But the lights were on in one cabin. Not many lights, but lights. And its chimney was trailing smoke.

The cabin was small, a traditional log cabin like Abe Lincoln and syrup, only with a satellite dish. Probably two bedrooms, a living room, kitchenette and a can or two. Only one car—the brown rental Ford.

My footsteps were lighter now; I was staying on the balls of my feet and the crunching under them was faint. I approached with caution and gun in hand and peeked in a window on the right front side.

Harry Something was sitting on the couch, eating barbecue potato chips, giving himself an orange-mustache in the process. His feet were up on a coffee table. More food and a sawed-off double-barreled shotgun were on the couch next to him. He wore a colorful Hawaiian shirt; he looked like Don Ho puked on him, actually.

Hovering nervously nearby, was Louis, a small, skinny, bald ferret of man, who wore jeans and a black shirt and a white tie. I couldn't tell whether he was trying for trendy or gangster, and frankly didn't give a shit, either way.

Physically, all the two men had in common was pockmarks and a desire for the other's ugly body.

And neither one of them seemed to need a sanitary napkin, though a towelette would've come in handy for Harry Something. Jesus.

I huddled beneath the window, wondering what I was doing here. Boredom. Curiosity. I shrugged. Time to look in another window or two.

Because they clearly had a captive. That's what they were doing in the boonies. That's why they were stocking up on supplies at a convenience store in the middle of night and nowhere. That's why there were in the market for Kotex. That's what I'd instinctively, immediately known back at the Welcome Inn.

And in a back window, I saw her. She was naked on a bed in the rustic room, naked but for white panties. She was sitting on the edge of the bed and she was crying, a black-haired, creamy-fleshed beauty in her early twenties.

Obviously, Harry and Louis had nothing sexual in mind for this girl; the reason for her nudity was to help prevent her fleeing. The bed was heavy with blankets, and she'd obviously been keeping under the covers, but right now she was sitting and crying. That time of the month.

I stood in the dark in my dark clothes with a gun in my hand and my back to the log cabin and smiled. When I'd come out into the night, armed like this, it wasn't to effect a rescue. Whatever else they were, Harry and Louis were dangerous men. If I was going to spend my sleepless night satisfying my curiosity and assuaging my boredom by poking into their business, I had to be ready to pay for my thrills.

But the thing was, I recognized this young woman. Like Harry, I spent a lot of hours during cold nights like this with my eyes frozen to a TV screen. And that's where I'd seen her: on the tube.

Not an actress, no—an heiress. The daughter of a Chicago media magnate whose name you'd recognize, a guy who inherited money and wheeled-and-dealed his way into more, including one of the satellite super-stations I'd been wasting my eyes on lately. The Windy City's answer to Ted Turner, right down to boating and womanizing.

His daughter was a little wild—seen in the company of rock stars (she had a tattoo of a star—not Mick Jagger, a five-pointed *star* star—on her white left breast, which I could see from the window) and was a Betty Ford clinic drop-out. Nonetheless, she was said to be the apple of her daddy's eye, even if that apple was a tad wormy.

So Harry and Louis had put the snatch on the snatch; fair enough. Question was, was it their own idea, or something the Outfit put them up to?

I sat in the cold and dark and decided, finally, that it just didn't matter who or what was behind it. My options were to go home, and forget about it, and try (probably without any luck) to get some sleep; or to rescue this somewhat soiled damsel in distress.

What the hell. I had nothing better to do.

I went to the front door and knocked.

No answer.

Shit, I knew somebody was home, so I knocked again.

Louis cracked open the door and peered out and said, "What is it?" and I shot him in the eye.

There was the harsh, shrill sound of a scream—not Louis, who hadn't had time for that, but the girl in the next

room, scared shitless at hearing a gunshot, one would suppose.

I paid no attention to her and pushed the door open—
there was no night latch or anything—and stepped over
Louis, and pointed the nine-millimeter at Harry, whose
orange-ringed mouth was frozen open and whose bag of
barbecue potato chips dropped to the floor, much as Louis
had.

"Don't, Harry," I said.

I could see in Harry's tiny dark eyes behind his thick
black-rimmed glasses that he was thinking about the sawed-
off shotgun on the couch next to him.

"Who the fuck . . ."

I walked slowly across the rustic living room toward the
couch; in the background, an old colorized movie was
playing on their captive's daddy's superstation. I plucked
the shotgun off the couch with my left hand and tucked it
under my arm.

"Hi, Harry," I said. "Been a while."

His orange-ringed mouth slowly began to work and his
eyes began to blink and he said, "Quarry?"

That was the name he'd known me by.

"Taking the girl your idea, or are you still working for
the boys?"

"We . . . we retired, couple years ago. God. You killed
Louis. Louis. You killed Louis . . ."

"Right. What were you going to put the girl's body in?"

"Huh?"

"She's obviously seen you. You were obviously going to
kill her, once you got the money. So. What was the plan?"

Harry wiped off his orange barbecue ring. "Got a roll of
plastic in the closet. Gonna roll her up in it and dump her
in one of the gravel pits around here."

"I see. Do that number with the plastic right now, for Louis, why don't you? Okay?"

Tears were rolling down Harry's stubbly pockmarked cheeks. I didn't know whether he was crying for Louis or himself or the pair of them, and I wasn't interested enough to ask.

"Okay," he said thickly.

I watched him roll his partner up in the sheet of plastic, using duct tape to secure the package; he sobbed as he did it, but he did it. He got blood on his Hawaiian shirt; it didn't particularly show, though.

"Now I want you to clean up the mess. Go on. You'll find what you need in the kitchen."

Dutifully, Harry shuffled over, got a pan of warm water and some rags, and got on his knees and cleaned up the brains and blood. He wasn't crying anymore. He moved slow but steady, a fat zombie in a colorful shirt.

"Stick the rags in the end of Louis' plastic home, would you? Thank you."

Harry did that, then the big man lumbered to his feet, hands in the air, and said, "Now me, huh?"

"I might let you go, Harry. I got nothing against you."

"Not . . . not how I remember it."

I laughed. "You girls leaned on me once. You think I'd kill a person over something that trivial? What kind of guy do you think I am, Harry?"

Harry had sense enough not to answer.

"Come with me," I said, and with the nine-millimeter's nose to Harry's temple, I walked him to the door of the bedroom.

"Open it," I said.

He did.

We went in, Harry first.

The girl was under the covers, holding the blankets and sheets up around her in a combination of illogical modesty and legitimate fear.

Her expression melted into one of confusion mingled with the beginnings of hope and relief, when she saw me.

"I've already taken care of the skinny one," I said. "Now Harry and me are going for a walk. You stay here. I'm going to get you back to your father."

Her confusion didn't leave, but she began to smile, wide, like a kid Christmas morning seeing her gifts. Her gift to me was dropping the blankets and sheets to her waist.

"Remember," I said. "Stay right there."

I walked Harry out, pulling the bedroom door shut behind me.

"Where are her clothes?"

He nodded to a closet. Same one he'd gotten the plastic out of.

"Good," I said. "Now let's go for a walk. Just you and me and Louis."

"Loo . . . Louis?"

"Better give Louis a hand, Harry."

Harry held the plastic-wrapped corpse in his arms like a B-movie monster carrying a starlet. The plastic was spattered with blood, but on the inside. Harry looked like he was going to cry again.

I still had the sawed-off shotgun under my arm, so it was awkward, getting the front door open, but I managed.

"Out on the lake," I said.

Harry looked at me, his eyes behind the glasses wary, glancing from me to his plastic-wrapped burden and back again.

"We're going to bury Louis at sea," I said.

"Huh?"

"Just walk, Harry. Okay? Just walk."

He walked. I followed behind, nine-millimeter in one hand, sawed-off in the other. Harry in his Hawaiian shirt was an oddly comic sight, but I was too busy to be amused. Our feet crunched slightly on the ice. No danger of falling in. Frozen solid. Kids ice-skated out here. But not right now.

We walked a long way. We said not a word, until I halted him about mid-way. The black starry sky was our only witness.

"Put him down, Harry," I said. The nine-millimeter was in my waistband; the shotgun was pointed right at him.

He set his cargo gently down. He stood looking gloomily down at the plastic shroud, like a bear contemplating its own foot caught in a trap.

I blasted both barrels of the shotgun; they blew the quiet night apart and echoed across the frozen lake and rattled the world.

Harry looked at me, stunned.

"What the fuck . . . ?"

"Now unroll Louis and toss him in," I said, standing near the gaping hole in the ice. "I'm afraid that plastic might float."

Horrified, the big man did as he was told. Louis slipped down the hole in the ice and into watery nothingness like a turd down the crapper.

"Slick," I said, admiringly.

"Oh Jesus," he said.

"Now you," I said.

"What?"

I had the nine-millimeter out again.

"Jump in," I said. "Water's fine."

"Fuck you!"

I went over quickly and pushed the big son of a bitch in. He was flailing, splashing icy water up on me, as I put six bullets in his head, which came apart in pieces, like a rotten melon.

And then he was gone.

Nothing left but the hole in the ice, the water within it making some frothy reddish waves that would die down soon enough.

I gathered the weapons and the plastic and, folding the plastic sheet as I walked, went back to the cabin.

This was reckless, I knew. I shouldn't be killing people who lived on the same goddamn lake I did. But it was winter, and the bodies wouldn't turn up for a long time, if ever, and the Outfit had used this part of the world to dump its corpses since Capone was just a mean street kid. Very little chance any of this would come back at me.

Nonetheless, I had taken a risk or two. I ought to get something out of it, other than killing a sleepless night.

I got the girl's clothes and went in and gave them to her. A heavy-metal T-shirt and designer jeans and Reeboks.

"Did you kill those men?" she said, breathlessly, her eyes dark and glittering. She had her clothes in her lap.

"That's not important. Get dressed."

"You're wonderful. You're goddamn fucking wonderful."

"I know," I said. "Everybody says the same thing. Get dressed."

She got dressed. I watched her. She was a beautiful piece of ass, no question. The way she was looking at me made it clear she was grateful.

"What can I do for you?" she said, hands on her hips.

"Nothing," I said. "You're on the rag."

That made her laugh. "Other ports in a storm."

"Maybe later," I said, and smiled. She looked like AIDS-bait to me. I could be reckless, but not that reckless.

I put her in my car. I hadn't decided yet whether or not to dump the brown rental Ford. Probably would. I could worry about that later. Right now, I needed to get her to a motel.

She slept in the car. I envied her, and nudged her awake when we reached the motel just inside the Illinois state line.

I'd already checked in. I ushered her in to the shabby little room, its floor space all but taken up by two twin beds, and she sat on the bed and yawned.

"What now?" she said. "You want your reward?"

"Actually, yes," I said, sitting next to her. "What's your father's number?"

"Hey, there's time for that later . . ."

"First things first," I said, and she wrote the number out on the pad by the phone.

I heard the ring, and a male voice said, "Hello?"

I gave her the receiver. "Make sure it's your father, and tell him you're all right."

"Daddy?" she said. She smiled, then she made a face. "I'm fine, I'm fine . . . the man you sent . . . what?"

She covered the receiver, eyes confused again. "He says he didn't send anybody."

I took the phone. "Good evening, sir. I have your daughter. As you can hear, she's just fine. Get together one hundred thousand dollars in unmarked, nonsequential tens, twenties, and fifties, and wait for the next call."

I hung up.

She looked at me with wide eyes and wide-open mouth.

"I'm not going to kill you," I said. "I'm just turning a buck."

"You bastard!"

I put the duct tape over her mouth, taped her wrists behind her and taped her ankles too, and went over and curled up on the other bed, nine-millimeter in my waistband.

And slept like a baby.

Primary Target

ONE

My big mistake was allowing happiness to creep in.

It's worse than complacency; or maybe it's just the same goddamn thing. But for somebody like me, for somebody with my sort of past, allowing the present to lull you into happy complacency is the surest fucking way to insure you'll have no future at all.

I met Linda when she was vacationing up at Lake Geneva, just another cute blonde among many cute college girls, many of them blonde. She wore white—a white tank top that made her seem flat-chested (which she wasn't, really) and white cut-off jeans, cut so short that the lower moons of her cute little ass showed through fringe of the cut-offs. She had china-blue eyes and short, very curly, white blonde hair, a tiny nose and the whitest teeth you ever saw; when she smiled, it was Dimples City—and you just had to like her. Or anyway I did.

I lived, at the time, in an A-frame cottage on Paradise Lake, a small, private lake with a scattering of summer homes. Paradise Lake held no truck with tourists, other than those visiting relatives in one of the cottages, and it afforded me plenty of peace, quiet and privacy. Nearby Lake Geneva, on the other hand, provided plenty of pussy, to put it bluntly, and when I first met Linda that was all she meant to me.

Maybe she made a little more impact on me than the av-

28

erage college girl I'd pick up, in those days; she was, after all, very innocent, or as innocent as a girl can be who goes to bed with you the day you met her. She wasn't terribly sexually experienced, and her idea of being daring was to smoke a little dope. She didn't strike me as terribly bright, but she was funny and cute and when she called me on the phone three months later, I remembered her almost immediately.

"Jack," she said. "This is Linda. Remember me?"

"Sure," I said, unsurely.

"You know. *Linda.*"

And the inflection in her voice brought her back to me.

"Well, Linda. Where are you calling from?"

"H-home."

The catch in her voice, and the static on the line, sent me a message.

"What's wrong?" I asked. "And where is home, anyway?"

"Home is Indiana."

As in back home again in.

"Okay," I said. "Now tell me what the trouble is."

"My folks. They're . . ."

And I could hear her crying.

"Linda, what is it?" I tried to be sympathetic, fighting irritation.

"My folks were killed last week."

"I'm sorry. What do you mean, killed?" That word meant something different to me than it might to some people.

"Automobile accident." She swallowed. "New Year's Eve."

It was the first week of January. Linda's parents were just another statistic.

"I'm sorry, kid," I said, trying to mean it, wondering why the hell she was calling me.

"Funeral was a few days ago," she said.

"Yes?" What did this have to do with me?

"I need to get away for a while," she said, in a rush. "I wondered . . . I wondered if I could come up and spend a few days with you?"

"Well . . ."

I mean, Christ, she was just some one-night stand. What the hell was this about? That was all I needed, was some college girl moping around my place for a week.

"I don't have anybody, Jack. *Any*-body. My friends are all back at school. My folks were all I had, except for my brother, and he headed back to San Francisco this morning. Now I'm all alone in this house and I don't have anywhere to go."

"Well, uh . . . go back to college with your friends, why don't you? Best thing in the world for you would be get back in the swing of things."

She paused. Then: "I flunked out. I'm not going back this semester."

She began crying some more.

I'm not particularly soft-hearted, but I remembered her being a good kid, and who knew? Comforting her might add up to my getting laid regular for a week or so. Would that be so bad?

"You can come stay with me, kid," I said. "Long as you need to."

"Oh, Jack . . . Jack, I *knew* I could depend on you!"

Why?

"Why don't you fly into Chicago," I said, "and I'll pick you up. At O'Hare."

We'd made the arrangements, and she came and stayed

with me for a week. Pretty soon the week turned into a
month, and a year later, in a little chapel at Twin Lakes, I
married the girl.

Here's the deal. I was thirty-five. I was getting bored
with one-night stands and my own microwave cooking. I
wanted some company, and she seemed pleasant enough.
She talked too much, but most people do. She was beautiful, a terrific cook, and she kept out of my way. What
more could I ask?

For many years the notion of living with one woman was
out of the question for me. I was in the wrong business to
accommodate what Donahue and the women's magazines
would refer to as a "relationship." But that business was behind me. I had retired, after socking away a hell of a nest
egg. I could live off my investments, one of which was an
oddball business called Wilma's Welcome Inn which was
just five minutes from my A-frame.

The Welcome Inn was a rambling two-story affair left
over from another era—gas station, restaurant, convenience
store, and hotel sharing one somewhat ramshackle roof. It
struck some chord in me, reminded me of something from
my childhood, a place I'd gone with my parents I think.
Anyway, I liked the place, for no good reason, and I also
liked the gal who ran the place, Wilma.

But Wilma—a nice fat woman who made great chili—
died a few years ago, leaving the place in the unsteady
hands of her boyfriend/bartender Charley. He was having
trouble keeping the business afloat without his porky pillar,
and Wilma's daughter, a zaftig babe in her late teens who
wanted nothing to do with the business except for any
money it generated, was not happy with Charley letting
things slip; she was threatening to can the ex-con and sell
the joint. So I bought it from the girl (who used the dough

to stake herself to a move out to California, where she planned to break into the movies—right) and kept Charley on.

When I was a kid back in Ohio, I tinkered around with cars and had worked in a garage when I was in high school and junior college; so I was able to get the gas station on its feet easily enough. I'm also fairly handy with a hammer and nails and paint brushes and such and was able to do some remodeling, make the Welcome Inn less ramshackle, though rambling it would always be. At first I hired a woman away from a place in Lake Geneva to handle the hotel and restaurant, but she was a smartass, and eventually Linda took over.

Linda was no rocket scientist (I handled the books) but people liked her, staff and customers both, and she was damn near as good a cook as Wilma had been.

So my life had settled into something not unlike normalcy. The vacation center we were a part of lent itself to water sport in the summer and skiing in the winter and there was plenty to do, including make a little dough at Wilma's Welcome Inn.

Both Linda and me got pudgy. Mine came from too much of her cooking, both at home and at the Welcome Inn, and from a general laziness—I ran the Inn like any good executive, delegating responsibility and filling my own life with relaxation. I listened to my stereo (Tony Bennett, Peggy Lee, Mel Torme) and read paperback westerns (they engaged my brain without taxing it) and watched old movies on TV (we had a satellite dish) and generally lived a life of leisure, acquiring the spare tire that went with it.

Linda's extra weight came from another source: my dick.

"You're pregnant?" I said.

"You sound . . . disappointed . . . or mad or something."

"Well, hell—how should I sound?"

We were discussing this at the A-frame, sitting out on the porch in deck chairs, looking out at a lake bathed in moonlight. Her eyes were a similar color—washed-out blue. I really liked the color of her eyes.

"You should sound happy," she said. Her eyes were tensing.

We hardly ever argued. In fact, I can't remember arguing with her. Sometimes I got mad at her when she was a little thick about some business aspect at the Inn, but when all was said and done, I cared more about her than any of that other shit, so I tended to cut her some slack. I mean, fuck, I didn't need the money. The Inn was just something to do.

"Happy isn't my style," I said.

"Sure it is," she said, and she got up and sat in my lap and smiled at me, dimples and all, though I could tell she was still sad.

"You want to break this damn chair?" I said.

She just smiled some more and hugged me around the neck and said, "I'm not that heavy yet. I'm only a month or so gone."

And she was a little thing, after all. I bet she didn't weigh a hundred pounds.

"I thought you were using something," I said.

"I was. I stopped."

"We should have talked about it."

"I thought you'd *want* a child with me. You said so once."

"I was drunk. And you know I don't drink, and when I do, I can't be held responsible."

"Well, you're responsible for this," she said, and patted her tummy, and her smile shifted to one side of her face, crinkling it.

Goddamnit, there's no way around it: I did love her, or as close to it as I'm capable.

I said, "If I was going to have a child, I'd want it with you."

"Well, I should hope to shout. I'm your wife, aren't I?"

"Only one I ever had," I said, which was a lie. I was married one other time, but that was in another life, the life she didn't know about.

"We'll be a family," she said sweetly. "Won't that be wonderful?"

This girl thought life was a fucking Christmas card.

"Linda, I don't know about bringing anybody else into this goddamn place."

She looked confused. "What goddamn place?"

"This world. This planet. It's no prize."

"Our life isn't so bad, is it?"

"We have a great life."

"So, why not let a third person in on it? A person who's part of us, Jack . . ."

I shook my head. "You don't understand, kid. This is a very protected life we got going here. We're the couple in the plastic bubble—nothing touches us. But a kid—he's going to have to go out in that world and face all the bullshit."

"How do you know it's going to be a he? And what's wrong with going out in the world?"

"For one thing, it's crawling with people."

"I *like* people!"

"I don't. I'm not so sure pulling another passenger onto this sinking ship is such a hot idea. What's he got waiting for him? Or, her?"

She gave me a sideways look, trying to kid me out of it. "Don't be such a Gloomy Gus."

"Read the papers. They're full of famine and AIDS and nuclear bombs."

"Jack, you don't read the papers."

"Well, hell, I watch TV. And I've been out in that world, baby. It sucks."

"I don't know why you feel that way."

"Well I do."

"Why? Have you had it so bad?"

"Not lately."

She cocked her head, gave me a smirky, pixie look. "When did you *ever* have it bad?"

I tasted my tongue.

"I never mentioned it before . . ."

Her eyes narrowed. "What, Jack?"

"I . . . I saw some combat."

"Combat? Where?"

"Where do you think? In the war."

"What war?"

I sighed. "Vietnam, dear. A distant event in history that happened during your childhood. Let's just say . . . I'm not wild about bringing somebody into this life when Vietnams are still a part of it—and they are."

She looked very troubled. She was sweet but she wasn't deep. "I never heard you talk like this."

"Sure you have."

"Not so serious, at such length. I . . . always thought it was a joke, the things you say, the way you see things. You always made me laugh. It was just, you know . . . sick humor."

"Defense mechanism."

"What . . . what makes life worth living then?"

She was really getting upset; I decided to smile at her. Said, "Life's worth living as long as somebody like you's in it."

She beamed and hugged me. I held her for a while. Listened to the crickets.

Then she drew away and said, "Jack, you don't really . . . you wouldn't have me get . . . rid of it, would you?"

Her lip was trembling and her china-blue eyes were wetter than the goddamn lake.

What else was there to say?

"Of course not," I said. "What do you think I am? A murderer?"

TWO

I was chopping wood, which was about as physical as my life got these days. The lake was placid and blue, surrounded by trees painted in golds and yellows and browns; the water reflected a soothing Indian summer sun. You could almost understand why somebody, long ago, chose to name the lake Paradise. There weren't even any mosquitoes this time of year.

I swung the axe in my two hands, building a rhythm, liking the pull on my muscles, enjoying the sweat I was working up, feeling alive. Wood chips flew and logs became firewood. When Linda got back from her yoga class at Twin Lakes, I'd prepare supper (still had a microwave) and the wine would be chilled and we'd sit before the fireplace and be "toasty warm" (as she put it) together. We would also undoubtedly have great sex, one of the major reasons I kept the ditsy little dish around.

Feeling winded but good, I sat out on the deck and unzipped my down jacket and relaxed with a cup of coffee. I was watching the lake when a cloud covered the sun and the gravel in my driveway stirred.

A chocolate BMW pulled abruptly up, making a little dust storm. I did not recognize the car—other than as the pointless and drab status symbol it was. I stood. My shoulders tensed and it had nothing to do with chopping wood.

From the edge of the deck I noticed two things: the driver of the car, a slightly heavy-set man of about fifty in a London Fog raincoat; and the front license plate of the BMW, which was covered with mud. There hadn't been any rain in the Midwest for several weeks.

He saw me perched above him on the deck. My expression must have been hostile because he smiled tightly, defensively, and put both hands out, palms forward, in a stop motion.

"Just a few minutes of your time," he said, "that's all I ask."

He had a mellow, radio-announcer's voice and a conventionally handsome, well-lined face, a Marlboro man who rode a desk.

"Whatever you're selling, I'm not buying."

His smile twitched nervously. "I'm not a salesman, but I am here on business."

I motioned off toward the highway. "Talk to Charley up at the Inn. If he can't handle it, make an appointment to see me, there, later. I don't do business at home."

"This doesn't have anything to do with the restaurant business, Mr. Quarry."

I said nothing. A bird cawed across the lake. My sentiments exactly.

"I, uh, realize that isn't the name you're using around here . . ."

"Explain yourself."

The outstretched hands went palms up, supplicatingly. "Please. There's no reason to get your back up. There's no obligation . . ."

"You *sound* like a salesman."

"Your wife won't be home for another hour. I didn't want to bother you while she was here . . ."

Mention of Linda made me wince; this guy, whoever the fuck he was, knew entirely too much about me. He didn't know how close he was to spending eternity at the bottom of one of the area's scenic gravel pits.

"Come up here and have a seat," I said.

He smiled tightly again, nodded, and came around and up the stairs.

I sat in one of the lounge-style deck chairs, legs stretched out, and he took one of the director-style chairs and pulled it up near me. His salt-and-pepper hair was heavy on the salt and thinning a little, though some fancy styling minimized it; you could buy a week's groceries for what he spent on that haircut. He smelled of cologne—some expensive fragrance, strong enough to blot out that of the pines around us.

"May I smoke?" he asked.

"It's your lungs."

He lit up—something unfiltered from a flat silver case drawn out from under the London Fog; I had a glimpse of dark, vested, well-tailored suit with blue striped silk tie.

"I know this is an intrusion," he said, deferential as all hell, "but I think, when everything is said and done, you'll be pleased. This is the opportunity of a lifetime."

"Does this have anything to do with Amway?"

A short, harsh, nervous laugh preceded his response: "Hardly, Mr. Quarry. This is more on the order of . . . Publishers Clearing House." The constant if slight smile turned wry, smug. "Mr. Quarry, I'm in a position to make you a very wealthy man."

"Drop the name, all right? I haven't used that in almost ten years."

He made a small open hand gesture. "A man known as the Broker gave it to you, a long time ago."

"That's right." I looked at him, locked his eyes. They were gray, like his cigarette smoke. "What else do you know about me?"

His smile faded, and he shrugged facially. "I know that you were a hero. That you served your country honorably and well."

"Yeah, right. Is there more?"

"I know that you were married once before. You returned from a tour of duty in Vietnam to discover your wife had been untrue."

"Untrue? I found her in bed sitting on a guy's dick."

"You killed him."

I shrugged. "Not on the spot. I came back the next day, after I cooled off, and he was under his sporty little car, making some minor repairs. I made one, too."

"You kicked the jack out."

I shrugged again. "He called me a 'bunghole.' What would you do?"

"You were arrested."

"But not tried, except in the papers."

"The unwritten law."

"There are two times society puts up with murder."

"War is one," he said, nodding.

"Finding somebody fucking your wife is the other."

He gestured with cigarette in hand. "Nonetheless, you were looked down upon in certain quarters."

"I had trouble finding work. I was a Vietnam vet, remember? We were all assumed to be unreliable dope addicts. And I was a 'disturbed Viet vet' before it was fashionable. Before it was a cliché even."

I killed a guy, after all. Nobody minded the numerous

yellow people I killed for no good reason. The one white asshole I killed for a good reason got people bent out of shape.

"Shortly after that," he said, carefully, quietly, the gray eyes studying me but pretending not to, through a haze of cigarette smoke, "you met the Broker."

"Did I?"

"I don't know the circumstances, but you began taking contracts. Working as part of a team."

Did I mention I had brought the axe up on the porch with me? Well, I had. It was leaned up against the front of the house, near the door. Not far away at all.

"Are you sure," I said, with a gentle smile, "that you want to keep this line of conversation going?"

"I just want you to know that I'm familiar with your background."

"Why?"

"Because I have a contract for you."

"I'm not in that line of work anymore."

"Mr. Quarry, you are an assassin. It's not something you can leave behind."

I nodded. "Well, I'm willing to kill again, under certain circumstances."

"Such as?"

"Assholes coming around fucking in my life."

He smiled again, another tight nervous twitch, and he said, "I'm not here to make trouble in your life. I'm here to improve your life."

"Say it. Whatever it is you've got to say, say it."

"Mr. Quarry, this isn't something one can . . ."

"Say it. I sat through 'This Is Your Life' patiently enough. But now the show's over. Cut to the commercial."

He cleared his throat, as if about to make a speech.

Maybe he was. "You are said to have been the best at what you do. But you dropped out."

"I dropped out. My partner bought it, the Broker bought it, and I dropped out. Say what you came to say."

He let the cigarette fall to the deck and ground it out with his heel.

Then he said: "One million dollars."

There's only one thing you can say when somebody says that, and I said it: "What?"

"One million dollars," he repeated.

"In regard to what?" I asked, dumbfounded and a little annoyed.

"One contract."

"A million-dollar contract."

He nodded, his smile confident now, not nervous at all. "One hundred thousand down. In cash. Unmarked twenties. It can be delivered to you in twenty-four hours."

"I'm . . . retired."

"I noticed you hesitate before saying so."

"Anybody would hesitate, offered a million bucks."

"You could go anywhere in the world. You and your wife. Nothing could touch you."

"Don't mention my wife again."

"No offense meant."

"Don't mention her. Don't speak of her. Or I'll cut your fucking heart out."

He swallowed and nodded. He'd noticed the axe. "I just wanted to emphasize what a rosy future you could paint for yourself with that kind of money."

"I don't believe in the future, and I don't give a fuck about the past. And my present is rosy as fucking hell. So why don't you just go away."

"Mr. Quarry, it's a million dollars."

"I know it is. But . . . I'm retired. What do I need with it?"

"One job. One simple job."

"I doubt it would be simple."

"You'd be surprised."

I stood. I walked to the edge of the deck and looked out at the lake. The sun was still under a cloud and a light breeze was blowing in. The water looked gray. I was going to have a son, or a daughter, before long. With my past, maybe it would be a good thing to get out of this country. With a million bucks you could live like a king in Mexico or South America. Maybe on a beach, the ocean your front yard. A protected life. A safe life for me and mine. In a year, I would be forty years old.

I turned and looked at him. "What's the contract?"

"Have you heard of Preston Freed?"

"I've heard the name . . . he's some sort of right-wing loon, isn't he?"

His face cracked with the first of his many smiles to reveal teeth; too white and too perfect to be real.

He rose and walked over to me. "That's exactly what he is," he said, folding his arms, seeming at ease with me for the first time. I'd have to do something about that. "He is the founder and leader of the Democratic Action party."

I made a sound in my throat that wasn't quite a laugh. "Just another one of these homegrown would-be Hitlers."

He shook his head no. "He's not a Nazi. His politics are a grab-bag mixture of extreme right and extreme left, but he's relatively young and genuinely charismatic, a Kennedy of the lunatic fringe if you will . . . and he's gathering real momentum for his movement. Do you follow the political scene in the papers?"

"I catch it on TV. But, look . . ."

He raised a hand in a gentle stop motion. "Freed has several key issues that have rallied conservatives around him—he's strongly anti-abortion and pro-school prayer, for instance. That's all some people need to hear."

"I suppose, but . . ."

"You don't have to know much about politics to understand that the coming presidential election will be a volatile one. We have a once popular, now somewhat tarnished president ending his two terms in office. Supposedly a conservative, this man has raised the national debt to a record high."

"Politics don't interest me."

"Even so, we are coming into a fascinating election year. The two parties—depending upon whom they choose as their standard bearers of course—should be in for a real battle. Think of it: the highest office in the land up for grabs . . . we could have a true conservative in the White House, or our most liberal president in years . . ."

"What does this have to do with anything? If this contract is political, you can really forget it."

His gray eyes pleaded with me, his brow knitting a goddamn sock. "Mr. Quarry, Preston Freed is a presidential 'spoiler' in the truest sense. The way his movement, his 'party,' is gathering steam, he will throw the entire election off kilter."

"Yeah, I suppose. I don't know much about it, and I don't want to, either."

"At this point, it is hard to say whether the Democrats or the Republicans would suffer the most, but . . ."

"I think you should leave. This is a civics lesson that I just don't want to hear."

"I represent a certain group of private citizens, responsible, powerful, patriotic citizens, who want Preston Freed stopped. Who want the natural order of our political system restored, and this madman—this potential American Hitler, as you aptly described him—destroyed like the rabid animal he is."

"That's very colorful, but I don't do politicals. I don't do *any* contracts anymore, as I tried to make clear . . . and I shouldn't have let you get into this at all."

"Mr. Quarry . . ."

"I don't do windows, and I don't do politicals."

"Why not?"

"You can offer me two million and I'd turn you down."

He was astounded; shaking his head. "Why, do you think it would be difficult to get near the candidate? True, Freed is somewhat reclusive, but with the first primary in January, there'll be plenty of opportunities, starting with a major press conference next month, which . . ."

"Stop. It's not hard to kill a politician. It's the easiest thing there is. You got a public figure, an egomaniac who thinks he's immortal, going out kissing babies and shaking hands and it's the easiest hit in the world."

"Then what is your objection?"

"I wouldn't live to spend the money."

"Are you implying that . . ."

"That you would have me killed? Why, I don't know what got into me. You and your concerned patriotic citizens wouldn't *think* of being party to murder, now would you?"

"Mr. Quarry, we *are* men of honor."

"Sure. I'd be an instant loose end, pal. You don't get away with shooting presidents or even would-be presidents. Oh, the guys who *hire* you can get away with it. In fact they always do. That's 'cause the poor bastard who squeezed the trigger is either dead, or locked in a cell and written off as a madman."

"I assure you . . ."

"I'm retired. I don't want to get back in the business, not even once, not even for your big bucks. This is a real good place to call a halt to this conversation . . . I still don't know your name, and that's how I like it."

"You won't reconsider?"

"No. And I don't want to see you again. You know far too much about me. I ought to kill you on general principles."

He sucked breath in, hard; till now, talk of death had seemed abstract to him, I'm sure. "But . . . but you won't."

"Not unless I see you again."

He nodded, sighed, extended his hand for me to shake. I ignored it.

Withdrawing the hand, he smiled gently and said, "No hard feelings, Mr. Quarry. It's too bad. I think you'd have been the right man for the job."

I didn't say anything.

His smile disappeared and, shortly, so did he, in a cloud of gravel dust; the BMW's back license plate was covered with mud as well.

I went inside and started a fire.

I sat before the glow of it, by the metal conical fireplace in one corner of the A-frame's living room, and waited for Linda, wondering if I should've killed the son-of-a-bitch.

THREE

I couldn't shake the feeling that I'd made a mistake. A week crawled by, my every moment filled with a sense I'd fucked up. No way I should've let that guy walk away from my place. He knew too much about me: where I lived, who I was, who I used to be. I should've followed the old instinct

45

and iced him on the spot and dumped him in a gravel pit.

But my caller in the London Fog raincoat didn't exist in a vacuum, and he wouldn't die in one, either: he was clearly just a messenger, a fancy one maybe, but a messenger. Which meant somebody else—your classic person or persons unknown—had sent him; knew as much, or more about me, as he did.

So killing him would *still* have left somebody out there knowing more about me than was healthy.

There were options. I could've dropped everything and followed the messenger home, and done what needed doing, to all concerned.

But I didn't.

I could pack up and disappear. Walk out of Linda's life and leave her and the child inside her and the Welcome Inn and the comfortable life I'd somehow managed to contrive for myself forever behind me. Go and start over somewhere. I had money stashed under several names, including my real one back in Ohio; I had buffers built in to allow this sort of contingency.

Or I might risk taking Linda with me. She loved me. She was as loyal as Tonto, or anyway Pocahontas. And, with the exception of her brother, she had no ties, family or otherwise, to prevent her from disappearing with me, the two of us starting up and over somewhere, under new names.

She would probably go along with that. It wouldn't even be necessary to tell her the truth about my past; she would, most likely, accept it when I told her that something in my past required it. Something "bad" that she didn't need to know.

So why hadn't I sprung it on her?

Because, goddamnit, I liked my life. I liked it just fine the way it was. I was fat and comfortable and, fuck! I didn't *want* to start over. Why should I start over if I didn't want to?

I had turned these people down. They knew I wasn't interested, and if I wasn't interested, what was I to them? Certainly no threat—what could I say to anybody about what they were up to? Nothing, without risking seriously screwing up my own life.

They would simply go elsewhere for their hired help. I was retired, they asked me to come out of retirement, I declined, their messenger in the London Fog tipped his figurative hat and went. No hard feelings, he'd said.

So why *shouldn't* I go on about my business, go on with my life?

And, so, I had, but I still couldn't shake the thought, the feeling, I'd made the wrong decision. The visit, from the man's smooth but nervous manner to his muddy license plate, lingered like a bad dream, leaving a mental aftertaste and not a pleasant one.

The days themselves had been ordinary enough—I divided my time at the Inn between the garage, where for the hell of it I helped work on cars from time to time, and making sure the restaurant and hotel operation was operating smoothly. That was slightly weird, because half the time I'd been in greasy coveralls, the other neatly attired in suit and tie, an executive with a wrench in his back pocket.

I'd spent some time with Linda, quiet evenings, watching the tube, curled by the fire. We were both readers—I stuck with my westerns, while she read these dismal sappy romance novels, sitting there lost in them, smiling dreamily. The girl saw the world through rose-colored glasses—prescription rose-colored glasses, at that.

Another week passed, and the unsettling feeling that I'd fucked up began to fade. It didn't disappear; but it did fade.

Nonetheless, I took precautions. I owned three nine-millimeter automatics, and was carrying one, a Browning, with me everywhere I went now, instead of just in the glove compartment of our sporty blue Mazda, and the drawer of the nightstand next to the bed.

Early on, Linda had wondered about why I owned so many guns, particularly handguns, keeping them stashed about.

"I'm just a little paranoid," I said. "Both my parents were killed by an armed robber."

Her eyes had gone wide and round; that, added to their light blue color, made her look impossibly innocent. "Jack . . . I knew your parents were . . . gone . . . but I never . . ."

"They ran a little neighborhood market," I said. "You know, mom-and-pop kind of deal. And they were both killed."

"Oh, Jack," she'd said, eyes full of tears, holding me tenderly.

It was all lies of course, but it led to some immediate great sex and some long-term understanding. She never asked me about the guns again, until just recently, when I started carrying the nine-millimeter around with me.

"Why are you wearing that?" she asked, concerned, as I was slipping my sportcoat over the shoulder holster, on my way up to the Inn.

"There've been a few robberies in the area," I said. "It's been in the papers."

And there had been, but so what? That was almost always true.

"I understand," she said, nodding sagely, and came over and hugged me, gun and all.

The girl's new insight into me apparently came from her adding the truth that I'd been in combat to the lie about my sainted mom and pop being shot down in their grocery store. I was just a poor, sensitive, traumatized soul, wasn't I?

I wasn't packing the gun when we drove down to Chicago for the day, however, though one of the three automatics was in the glove compartment. We were picking up her brother Chris at O'Hare early that evening—he was coming in from Atlanta, Georgia—and Linda suggested we go in early, spend a day in the city Christmas shopping. Even mid-week, the city was jammed with traffic, sidewalks packed with people, and was a good reminder of why I lived on a quiet lake.

She shopped at Water Tower Place, six floors of trendy expensive nonsense, equal parts marble, glass, plants and people; it was the sort of shopping center where women in mink coats rode escalators. I quickly found my way to the theater complex and parked my butt in a fairly comfortable seat and watched Clint Eastwood pretend to be a marine for a couple of hours. I met Linda for lunch at a cafe next to the theater—where two people could have pie and coffee and get just enough change back from a twenty to leave a tip—and she was bubbling over about the things she'd bought, including several hundred bucks' worth (using the word "worth" loosely) of metal signs, replicas of vintage advertisements for Coca Cola, Crackerjacks, Heinz pickles and so on, for decoration in the Welcome Inn's rustic dining room. She'd also bought some presents for me, which she was dying to tell me about but managed to contain herself. She was a sweet kid. I didn't deserve her, but then who does deserve what they get in this life, good or bad?

We walked to Gino's East a few blocks over and shared a medium pepperoni pizza, the best deep dish pizza (so they said) in a town famous for deep dish pizzas. The walls were carved up with graffiti (it was encouraged—it gave the place atmosphere, and having your customers provide the decoration made more sense than buying little tin advertising signs yourself) and she coaxed me into carving our names there. Too many romance novels. What the hell, I did it, using the serrated part of a table knife, a heart with Jack and Linda in it, squeezed between THE BOSS FOREVER and BON JOVI SUCKS.

I never met her brother before, and when he showed up—his flight an hour late, his only bag a tan leather carry-on—I wasn't sure I wanted to. He was very blonde, very tan, and prettier than Linda. He wore a loose-fitting pastel blue shirt and off-white, baggy, pleated linen pants; he also wore huaraches and no socks.

"Sis!" he said, beaming, and hugged her. Then he backed away, with her still in his arms and said, "I'm freezing my *nuts* off."

What kind of dildo would fly into Chicago in November dressed like the fucking beach? This kind of dildo.

"Here," I said, and gave him my plaid hunting jacket. "It isn't Ralph Lauren, but it'll keep you warm."

"Why, thanks, sport," he said, and he had a nice smile, white teeth in a face as tan as his Gucci carry-on. He slipped the jacket on and it fit him fine. Well, in terms of size it fit him fine.

"I thought I'd *never* get here," he said, slipping his arm around her shoulder. She looked up at him adoringly. I fell back, following them down the wide aisle toward the main concourse. "All these delays, and the turbulence? I'd have lost my lunch, if I'd eaten any."

"You look *great*, Chris."

"I feel terrific."

"Are you being careful?"

"I'm being careful."

She'd never mentioned her brother was gay, but I had figured it out. First he lived in San Francisco, then in Atlanta—both centers of such activity—and he was thirty-five and unmarried. I know you can be thirty-five and unmarried and live in one of those cities and *not* be gay, but not when you have a succession of male roommates, and particularly not when you have a sister who cries every time she reads about AIDS in the papers.

"Safe sex," she said, shaking a lecturing finger at him.

"I know, I know."

"But you broke up with Ray . . ."

"I'm looking for a monogamous relationship. I'm not by nature promiscuous."

I stopped listening about then. I wasn't interested in the conversation, and I was distracted by the sight of Preston Freed's clean-cut disciples peddling his Democratic Action party magazines and bumper stickers (the latter seemed pro-nuclear energy and anti-Jane Fonda).

I went and got the car, not minding the cold at all, and picked them up amongst the cabs. He squeezed in back, behind me, with Linda's many packages, and she sat in front but looking his way. They chattered all the way back, mostly about his work (he was an artist, and had had some gallery showings in several cities—an abstract painting in pastels of his hung at the A-frame, and I didn't mind it). Later in the conversation Linda revealed that she was "expecting," and he seemed thrilled, maybe even envious. He patted me on the shoulder and I smiled at him in the mirror.

"I'll make a fabulous uncle," he said. "I just love kids."

I wasn't sure I wanted the details.

Finally, I pulled in the restaurant parking lot, and Linda said, "It's getting a little late—I'd rather wait till tomorrow to show Chris around the Inn."

"Why don't you kids go back and chat," I said, getting out of the car. "I have something here I want to work on."

"Jack," she said, "come with us—we'll make a fire, have some drinks . . ."

"I'll be home by midnight," I said. "You have a lot to talk about. Family stuff. You'll both see plenty of me over the next week."

She seemed a little disappointed, but she smiled anyway, said, "Okay, honey," and slid over into the driver's seat. Chris got out of the back and got in front next to her.

Gravel stirred as they pulled out of the parking lot and onto the road. I went into the Inn and settled myself at the bar and watched the "Tonight Show" and then "David Letterman" and drank a couple of caffeine-free diet Cokes. I wanted to sleep tonight.

"You okay, Jack?" Charley wondered. Business was slow and he was sitting on a stool behind the bar, watching TV, too. He was bald and round and wrinkled, a friendly old hard-ass.

"Ungh," I said.

"Your wife's brother's arrived," he said, smiling on one side of his face, nodding.

"Yeah." I shrugged.

"That comes with the territory. In-laws."

"He seems like an okay guy."

"I'm sure he is."

"His idea of a good time is sticking his dick in some guy's hairy asshole, but hey, who am I to judge?"

"Don't be an asshole, yourself, Jack. We can't choose our relatives. Besides, maybe he prefers bein' the stickee."

"I know, I know. I got nothin' against the guy."

"You just don't like fags."

"I don't give a shit about that."

And I didn't. I worked with one for many years, and he was, for the most part, as good a partner as any. Why somebody's sex life should be of concern to somebody else is beyond me, anyway.

"You just like your privacy," he said.

"Why don't you polish a glass or something? Do I pay you to watch television?"

"Fuck you, Jack," he said cheerfully. "You're just like anybody else. You don't like being invaded."

I shrugged again. "Our place isn't big. Having another human being under foot for a week, well . . . fuck it, I'll live."

"Sure you will. Why don't you put him up here at the Inn? Business is slow."

That perked me up. "Not a bad idea. Of course, we got room for him at the A-frame—he was going to crash on the couch in the loft . . ."

"You want my advice? You got a sweet little girl there. Don't cause her any trouble. Show her and her brother a nice time—take 'em to Lake Geneva, and Twin Lakes, and do touristy shit—eat at a nice restaurant every night. Days, find work to do up here, give 'em some space. She can drive him around and show him antique shops and shit. She's going to want to spend time with him, and you can cover for her at the restaurant, or work on cars or do any damn thing you want. We got plumbing problems upstairs, y'know, if you're ambitious."

"That makes sense, Charley."

"And at night, well you send the boy up here where he has a private room. He can even entertain an occasional guest, if he likes. Beats sleeping on a couch."

"Charley," I said, and smiled a little, climbed off the stool, "forget about polishing a glass. Watch TV till your eyes burn, if you want. You just earned your keep."

"No problem, Jack. Just remember that faggot is all the family your little wife has in the world."

"Well," I said, thinking about what was growing inside her, "that's not entirely true, but I appreciate the sentiment. I know I got a good thing going. I'm no fool. I'm not about to fuck it up."

He nodded and turned his attention back to the tube.

I walked outside and started back home. It was less than half a mile to the turn-in, off of which was my drive. The night was cold, particularly with me minus my hunting jacket, and overcast; the moon was glowing behind some clouds up there, not having any luck getting through. About half-way home I noticed a car parked alongside the road. Headed north. I was walking north, but on the other side of the road. It was a dark blue late-model Buick and the man behind the wheel was pale and blonde and skeletal. He wore a black turtleneck sweater. He didn't look at me as I passed.

There was no reason for him to be parked there. He wasn't parking in front of a house or anything.

The house he was parked nearest to belonged to Charley, a quarter-mile away, and no other houses were immediately around; it was a gently wooded area near the lake, after all.

His plates were Illinois. Rock Island County.

The Quad Cities.

Where the Broker had lived.

Without picking up my pace, I walked into the brush lining the road, wanting to make myself less of a target. I was not armed. My shoulder holster was in the closet; the other guns were in their usual positions in glove compartment and nightstand drawer. But the house was nearby, and all I had to do was get in there first.

My past had come looking for me; the lingering feeling I'd had that I'd fucked up had been valid. I'd chosen the wrong fucking option.

Well, it wasn't too late. All I had to do was get inside that house and get one of my guns, and I'd start exploring other options.

I went in the side, rear door, quietly as I could; it was after midnight, but I figured Linda would still be up, talking to her brother in front of the fire. Lights were on in the front part of the house, so that seemed a safe assumption. I hoped to get in and get my gun and go back out, without alerting Linda or our house guest I'd even been home.

I opened the drawer of the nightstand, felt inside; my hand touched the cold gun.

That was when I noticed that Linda was in bed already, but she hadn't made a sound; I hadn't disturbed or frightened her, either, coming in as I had.

Because she was dead.

FOUR

He didn't hear me come up behind him.

I had slipped out of my shoes. Left them in the bedroom, next to the bed, where what had been Linda was soaking up the sheets, getting them red. She hadn't suffered; that was something. My guess is she'd been asleep. He'd put one in her head, and three more in her chest and stomach. But it was clear she hadn't stirred. She was on her side, like a fetus. His first shot, the head shot, had been enough. Why the other three?

And so I had walked on shoeless feet in the darkness through my familiar house and had made not a sound. It was something I had learned to do a long time ago and apparently, like riding a bike, it sticks with you. I was right up behind him, before he sensed me, and before he could turn, my gun was in his neck.

"You fucked up," I said. My voice sounded strange to me. Probably to him, too. But to me it sounded distant. Like something playing on television in another room.

He didn't know what to say. I couldn't blame him. He was just a dark shape standing over the corpse of my brother-in-law. Chris was seated in my big soft leather chair, facing the dying fire, which was the only light in the room; a beer that had been in his hand had spilled onto the floor, soaking our new carpet. Linda had picked it out just a few months before; carpet samples had littered the floor for days.

"You killed the wrong man," I said.

"Please," he said.

"He was my brother-in-law. I loaned him my jacket, and you took him for me. Nice piece of work, dipshit. Toss the gun to the floor. Underhand toss. Now."

He did. It was a nine-millimeter, too, but not a Browning: a Luger with a rather bulky homemade silencer attached.

"Turn around, slow."

He did, and as he did, I stepped back and had a look at the man who had taken so much from me. He wasn't big, he wasn't small—about my size, five-ten, heavy-set but not fat; he was perhaps thirty. He was in a black sweatshirt and black pants and black gloves. He had short dark hair and dark frightened eyes in a round, pale face dotted by several dark moles. His cheeks had Nixon shadow.

"He doesn't even look like me," I said, gesturing to dead Chris. "He's got blonde hair, for Christ's sake."

He didn't know what to say. His lower lip was trembling. He knew he was going to die. He knew there was nothing he could say that would change that. Maybe I could make him believe otherwise.

"I understand," I said.

"What?"

"I understand."

"Understand?"

"That you're just hired help."

His eyes tensed.

"That this is nothing personal. I used to be in this business myself. I was a hell of a lot better at it than you, and I never killed a whole fucking family, but . . ." I got a hold of myself and smiled tightly at him. ". . . but I want you to think about telling me who sent you. If you do that, I might give you a pass."

He shook his head. "They'd kill me."

"What do you think I'll do?" I said, and I whapped him on the side of the head with the nine-millimeter. He went down on the soft carpet, hard. He was out, or pretending to be, a trickle of blood like a red thread down his temple. I took off my belt and quickly lashed his wrists behind him. I kicked his gun under the sofa. I could have used the thing, the silencer would've come in handy, but I didn't want to touch it. Not that gun.

I went to the door. Before I dealt with him, I had to deal with the back-up man. The man who'd been parked alongside the road. He might be gone, now. Seeing me come bopping along, when I was supposed to be home getting shot, might have sent him running. Or he might be coming in any minute now to help his partner. Those were pretty much the probabilities.

Thinking it over, I went back through the dark house to the side door. You could smell death in that house. I'd forgotten that, or anyway hadn't thought about it in a long time. The smell of it. Of blood. Of shit. Of death.

I opened the back door and he was standing there, on the steps, about to come in, a ghostly pale presence in black, skinny and taller than me and with a revolver in his hand. A fucking revolver! Even his idiot friend knew enough to carry a silenced automatic . . .

Him standing there was a surprise to me, but then he was surprised to see me, too, so we both lost about the same amount of time and before he could raise and fire his revolver, I kicked his balls up in him. He howled and doubled over and I kicked the gun out of his hand, thankful that he hadn't fired it reflexively. Then I slapped him with the nine-millimeter and he looked up at me with a face as pale as a sick child; cheek streaked with blood, eyes begging, he said, "No . . . please no . . ."

I slapped him again with it and he went down on the small cement area, like so much kindling.

I really didn't want to shoot him with the nine-millimeter. I hadn't had time to map any of this out, but I knew I wanted to contain it; I knew I didn't want to fill the night with gunfire. I was hovering over him indecisively when he reached out and grabbed my ankle and sat me down hard on my ass.

He didn't want to stick around to fight; he didn't even bother looking for the revolver he dropped. He just wanted to get away from me, from here, from everything. He ran, ran back toward the brush and trees that separated my house from the road, where his car waited. He was perhaps fifty feet away when I hefted the nine-millimeter and hurled it, hitting him in the back of the head, sending him face down to the ground. He didn't move. Maybe he really was unconscious this time.

Enough fucking around. I went over to the woodpile and got the axe and went over to him and swung and it split his head like a melon.

Some of him splashed on my face and I knelt and untucked his sweatshirt in back and wiped myself off. On the ground around him, I felt around for the nine-millimeter; found it. Over nearer the house I found his revolver, which I heaved into the trees. Then I went back in the house where his partner was waking up.

"Your partner seems to have taken off without you," I said.

"Oh God," he said, quietly, pitifully. He was sitting up, hands still behind him. He was sitting next to Chris, who sat in my big comfortable chair staring with vacant eyes at the fire, which was damn near out by this time.

I untied his hands, put the gun in my waistband, slipped my belt back on. I stood over him, but didn't want to wave the gun in his face. Wanted him to think he might have some chance, at some point, to overpower me.

"And now," I said, "you're going to tell me who sent you. I think I know. But you're going to tell me . . ."

He shook his head. "You're going to kill me anyway."

"Let's suppose that's the case. What do you have to lose by telling me?"

"What . . . what do I have to gain?"

Good point.

"Well . . . you could buy some time. Maybe your partner is still out there, waiting to make his move. Waiting to come in and blow me away and get you out of this."

He thought about that.

"You're not a pro, are you?"

He said, "No . . . not really."

"You didn't stake me out or anything. You just had information about me, where I lived, and you came and did this."

He nodded.

"No careful planning. No surveillance. No days on the scene ahead of time. Just one day, or night rather. In and out. Just the hit."

He nodded again.

"Were you told to do the woman?"

He swallowed.

"Answer me. It'll go easier if you answer me."

"Whoever was here."

"And she was here."

He nodded, looked at the floor.

"You shot her four times."

He didn't say anything.

"Ever kill a woman before?"

He shook his head no. Then added: "Not a white one."

Seemed I was in the presence of another Vietnam vet.

"How did it feel?"

He swallowed.

"Just answer me."

"It . . . didn't feel like anything. It was no different."

"Than killing a man, you mean."

"Yeah . . . yeah, than killing a man."

"Or some slant."

"Or . . . or some slant."

"She was pregnant."

He looked at me sharply. "Really?"

"Really."

"I . . . I didn't know that."

"Would it have made a difference?"

"Sure . . . sure it would."

"Why did you shoot her four times?"

"To . . . to make sure."

Nam or not, he wasn't a pro. Didn't claim to be.

"Who hired this?"

"I don't know."

"Who hired this?"

"I can't say. They'd kill me."

"They can't kill you any deader than I would."

"They . . . they could kill my family. You don't know who I am. You can't do anything to my family."

"Yeah, but on the other hand, I could cut your nuts off with a steak knife."

He was shaking. "I can't stop you from whatever you do to me. That was . . . was your wife in there."

"That was my wife in there."

"Then there's no getting out of this. You killed my partner, didn't you?"

I said nothing.

"You killed him," the guy said, shaking his head. He was crying; quietly crying.

"I killed him," I said.

He looked at me, his face slick. "I didn't hear a shot."

"I used an axe."

He shivered. "God, oh God . . ."

"Are you praying or swearing?"

"Why don't you just do it?"

"It's political, isn't it? It's because I turned that job down. It's because it's political and I'm a loose end."

He shook his head no, emphatically. "I don't know. I

don't know. I have nothing to say to you." He was staring at the floor.

"You're going to say it all," I said, trying to control the rage, and I reached down and pulled him up to a standing position, by his sweatshirt, and yanked the gun out and buried it in his stomach. He made a sucking-in sound; I was looking right at him, I could smell the minty mouthwash on his breath, see the hysteria in his dark eyes. "You won't die in your sleep, like she did. You'll crawl around the floor trying to keep your intestines from falling out, but all you'll get out of the effort is bloody fucking hands. Now talk."

"Fuck you," he said, sobbing.

"Now you've done it," I said.

"W-what?"

"Gone and made me mad," I said, and squeezed the trigger. His body muffled the sound and I let him drop and stood over him and watched him die. It took a while.

I went in the bedroom and sat on the bed next to Linda. What had been Linda. Put my hand on her stomach. My hand came away red.

I got a suitcase from the bedroom closet; when I opened it, I found several brightly wrapped packages. Christmas paper and bows, little cards inscribed by her hand, "Love you, Jack—your Linda," and so on. I left the gifts in the suitcase but filled in around the sides with a few more things: pair of jeans, couple sweaters, socks, underwear, some toiletries. Just enough to get me by for a few days. I'd pick up some new clothes. Linda had some sleeping pills, Seconal, and I took the bottle with me. I had a few business papers I wanted to take along—from the old days, the Broker days— and from the safe in my little office I took my stash of emergency cash, ten grand, in twenties and fifties. Tucked those packets into the suitcase, as well. I left the safe open.

I went outside and took the axe out of the back of the guy's head, which made a sound like pulling your foot up out of mud, and dragged him by the feet in through the back door, all the way into the living room; he left a snail-like trail of blood and brain matter, even though the mess was facing mostly up. In his pants pocket I found the keys to his car, which I kept. He had no I.D. of any kind, of course. Like a department store window dresser, I arranged my mannequin so that his head was against the metal lip of the fireplace. Near his open right palm I placed the nine-millimeter I used on his partner. I found my hunting jacket hung on the hook by the front door; my car keys were on the kitchen counter and I put them in the right-hand jacket pocket. As if dancing with a clumsy partner, I put it on the other corpse, and draped him near the fireplace as well. I removed his leather gloves; put them on—they fit perfectly—and reached under the sofa for the silenced Luger, leaving the gun near the two dead men. Then I stepped back to look at them, an artist checking his composition. As an afterthought—and with some reluctance, I admit—I removed my Rolex, engraved on the back "To Jack—Love Linda," and placed it on the left wrist of the corpse wearing my hunting jacket. Now satisfied, I went back out to my little tool shed and got a can of gasoline. Still wearing the gloves, I soaked a good deal of the living room down, dousing the two corpses, and particularly the fireplace, whose dying embers flared into life. I didn't douse Chris at all—I hoped he would eventually be identified. I splashed some in the hallway. Couldn't bring myself to splash any around the bedroom. The smell of the gas began to override the death smell.

I went in the bedroom one last time. I was going to kiss her goodbye, but she really wasn't there anymore, was she?

She was gone. I'd fucked up, chose the wrong option, and she was gone. Somebody screamed. Me.

I had lived here a long time. But I could never live here again.

Then I went out the front door, suitcase in hand; I stood on the deck for a moment and held the door open with my foot. Put the suitcase down and lit a kitchen match.

Tossed it in.

The heat rushed back at my face, like an oven door opening.

"Bye, baby," somebody said.

Me.

Behind me the world turned orange; ahead the world was dark. I walked toward the darkness.

FIVE

The phone rang until it woke me. It rang a good long time, because I was way under, but it finally did wake me, and my eyes opened, tentatively, to a darkened motel room, just enough light filtering in around the drapes to let me know it was day.

"Hello," I said. My mouth was thick and foul from sleep and Seconal.

"Mr. Murphy?"

The voice was male and sounded official and unsure of itself at the same time.

"Yes. What is it?"

"We were, uh . . . worried about you, sir."

"I'm touched. Why."

"It's . . . Friday, sir. Friday afternoon, and you arrived early Thursday, in the early A.M. Which is to say,

Wednesday night, very late."

I yawned and sat up. Not terribly engrossed in this conversation.

"Yeah, right," I said. "So?"

"Housekeeping informs us that you haven't been out of your room since you arrived. You've taken no meals, and . . ."

"Is babysitting your guests part of the service here, at . . . where am I?"

"The Ramada Inn. Near O'Hare."

Yesterday I'd been here with Linda. Not here exactly— at O'Hare, picking up her brother . . . and maybe it *wasn't* yesterday, exactly . . .

"So it's Friday," I said. Blinking my sleep-crusted eyes. Tasting my gym-sock tongue.

"Friday afternoon," he said. "Three o'clock, and no sir, we don't 'babysit' our guests. We as a policy respect the privacy of our guests. But housekeeping has checked in periodically —you didn't put out the 'do not disturb' sign—and, frankly, reports were that you were sleeping very soundly . . ."

They thought I was in a coma or something.

"Look," I said, "who am I speaking to, anyway?"

"My name is Hollis," he said, somewhat defensively. "I'm an assistant manager."

"Is that your first name or last name?"

"Last," he said.

"Well, Mr. Hollis, I appreciate your conscientiousness. But I'm really quite all right. I was just very tired, and needed a good deal of sleep."

Long pause.

Then: "I understand. I'm sorry to have disturbed you, Mr. Murphy."

"That's all right. I like to get up every few days, anyway. Thanks again."

"You're welcome, sir."

His voice still sounded doubtful, suspicious.

"I'll be sure to recommend your facility to my company," I said.

"Well, thank you, sir," he said, brightly, mollified.

I hung up.

I sat on the edge of the bed and ran my hand over my face. The grease and growth of beard there confirmed that I had indeed slept for a day and a half. I'd taken too many of those fucking pills. What was I trying to do, kill myself?

That wasn't in me. I'd worked too hard, for too many years, to survive, to ever throw it away. Even yesterday's losses—or the day before yesterday or whenever the fuck—weren't enough to change that. This planet, without Linda on it, was pretty much worthless, but what else was new? It all fit in with the Almighty's master plan, which was that there was no master plan, or Almighty either.

I'd learned two lessons in Vietnam: the meaningless of life and death; and the importance of survival. They seem to contradict each other, those lessons—but they don't. I can't explain it to you. I won't try.

I got up, feeling woozy from all that drugged sleep; shuffled into the bathroom on rubbery legs and leaned on the sink with one hand and threw water on my face with the other. I looked at myself in the mirror. My eyes were red and dead. My face held no expression at all. There was gray in my beard. I was getting old. Death was coming.

But not today. I went in the other room and dug the little bag with my toiletries out of that suitcase where Linda, in one of her last acts, had hidden my Christmas presents. I would have to open those presents to make room in the suitcase. Waiting till Christmas was out of the question. Death might be here by then.

I shaved; nicked myself twice. I smiled at the mirror, seeing if my face still worked. Seeing if I had the masks needed to go out in the world and mix.

I did.

I showered, cold to wake me up, and once awake, hot to relax me. My stomach was grinding. It had had nothing in it but Seconal for damn near two days.

I got into the jeans and a white Polo sweatshirt Linda had given me for my last birthday. The clothes I'd worn here would have to be tossed, preferably burned; there would be blood and fiber evidence and what have you. But in the meantime, I stuffed a few twenties in my pocket and walked out into an endless hallway connecting with other endless hallways, following various signs until I was in an equally sprawling lobby area, parts of which seemed under construction. It was one of those places that would always be under construction, I thought, growing constantly, like cancer cells. I ignored the hotel's own restaurants and went out the front door, into a starkly cold and sunny afternoon, a jet roaring overhead, making its descent into the out-of-sight but nearby O'Hare. Within easy walking distance was a Greek/American restaurant that, among other things, served breakfast twenty-four hours a day. I ate a Denver omelet with pancakes on the side; also orange juice and iced tea. It tasted good, all of it, and made me feel alive again. It was a deceptive feeling, I knew, but even a beat-up wreck of a car needs some gas in it, if it's going to struggle down the road.

And speaking of cars, in the motel's vast parking lot, I found the dark blue Buick immediately, something leading me there though I had no conscious memory of where I'd left the thing. Before driving it away Wednesday night I'd taken only the time to check for registration and, not surprisingly, had found none. Now it was time to go over the car more thoroughly.

Not that I expected to find anything: it was a new car. It still had the new car smell; the ghost of the price sticker was on the driver window, several bands of paper and glue. But I looked anyway.

In the trunk I found nothing but the jack and spare. It was spotless; nothing had ever been stowed here.

In the backseat, even pulling the cushions out, I found nothing at all. Not even the usual spare change.

Nothing on the floors in back except paper mats.

In the glove compartment, I found three maps: Wisconsin, Illinois, Iowa. There was also a silver flashlight. And a pair of flares.

Also an owner's manual, warranty literature and such, the likes of which come with any new car. But no name of the car's owner.

However, there was, on the manual, the rubber-stamp imprint of the car dealership from which the car apparently came: BEST BUY BUICK & OLDS, DAVENPORT, IOWA. Davenport was on the Iowa side of the Quad Cities; Rock Island—the county and the city, and the source of the Buick's license plate—was on the Illinois side. Interesting.

I found nothing under the front seat, but digging down in the seat, in front, my fingers touched something small and cool. I withdrew a matchbook. It was bright red. In black its shiny surface said THE EMBERS. There was no address, but there was a phone number, and the area code—309—was an Illinois one—that included the Quad Cities.

I pocketed the matchbook and felt my face make something that might have been a smile.

Pros these boys had not been. Even driving a brand-new

car, they had managed to leave a trail of stupidity all the way back home. They were lucky they were already dead, or I'd be killing them again.

One at a time, I spread the Illinois and Iowa maps out on the hood of the car; there were no markings on either. On the Wisconsin map, however, highways and roads en route were traced in pen and Paradise Lake was circled.

I folded the maps back up and tucked them under my arm. I walked back into the hotel, the cold air whipping at me, a jet screaming overhead. In the gift shop I found a blue Chicago Bears windbreaker, inappropriate for the time of year, but it would do till I had a chance to stop and buy a real jacket.

Not a hunting one this time, even though that *would* be appropriate.

I also picked up the *Sun Times* and the *Tribune*. The latter had a small inside story about the incident, but in the former, in true tabloid tradition, MULTIPLE MURDERS FOLLOWED BY FIRE had made page two, and had some details, including a few pictures: what seemed to be a high school picture of Linda looking impossibly young, pretty and innocent (like usual) and a shot of firemen working hoses on the burning house; fire must've lasted a while, because it was a daylight pic. No pictures of me. There weren't any, that I knew of, under that name; or dental records or anything else, if they went looking.

I was sitting on the bed, reading the articles a second time, the TV tuned to the "Eyewitness News," when an update came on.

The glow of the TV was on my face like the set was a hearth I was sitting in front of. A black reporter in a gray topcoat and a black tie was speaking earnestly into a microphone, his breath smoking with cold. Behind him was my

A-frame, not recognizably an A anymore, smoking with heat. Even now.

"No official statement has been made," the reporter was saying, "but one Twin Lakes fire department investigator, who wished to remain anonymous, speculated that the blaze may have begun as an accidental side effect of a 'fight to the death' between the man of the house and an intruder. That as yet unidentified intruder apparently stole an undisclosed amount of cash from a safe in the Wilson home, after killing Mrs. Wilson and her visiting brother, Christopher Blakely. Apparently Jack Wilson, the husband, came upon the scene and struggled with the intruder. Both Wilson and the intruder were killed; their struggle, near a roaring fire in a fireplace, may have led to the conflagration."

Cut to Charley, behind the bar at the Inn, looking haggard, shattered.

"Jack did keep money in his house," Charley said. "How much, I don't know. I do know that his brother-in-law and wife were alone in that house that evening, before he joined them about midnight."

Cut to a closer-up shot of the black reporter. "Wilson apparently killed the intruder by smashing his head against the edge of the metal fireplace. But Wilson was shot during the struggle and was probably dead before the fire flared up."

Cut back to Charley.

"I don't know much about Jack's background," he said. His voice was quavering. I felt bad about putting him through this. Well, when he discovered the Welcome Inn's ownership reverted to him upon my death, that would cheer him up some.

"I do know that he saw combat in Vietnam," Charley was saying, "and he kept guns in his house. It don't surprise me Jack took the bastard with him."

Local news. They could leave words like "bastard" in. Was this one of those ratings "sweep" weeks, I wondered, or did they routinely go "in-depth" into exploitable tragedies like this?

"Locals say this is the first murder at Paradise Lake since the late 1800s," the reporter was wrapping up, "when two trappers fought over fur-trading rights. And it may be the most bizarre and tragic multiple homicide the Lake Geneva area has ever seen. Len Myers, Eyewitness News."

Then some asshole came on and talked about the weather. It was going to get colder.

SIX

I left the Buick in one of the parking ramps at O'Hare, where it could sit for a good long time before anybody discovered it had been abandoned. Then I paid cash for a seat on an evening flight, via Air Wisconsin to Moline, Illinois. On my way to the concourse I paid five bucks to the clean-cut young men hawking Preston Freed's Democratic Action party literature. The forty-five-minute flight allowed me to inform myself on the evils of abortion, the need for prayer in school, the Royal Family's role in global drug traffic, the Zionist-inspired banking crisis and the approaching nuclear apocalypse. All Freed's world outlook lacked was a white rabbit looking frantically at his watch.

The Moline airport terminal was a massive modern rambling structure, ridiculously outsized for what it was. The structure was relatively new—in the old terminal, which was still standing nearby, a building that was modern in the 1950s sense, I had done a job once. One of my last jobs for the Broker. Killed a priest in the men's room, only he was just a guy passing for a priest.

I was passing for John Ryan, a name I had I.D. for, including a driver's license. Even though I was out of the business all those years, I kept a spare identity active. One never knew, did one, when it would come in handy.

Ryan was supposed to live in Milwaukee, though the address was just a P.O. box. He had money in the bank—time certificates, mostly. His profession, should anyone ask, was sales. He owned his own small company and sold auto parts. That was the story. It wouldn't hold up if I was in serious trouble, but if I was in serious trouble, I'd be past needing it to hold up.

But I had my driver's license, social security number, and several credit cards. And that's all anybody needs in the United States to qualify as a real person. It felt great being a real person. Real persons can rent cars, and I did, from National, another Buick, this one light blue. I wondered if National bought their cars locally, in which case it may have come from Best Buy over in Davenport. Everybody sing: it's a small world after all, it's a small world after all . . .

It was eleven when I checked in at the Howard Johnson's near the airport. I'd been here before, too, years ago, but it had been remodeled some, not that I gave a shit. Remodeling a Howard Johnson's is like a homely woman getting a facelift; sure she looks younger, but why the fuck bother?

I was feeling alert and awake, the Seconal hang-over easing off. I had slept some on the plane, nodding off halfway through a Freed article explaining the link between the Zionists and the Illuminati. But before I'd dropped off, I learned something extremely interesting about extremist Freed: his home base was right here in the Quad Cities. His campaign headquarters for the coming presidential election was a suite of offices in the Blackhawk Hotel. His private estate was nearby, "just outside Buffalo, Iowa, in America's heartland."

Well, somebody in America's heartland wanted Freed dead. And if I could figure out who that was, I'd know who *I* wanted dead.

I sat on the bed in the motel room, knowing I wouldn't need to sleep for a while, and decided to get to work. I checked the phone book for Victor Werner, but there was no listing. It figured that he'd be unlisted. I had an address for him, in the Broker's papers, but it was ten years old, that address. Would he still be there?

Only one way to find out.

I had left the Browning nine-millimeter behind, of course, but the other two, a matched pair of Smith and Wesson's, were still with me. So was an Automatic Weapons Company HP-9 suppressor, a dark round tube that attached to the end of about any nine-millimeter, my S & W's included. With a silencer like this, all a nine-millimeter made was a little *thump* you could sleep through. Forever, if necessary.

I attached the suppressor to one of the nine-millimeters and rolled the gun up in a bathroom towel. I still had my shoulder holster, but the silenced weapon was too bulky to wear that way. I had a dark blue sweatshirt along, which I put on, still wearing the jeans, and threw the lighter blue CHICAGO BEARS windbreaker over that. With the rolled-up towel under my arm, I looked like I was going to the Y for a work-out.

I wasn't. I was on my way, in my rental Buick, to Davenport, via the free bridge at Moline; traffic was brisk, but that was to be expected on a Friday night. In Moline I made a stop at a 7-11 and bought a roll of wide adhesive tape and a plastic-wrapped packet of clothesline. Soon I was cruising four-lane River Drive, which connected Moline and Davenport, and to my left was the Mississippi, its shiny black surface reflecting the lights of the cities across the way, and to my right was a slope on which perched various homes, many of them mansions or anyway near-mansions.

Werner's was a big white would-be Tara, with six pillars in front, its slope of lawn winter-brown at the moment, unmarred by sidewalk. I drove up the nearest side street and found you entered via an alley, off of which was the house and its three-car garage. But the place was dark. Well, it figured. Friday night.

I left the car several blocks away and walked back to Werner's and waited. I waited in the shrubs near the garage. I never did do home invasions. That wasn't my style. I always worked as part of a two-man team, one of whom would do most of the watching, the surveillance, getting the target's pattern down before choosing the right time and place, when the other team member would do the actual hit. Which was usually me.

But home invasions, no, and so I had only the most rudimentary experience with things like alarm systems. A connected guy like Werner would have a sophisticated one, too, and possibly a live-in bodyguard or two, though after an hour no one checked the grounds.

The night was overcast and cold and a little foggy up on this higher ground; the streetlamps in the alley glowed like halos. I should have been chilled, in the light jacket, but for some reason I couldn't feel it much. I felt dead, even if my breath in the cold air indicated I wasn't.

Finally, just after midnight, a security company car crawled down the alley. One of the two uniformed, brown leather-jacketed men got out and walked the grounds with a flashlight, while the other waited, sipping steaming liquid from a Styrofoam cup. It was only a half-hearted effort, the one with the flash not even brushing the bushes where I hid with his beam. Good thing. Cold-inspired laziness had saved a couple of lives.

And at one-thirty-something, a jade green Lincoln coasted down the alley and pulled in the drive; one of the three doors of the garage swung up upon electronic command, and the big boat of a car docked itself within.

The door shut itself, and a man in a camel's hair overcoat and a woman in a mink exited the garage via a side door. The woman was in the lead, a harshly attractive blonde in her late forties who was staying perhaps too thin in an effort to hold onto her youth. The man was shorter than his wife, and in his mid-fifties though his hair was jet black; he had a round, youthful face, but his mouth was a tight gash. He was pulling on his gloves.

"We're going to the game," Mr. Werner said, irritably.

"You'll go alone," the apparent Mrs. Werner said. Her voice was as icily crisp as the air.

"Isn't it enough I give those phony bastards my money? Do I have to . . ."

She turned and pointed a finger in his face; she was wearing black leather gloves. "The Arts Council is the most important thing in my life. Don't louse it up!"

"We don't have to be at every goddamn meeting . . ."

"Well, I do," she said.

By this time they were at the back door. The woman stood with her arms folded, tapping her foot as if to some inner and no doubt unpleasant tune while Werner worked a key in the lock.

"I'm going to that game," he said. "I didn't spring for

season tickets to stay home."

"I'm co-chairperson, Vic. Don't forget that."

"Would that I could."

He had the door open, now. The whine of an alarm system sounded.

"Doesn't mean a thing to you the Hawks are number one in the nation, does it?" he asked, as he reached around inside to work another key in a wall socket, turning off the alarm.

With a patrician downward glance at him, she said, "I enjoy the games. Driving all the way to Iowa City doesn't thrill me, but I'm as much a Hawk fan as you are . . ."

"I doubt that."

"I just have my own priorities."

So did I.

They stepped inside and I stepped in with them, putting the nine-millimeter's silenced nose in the back of the woman's neck.

"God!" she said.

Werner was looking at me through narrow eyes, as if trying to comprehend that I was really standing there. The kitchen was dark, but the alley was well lit and that made for some visibility.

"Don't turn on the lights," I told her, "and don't turn around."

"Don't rape me," she said. "Please don't let him rape me, Vic!"

"Shut up," he said.

I tossed him the packet of clothesline.

"Tie her in that chair," I told him. To her I said, "Keep your back to me. Don't see me."

"All right," she said timidly.

"Sit," I said.

She sat.

Werner, moving with slow, quiet disgust, tied his wife into the chair. I watched him carefully and he performed his task well, making it tight enough and knotted well enough to get her bound, but not hurting her. Despite their bickering, he seemed to care for her.

While he was doing that, I asked him: "Anyone else in the house?"

"No."

"No children?"

"We have two kids, both at college."

"Neither home at the moment?"

"Neither home at the moment."

"Any live-in help?"

"No."

"No bodyguards?"

"No. I used to have live-in help like that. No more."

"Why?"

"I'm a respectable member of the community. Respectable members of the community don't go around with bodyguards."

He got up from where he'd been kneeling to tie her legs to the chair and said, "Now what?"

"Her mouth," I said, and tossed him the adhesive tape.

He sighed and put a slash of tape across her mouth. I saw him smile reassuringly at her, squeezed her shoulder once. Said, "Don't look at him, Virginia."

She nodded.

"Now what?" he asked.

"How often does the rent-a-cop car come by? Don't lie."

"Twice a night."

"When?"

"It varies."

"Usually."

He shrugged. "About midnight. Then again around three."

"Let's go outside."

"Why?"

"I have the gun. The one with the gun gets to ask the questions."

"Right," he sighed. He turned to his wife, whose back remained to us. "Just sit there," he said pointlessly. "Don't try to do anything."

She nodded again, which was about all she could do, anyway.

And her husband and I went out into the cold foggy air. The distance from house to alley was moderate, but the yard was wide and protected from neighboring houses and their big yards by walls of shrubbery.

"What's this about?" he asked. He didn't seem very afraid.

"I used to work for the Broker."

That only seemed to irritate him. "Well, what are you coming around here for, then? And what's the idea of the gun, and tying up my wife?"

"Simple precaution," I said; he seemed to have taken me for somebody else, which could prove interesting.

"Look . . . Stone, is it? None of this has anything to do with me, and I don't want to have anything more to do with it. You can tell that to Ridge." He sliced the air with the side of his hand, karate-chop style, in a gesture of finality. "I've done all I'm going to do."

"I may not be who you think I am."

"Well, you're Stone."

"No, I'm not. I know who you mean. I worked with Stone, a few times. But I'm not Stone."

"You're not."

"I'm someone else who used to work for the Broker."

"Someone else? Who?"

"What's in a name?"

"Look, a lot of people worked for the Broker. But that's ancient history. That cunning old son-of-a-bitch died years ago."

"I know," I said. "I was there."

He wasn't impressed yet. "Were you really." It wasn't a question.

I said, "He pointed you out to me, once, Mr. Werner. He said you were a rising star who fell."

He laughed humorlessly. "That sounds like him."

"He said you were destined for big things in the Outfit, but that you made some mistakes. You were lucky to stay alive, actually, let alone hang onto your vending business, hotel interests and other holdings locally."

"I have very little to do with those people anymore," he said. "I am, as I told you, a respectable member of the community. What are you, down on your luck? Looking for work? If you're auditioning, you've come to the wrong place. If you're just a thief, now, well, there's little of value in my house, but I'm willing to lead you to what there is, if you'll be done with this and go. We have perhaps a thousand in cash, some negotiable securities, some jewelry, a few paintings, though the latter might not be anything you'd want to fool with."

"Well, you've seen me, Mr. Werner. You'd give my description to the authorities."

"But I wouldn't. I'm still connected enough that I don't relish investigation of any sort. If they caught up with you, you might tell them what you know about me, and while I don't think much would come of it, it could prove embarrassing."

"Embarrassment is the least of your problems. I said I used to work for the Broker."

He looked at me sideways, drawing back a bit.

And then it hit him. The blood left his face.

"You . . . you're not the one he called . . . *Quarry,* are you?"

"That's right."

And now he was scared. He was starting to breathe heavy, his country club cool melting on him, even in this weather. He started backing up.

"Don't do that," I said.

He stopped; suddenly his breath was smoking up the place. "I thought . . . I thought . . ."

"You thought I was dead? And why is that?"

"Look—I was just doing a favor for a friend . . . I . . ."

"What friend? What favor?"

He patted the air with his palms. "Let's be reasonable. Let's just be reasonable. I can explain."

"I'll explain. Someone came to you, someone who knew you had mob connections, and requested the name of an assassin. And you used to be the Broker's mob conduit, so you knew the names and even the whereabouts of some of his people. What made you pick my name out of the hat?"

A swallow and a sigh. "Broker said . . . he said something about you once."

"What's that?"

He looked at the ground. "I don't remember. I just remember he singled you out."

"No, really. I'm interested."

He swallowed again, reluctantly met my eyes with his. "He said you were his best man. If I ever had anything . . . out of the ordinary, anybody important, you'd be the man for the job."

Even dead, all these years, that cocksucker was still causing me problems.

"Well, I'm flattered," I said. "And that's why you gave out my name for this political contract, is it?"

He shook his head no, repeatedly. "I don't know anything about the contract. I just know who put it in motion."

"And who would that be?"

He thought.

Then said: "If I tell you, you have to promise me something."

"Which is?"

His eyes were slits. "You'll kill this man at your first opportunity."

"No problem."

"He's . . . a friend of mine, you see, but he's . . . he wouldn't stop at anything, to reach his goals. If he knew I'd told you who he was, I'd be dead."

"Who is he?"

"He's a self-made millionaire. Real estate."

"What's his name? Ridge?"

"Ridge," he nodded. "George Ridge."

"Lives here in the Cities?"

"In Davenport. That's where his business is, too. It's in Paul Revere Square on Kimberly."

"I see. You've been helpful, Mr. Werner."

He smiled. "You don't have to worry about me keeping my mouth shut," he said.

"Oh, I know," I said, and raised the nine-millimeter.

"Wait! Wait. That's not necessary!"

"You thought I was dead, Mr. Werner. Why?"

"George . . . George told me you hadn't worked out. He asked me if I could give him another name. I . . . I gave him one."

81

"Stone."

He thought for a moment, then shrugged, what the hell. "Stone. I . . . guess I let that slip before."

"That's right."

"But that's just what the Broker called him. He was living under another name. Brackett, I believe."

"I know that, too," I said.

"Oh, you do. But I have been of *some* help . . ."

"You have. Only something doesn't track, here."

"What?"

"The two men who tried to hit me. Neither one was this man Stone, Brackett, whatever. I don't think they were pros, those two."

He lifted his eyebrows. "Well—I think Stone was going to get offered the job you turned down. George has people working for him who have pretty rough backgrounds. He might have used some of them."

"How educated a guess is that?"

"Pretty educated. He did say to me . . . well, he said he was going to have to do something about you."

"Because I was a loose end."

"Something like that. He . . . I admit he makes me more than a little uneasy."

"And why is that, Mr. Werner?"

"Well, hell—I didn't want to be a 'loose end' myself." He shrugged, lifted his eyebrows. "But I don't really think George looks at me that way."

"Why's that?"

"He thinks of me as Outfit. Which I still am, to a degree. It's just that I'm strictly legitimate these days."

"Do you love your wife, Mr. Werner?"

"What sort of question is that?"

"Do you love your wife?"

82

"Of course I love her."

"Well, thanks to you, my wife is dead, and my unborn child. So when I've done you, I'll do Mrs. Werner."

"No!"

"And I may just look those kids of yours up for the hell of it."

His eyes went wide with a terror like none I'd ever seen; I let it linger there a few moments, then shot him between them. The heavy camel's hair overcoat cushioned his fall and he lay on his back staring up at the overcast sky, eyes and mouth open, in a look of empty yet reflective horror.

I had no intention of killing his wife or kids. I didn't want to lower myself to that level.

I just wanted him to think I would.

There's no reason to believe there's anything after this life but darkness, and I wanted to make sure the son-of-a-bitch spent at least a few seconds in hell.

SEVEN

The wide one-way of Brady Street burrowed through a valley of plastic and metal and cement that was America in all its fast-food, discount-chain glory. It was Saturday afternoon, and the four lanes were thick with cars; even in the unemployment-stressed Quad Cities, people seemed to have income to dispose of, as car after car would leave the pack and disappear into the jammed parking lot of this temple of Mammon or that one. And on the right, as the valley dipped, between McDonald's and Payless Shoe Source, an auto lot sprawled, a virtual football field of vehicles, new and used: BEST BUY BUICK & OLDS.

I pulled the rental Buick into the lot and stepped out,

looking (I hoped) fairly prosperous in my suit and tie and brown leather overcoat. These, as well as a second suitcase and enough clothes of various sorts to fill it and my immediate needs, I'd bought at shops on the Illinois side of the Cities, at South Park Mall, which hadn't been far from the Howard Johnson's I'd checked out of. I had checked into the Blackhawk Hotel, just before heading out Brady Street, and all of this had eaten up most of the morning. It was now approaching noon, the sun bright and reflecting off the shiny new (and used) cars.

I began nosing around. Buicks and Oldsmobiles and Pontiacs. Sporty cars and conservative ones. Expensive ones and less expensive ones. Here a two-tone barge with a vinyl top; there a low-slung number with a garish bird spread over its crimson hood. Symbols of status that told you who you were, in case you didn't know.

A Mexican blue-collar type was chatting with a heavy-set salesman in a red blazer; the blazer blurred into the red Firebird they were discussing in puffs of smoky breath. A middle-class family was looking a station wagon over; the father was about my age, the mother perhaps ten years younger—two well-behaved kids, a boy and a girl, six and four I'd guess, tagged along. A younger red-blazered salesman was pointing out the benefits of these practical wheels; but I caught the father gazing wistfully at a sporty little two-seater.

I heard the swish of nylon and turned to see a beaming, very blonde, startlingly beautiful woman in red blazer and white pleated skirt and blue shoes approaching. Her lipstick was bright red, teeth a dazzling white, and her eyes a deep resonant blue. She was a human American flag, her arms moving like a soldier on parade, waving her hips by way of patriotic greeting.

I couldn't help but smile; first time in days I'd done that. Her manner was a skillful blending of cheerleader sexiness and no-nonsense businesswoman. You wanted to fuck her, and she implied she'd love to fuck you, as well—only business before pleasure.

"What do you see that you like?" she said, in a tone utterly devoid of innuendo, or for that matter irony.

"Nothing yet," I said, smiling blandly, and moved along the row of cars, ignoring her, as if I didn't know she was following along at my side, like a beauty pageant contestant on a runway.

"Do you have something in mind?" she said, pleasantly, her breath visible in the cold. None of the sales staff was dressed warm enough.

"I was here about a week ago," I said, giving her a casual glance. "I don't believe I remember seeing you, and I think I'd remember." A quick smile to acknowledge her attractiveness. "You new here?"

"Why, relatively new," she said, the question throwing her just a bit off guard. "But I've been with the firm several months. Were you here in the evening?"

"Why, yes."

She smiled like a stewardess. "Well, that explains it. I'm only here mornings and some afternoons."

"You don't often see a woman working a car lot."

"Times are changing," she said, perkily, not insulted, or anyway not showing it.

"I noticed. But car lots—particularly used car lots—seem one of the last male strongholds. When did you last hear someone say, 'Would you buy a used car from this woman?' "

"Never," she said, something warm and more real in her voice now, "but then I almost never get mistaken for Nixon."

That made me smile again and look at her, in a different way. The Nixon reference was surprising, because it was something you'd only say if you were about my age, and I'd thought her younger than me. And she was, but only a few years, though if you looked past the deft, sparingly applied makeup, you could see it. She'd been a cheerleader, all right, and probably a beauty queen too—but fifteen years ago.

"What's your name?" I asked her.

She pointed to her bosom; on the blazer it said, ANGELA, in blue stitched cursive. Her tapering hand wore no wedding ring, but I could see the smooth shadow where one had been.

"Angela what?"

"Jordan." And she extended her hand.

I shook it and said, "I'm Jack Ryan. From Milwaukee. I get through here from time to time."

"Really?"

"That's right. And, like I said, I stopped by your lot, here, not long ago. Had my eye on a buggy. A Buick."

"And you don't see it here? Do you know the model?"

"No. It was a big car, or as big as they make 'em now. Dark blue, with a sky-blue interior, white walls . . ."

"I think I can show you a similar car, but not with that color combination . . . funny."

"What is?"

"I think I know the car you mean. A Regency. Beautiful car." She lifted her eyebrows. "It's just funny that you should ask about that particular unit."

We were walking into the used car area now. There was a gentle but chilly breeze; pennants flapped above us.

And I asked her again: "What's funny about it?"

She sighed, crinkled her cheeks with a wide, closed-mouth smile. "It was stolen."

I shook my head and made a world-weary face. "Really. That's terrible."

She grunted agreement, then said, "Of all the cars on the lot, that one was the only one taken."

"I suppose somebody hot-wired it and just took off."

"I suppose. We never had a car stolen before. I mean, I'm pretty new, like I said, but Don has been here for years, and he said he never heard of such a thing."

"Really."

"Yes. And it just happened, you know."

"Really."

"Actually, I . . . well. Why don't you let me show you something similar to the unit you had your eye on."

"You started to say something. About the stolen car."

"Well, Lonny—Mr. Best—just reported it stolen, yesterday."

"Mr. Best? You mean the 'Best' in BEST BUY is a name?"

"Sure." She looked at me with just a tinge of suspicion, or maybe it was just curiosity. "I thought you said you got through this area from time to time."

"Well, I do, but only recently. I've only been working in Iowa and Illinois since the beginning of October."

"I see," she said. "Now, I know we have a like-new Regency, it's a copper-brown, but . . ."

"Excuse me, Angela. Mind if I call you Angela? You said that car I wanted *was just* reported stolen, like that surprised you."

"Well . . . I noticed it was off the lot on Wednesday morning, and I asked Lonny who'd sold it. He said nobody, and I asked where it was, and he said he thought it was being serviced."

That was about as far as I dared push it.

I said, "What have you got in a smaller car?"

She gave me a puzzled, if good-natured, look. "I thought you wanted a big Buick . . ."

"I did. But it got stolen. What about that little black Sunbird?"

We walked over to it and she put her hand on the hood, gently, almost affectionately.

"It's a cute little car," she said. "It does have some miles on it—but a one-owner. The camel interior is lovely, don't you think? I drive a little Sunbird myself."

It had a cardboard sign in the window that said $2,500.

"What would you say to two grand cash?"

She raised an eyebrow, smiled. "I think that's a possibility. I'll have to check with Lonny. Mr. Best."

"That's fine. I'd like to meet Mr. Best. Lonny."

She showed her teeth and her dimples; they went well together. "I think that can be arranged."

I followed her back up the lot and into the showroom, where Cadillacs and other pricey barges were in dry dock. Soon I was inside a cubbyhole office decorated with GMC awards, classic car photos and, on a special shelf, golf trophies.

"Mr. Best," Angela said, "this is Jack Ryan. He's made an offer on the black Sunbird."

Lonny Best stood behind his desk and smiled, a big glad-hander's grin that let me know that no sale was too small to command the boss's attention. A few years older than me, he was nonetheless boyish, and fairly small—perhaps five-eight—and just this side of chunky, with short brown hair and apple-red apple cheeks that spoke of high blood pressure; his eyes were small and dark and bright, the eyes of a predator, or a salesman, if there's a difference.

His red blazer was thrown over the back of his chair; he wore the white short-sleeve shirt, red-white-and-blue striped tie and white slacks that seemed a part of the BEST BUY uniform. He thrust his hand out for me to shake and I did. He suggested I pull up a chair and I did. He gave Angela a nod, which I supposed was a silent command for her to gather the paperwork, and then turned his too-pleasant smile on me. If his smile had been any bigger, there wouldn't have been room in the little office for the two of us. If it had been any less sincere, I'd have lost all my faith in my fellow man.

"That's a nice little car," he said. "Mind if I smoke?"

"Go ahead," I said, and smiled meaninglessly.

He lit a filtered cigarette, one of those low nicotine and tar brands that let you die slower.

"You drive a hard bargain," he said, winking at me, giving me a sly ol' grin. "But I think two thousand is a reasonable offer."

"Well, this is a second car. For my wife. I also need to get something bigger, newer. Had my eye on that dark blue Buick that Ms. Jordan says got stolen out from under you the other day."

He shook his head, laughed, as if something were funny. "Damnedest thing. Almost fifty years since my dad started this business, God rest him, and never had a car stolen before. Right off the damn lot."

"Awful," I said, world-weary again. "How do you suppose they managed it?"

His smile turned curious and perhaps a shade irritated; he cocked his head to one side like a dog and said, "Pardon?"

"How do you suppose whoever it was managed to steal it, right off your lot? On one of the busiest streets in the

Cities, I would guess. Constantly traveled, and your lot's well lit."

He shrugged elaborately, still smiling, said, "Well, folks are always driving through the lot, after hours, browsing. Probably wouldn't be so tough to do. Maybe we're lucky it never happened before."

"Don't you have security?"

His smile showed some strain. "Not on the lot, no. But the boys in blue swing by, and a local security company has us on their route."

I made a tch-tch sound. "Yet you still get a car swiped off your lot."

"I guess there isn't anything they wouldn't steal these days. What do you expect?"

"I know," I said, shaking my head in disgust.

"That's what you get," he explained, no trace of the smile now, "in a welfare state full of dope addicts."

"That's what you get," I nodded.

"Country's going to hell in a handbasket," he said. "But don't get me started on politics."

"I don't mind. I like a lively political discussion."

His smile drifted to one side of his face. "Well, I got to warn you, Jack—my views are a little on the conservative side."

"That's fine with me, Lonny. I'm just a little to the right of Genghis Khan myself."

He laughed, though I wasn't entirely sure he understood the remark. "You have to *expect* wholesale theft in a society where the police are hamstrung, and the courts are soft on crime."

"I couldn't agree more," I said. "How do you feel about this fella Preston Freed? Isn't he from around here?"

He frowned. Swallowed. "I draw the line where that

bastard is concerned—if you're a supporter of his, I don't mean to offend you . . ."

"I'm not and you haven't."

"He goes just too far. Too damn far."

"I don't know," I said. "He sure makes a lot of sense where prayer in school is concerned, and abortion. He's got a healthy anti-drug posture, don't you think?"

"Maybe so, but . . . well, here's Angela."

She came in, smiling sunnily; she had indeed got the paperwork together, and handed it to Best. He looked it over, informed me matter-of-factly that license and tax and so on would be on top of my two grand, and I didn't bitch. I handed over the cash and we shook hands and I said, "I had an ulterior motive, coming to see you."

"Oh?"

"Could we have a word in private?"

He nodded, then nodded to Angela, who disappeared in another swish of nylon, closing the door behind her. "What can I do for you, Jack?"

"Maybe I can do something for you. I'm in the auto parts business. Used."

"Well, I'm afraid I'm not in the market . . ."

"Hear me out. I think I can provide you with *like-new* auto parts. Regularly."

His eyes narrowed; his smile was, for the first time, sincere. Which is to say crooked, in more than one sense of the word. "I may understand at that."

"I have people in Milwaukee and Chicago who can provide you with about anything you might need. Reasonably."

He was nodding slowly.

"I've been working all over the Midwest, from Missouri to Wisconsin. But you're the first person I've approached in this area."

He lifted both eyebrows. "I'd need to be the only person you approached."

"Fine. I understand you have another lot on the Illinois side."

"Yes. And one in Clinton."

"Why don't you think it over," I said, rising. "I'll be in town a while. We can talk later."

He stood, too. "I have a business partner I'll need to discuss this with."

"Understood."

"Jack, if we do business . . . I don't want to know any more than what you've just told me. I don't know anything about you and/or your business. As far as I know, you're a reputable auto parts dealer from Milwaukee."

"Sure, Lonny. Far as we're both concerned, a chop shop is a Chinese restaurant."

He liked that. He laughed. Sincerely.

We shook hands and I left him in his cubbyhole office with his opinions about wholesale theft and the criminal justice system.

I had, I knew, in one stroke established myself with a cover story that was both believable and shady enough to serve my purpose, over these next few days. I had also learned plenty about Lonny Best.

Outside, Angela was waiting with my Sunbird and my keys. I arranged with her to have the car delivered to the Blackhawk Hotel; I had my rental to return. She was helpful and, the sale made, more relaxed, more real.

The sun bathed us, despite the chilly air; her congeniality seemed genuine, and so did her interest in me. My interest in her was pretty abstract. She was a beautiful woman, and I found her attractive and pleasant, but right now I had no plans for my dick except taking the occasional leak.

"I hope to see you again," she said, warmly, touching my hand.

The little flags flapped overhead.

I glanced around this lot where that dark-blue Buick had sat, just a few days before, the vehicle that had brought death back into my life.

"You will," I said, and got in the rental.

EIGHT

It was only ten minutes from Best Buy Buick to Paul Revere Square; I turned off Kimberly Road onto Jersey Ridge, a funeral home off to my right, and pulled in at the left, between the brick pillars, the wrought-iron gates standing open, as if welcoming me to a private estate.

Paul Revere Square was an ersatz slice of New England plopped along the frontage of Kimberly Road, a sprawling commercial strip on the western edge of the Cities, connecting Davenport and Moline. Mostly Kimberly was middle-class mini-malls, and franchise restaurants with "Mister" in their names; but Paul Revere Square seemed to cry out, "The wealthy are coming."

I parked my rental job in the side lot and walked toward the courtyard square where wooden signs extended from buildings on wrought iron, swinging in the gentle chilly breeze, and lampposts lit up the overcast afternoon with yellow electric lights that pretended to be gas. Despite the efforts to look old, these brick buildings were new, the mortar barely dry, and a good many of the storefronts had yet to be filled. Saturday afternoon or not, there weren't many people wandering the courtyard of shops, though those who were there were well-dressed.

Several handsome fortyish women in mink jackets over slacks outfits wandered into a shop where, a glance in the window informed me, fancy dresses were displayed on the walls like museum pieces.

Two- and three-story brick buildings—an anomaly on this commercial stretch where low-slung and cheaply built was the standard—loomed on the periphery, making me feel more like I was in a fortress than a mall. Of course, this wasn't just a mall; various medical specialists kept offices here, and Butterworth Tours, E. F. Hutton, several insurance firms, a massive bank. Building A, for instance, numbered among its occupants the Obstetrics and Gynecology Group, and Slices and Scoops. The latter had nothing to do with either obstetrics or gynecology: it was a deli restaurant with "home-made" pie. I ate lunch there. So did several pregnant women.

Just after one o'clock, I wandered into Ridge Real Estate World, on a lower level around the corner from the courtyard shops. I found myself in a waiting room where cream carpet and cream walls set a soothing tone, and a large elaborately framed picture of George Ridge, the company founder, was the dominant wall decoration. The wall was otherwise covered with plaques various civic and mercantile groups had awarded to Ridge and/or his company. A good number seemed to have to do with public speaking; several were from the Toastmasters, for instance.

I stood and stared at the picture of Ridge for a good long time, and finally I heard a pleasant voice say, "Could I be of help?"

She was brunette and she was petite and she was attractive; she wasn't as attractive as Angela back at Best Buy, but this woman, too, had most likely been a cheerleader and/or a beauty queen, only somewhat more recently than Angela.

She had money-green eyes and too much make-up and a forced, sparkling white smile. She also wore a blazer: a blue one with a RIDGE crest over a white frilly blouse.

This, apparently, was my day to encounter attractive women in blazers.

I put on a smile and walked over to the desk. "I had an appointment with Mr. Ridge," I said.

I thought that would send her scurrying to a desk drawer for her appointment book, but she only smiled and shook her head. "You must be mistaken," she said.

I took off the smile, put on a concerned, confused look. "I don't think that's possible. My secretary called . . ."

"Mr. Ridge is out of the country. I'm sorry if there's been a mix-up."

"I see. Where is Mr. Ridge, exactly?"

Her smile tightened. "He's in Canada. Giving a seminar. He will be back Tuesday, however."

"And available?"

"Yes. I can probably make an appointment for you, for then."

"I'd appreciate that." I dug for my billfold in my inside suitcoat pocket, removed a business card. "My name is Ryan, and I'm president of the company. I'm sorry for the confusion I've caused."

"That's fine, Mr. Ryan," she said, coldly pleasant. "And might I ask the nature of your business with Mr. Ridge?"

"I'd like to invest some money," I said. Her smile disappeared; she didn't frown, but she definitely was not smiling.

"I'm afraid I don't understand," she said.

Why?

"Well," I said, "I really would prefer to discuss it with Mr. Ridge." Her eyes narrowed, and she kept them narrowed as she examined the business card. Then she stood and twitched her cold pleasant smile and said, "If you'll excuse me."

"Certainly," I said.

She left the reception area and I glanced around some more, wondering why anyone in a real estate office would be confused that I wanted to invest. But then this was the damnedest real estate office I'd ever seen. It was more like a doctor's reception area, or a lawyer's. Where were the prominently posted photos of houses with their detailed listings? Where were the eager-beaver agents, in their fucking blue blazers, scurrying after my (after anybody's) business?

Nothing here but this big fat gilt-framed photo of George Ridge, and an attractive, icy receptionist. I walked over to look toward where she'd gone; down to the left was a hallway off of which were a few offices. The place smelled new, smelled of money, yet it was small for a real estate operation, particularly one that had (as the late Mr. Werner had told me) made George Ridge a millionaire.

Finally she came back, a small woman with a nice body under that blazer and skirt, not that I cared. She gave me the phony smile and a hard appraising look from the money-green eyes.

"Mr. Janes will see you," she said.

I gave her a phony smile back. "And who is Mr. Janes?"

"He's a vice president with the company. He'll be able to help you."

"I'd like to see Mr. Ridge."

"He's out of the country."

"Who's on first?"

"Pardon?"

"I'll talk to Mr. Janes. Point me to him."

She walked me there; she was wearing Giorgio perfume.

Linda had used that. Expensive fucking shit.

The office was small and rather bare. Janes was a young, thin, pockmarked man wearing dark-rimmed glasses and a big smile. I'd seen a lot of smiles today, but this one I almost believed.

"Mr. Ryan," he said, grinning, pumping my hand, like we were long-lost buddies. "Sit down. Please."

A chair opposite him was waiting.

His desk was filled with paperwork and he was in his rolled-up shirtsleeves, his tie loose. He had a coffee cup, from which steam rose like a ghost.

"Excuse the mess," he said, and sipped the coffee. "Can I have Sally get you a cup?"

"No thanks. Kind of you, though."

"Excuse my appearance. I don't generally deal with the public on Saturday. I'm only working because half our staff is on the road this week, and I'm up to my armpits in alligators."

"I know the feeling."

He put the coffee cup down and folded his hands on top of some of the paperwork and leaned toward me, his eyes tightening, his smile tightening. "I understand you're looking for an investment opportunity."

"That's correct."

"Sally tells me you're the president of your own company." And he grinned, and shook his head, as if amazed, as if it was all he could do to keep from saying, "Gosh."

And the hell of it was, he seemed sincere.

"Frankly," I said, "all I did was hand Sally . . . is that your receptionist's name?"

He nodded, but added, "She's an executive assistant, though."

"Executive assistant. Sorry. Anyway, I just handed her

my card, is all. She doesn't know any more about my business than you do, but in point of fact I'm president of an auto parts outfit in Milwaukee. My secretary was supposed to have called and made an appointment for me to talk with Mr. Ridge, but there was a screw-up somewhere."

He laughed. "These things happen."

Christ, this guy made "Up with People" seem glum.

"At any rate," he said, "investment opportunities."

"Yes."

"You do understand we're a privately held company, not offering any stock."

Huh?

"Certainly," I said.

"Mr. Ridge will, I'm sure, appreciate your interest, but that's just the way it is. You're not the only one who's been so inspired by Mr. Ridge's program, or impressed enough by the growth of our company, to make such an inquiry."

"Perhaps we've got our wires crossed . . ."

"Have we?"

"Isn't this a real estate office?"

He seemed puzzled. "In what sense?"

"Well, in the sense of offering properties for sale. Houses, land. You know. Real estate."

And now he was amused. He laughed like a bad impressionist doing Burt Lancaster. "You don't think Mr. Ridge actually *sells* real estate, do you?"

Well, that answered one question: *who* was *definitely* on first.

"What exactly does Mr. Ridge sell?"

"Why, advice, of course." He sat up. "Is *that* all you're interested in?"

I smiled, shrugged.

He smiled ruefully, shook his head. "My apologies.

When Sally informed me that you were the president of your own company, that you'd had an appointment with Mr. Ridge that had somehow fallen through the cracks, that you wanted to invest with us . . . boy, is my face red. Excuse me."

He rose and left the small office.

I just sat there wondering what the fuck this was all about. I wondered if the son-of-a-bitch would be so cheerful if I let him suck on the nine-millimeter a while.

Then he entered and we exchanged shiteating smiles and he sat and handed me across a tan book about the size of a dictionary, only it wasn't a book: it opened up into a carrying case for a dozen cassettes.

"The whole program is there," he said.

"Program?"

"Everything you'll need to know about no-money-down real estate. How to take advantage of distressed properties. The creative use of credit cards. That is how George Ridge became a millionaire by the time he was thirty."

No-money-down real estate! Is *that* what this was?

"You don't sell real estate here," I said. "You're strictly in the business of selling books, tapes. Putting on seminars. How-to stuff."

"Certainly. Surely you knew that."

"Of course," I said. "But I was under the impression that you were also in the real estate business proper."

He shook his head no. "Not at all."

I didn't blame them. This scam was much safer.

"I was also under the impression that Mr. Ridge was available for private consultation."

"You desire direct advice on investing?"

"That's right. Excuse me, but I can't talk to a goddamn tape."

And I patted the tan carrying case.

He nodded, eyes narrowing, seeing the wisdom of that. "You'd like to sit at the feet of the guru of real estate, so to speak."

"You took the words right out of my mouth."

"I can understand your desire. And from time to time Mr. Ridge *does* do personal consulting. But it is expensive. He's a very busy man."

"I know. I understand he's in Canada, at the moment."

"Yes, Toronto, with two of our other top people."

"And he'll be back, on Tuesday?"

"Yes."

"I'd still like to arrange an appointment. Even fifteen minutes of his time would be appreciated."

Janes stood, increased the wattage on the smile, extended his hand. "I'm sure Sally can arrange that. Just tell her I've given my okay."

"You've been very helpful. What time Tuesday is Mr. Ridge getting back from Canada?"

"Oh, he isn't getting back on Tuesday. He's flying in Monday night."

That's all I wanted to know.

"As I say, you've been very helpful," I said, and left him and his positive attitude behind.

I stopped at the desk of the "executive assistant" and told her Janes had approved an appointment, and made one for eleven o'clock Tuesday morning. Fifteen minutes was all I got, but what the hell. I'd make and keep my own appointment with him, Monday night, when he arrived by plane from his Canadian seminar.

On my way out I paused again to stare at the portrait of George Ridge.

A friendly-looking, slightly heavy-set man of about fifty,

a smile cracking his well-lined face.

It had to be a recent picture. He had looked much the same when he came to my A-frame to offer me that million-dollar contract.

NINE

I dropped the rental Buick off at the airport, where I stopped in to check available flights to Toronto. There was nothing direct—all flights had O'Hare connections, with return trips likewise routed through Chicago. That meant anybody coming back from Toronto Monday night could be on one of half a dozen flights offered by a trio of small, shuttle-service airlines. This would make it easy for me to be on hand to welcome George Ridge home.

An airport shuttle bus dropped me at the Blackhawk Hotel, but I didn't go up to my room. I didn't even go into the lobby. Instead, I stopped in at the DEMOCRATIC ACTION PARTY NATIONAL CAMPAIGN HEAD-QUARTERS, which was located in one of the street-level storefronts that were a part of the hotel's eleven-story building.

A banner in the window wondered PRESTON FREED—WHY NOT A *REAL* PRESIDENT?, and so did several other smaller red, white and blue posters, without obstructing a view of the bustling activity within the modest boiler room set-up: two rows of half a dozen banquet tables on either side, with staffers manning (though more frequently woman-ing) the many phones, all of which were red, white or blue. The patriotic color scheme extended to the various posters on the white walls, which pictured Freed himself, a smiling, boyishly handsome man in his vague forties, with rather long stark white hair. On one side wall, where it could be viewed from the street through the front window, a large color portrait of the candidate revealed eyes that were spookily light blue in a well-tanned face. He was wearing a tan suede jacket and a riverboat gambler's string tie and looked, in the massive color blow-up, like a cross between Big Brother and Bret Maverick.

The busy campaign staffers were mostly young, between twenty and thirty, closer to twenty in most cases. It surprised me, somehow, though it shouldn't have. Vietnam-era relics like me have trouble believing the stories about a conservative younger generation, but here was the proof, as clean-cut and persistent as those Mormons who periodically show up at your door.

And so many of these zealots were young women. Girls. They weren't wearing blazers, like Angela at Best Buy and Sally at Ridge Real Estate; but they were color coordinated, like their phones: blouses of red, white or blue, skirts of the same; the designer label on these threads, if there were one, would most likely read Betsy Ross not Betsey Johnson. The men—boys—wore white shirts and red or blue ties and navy slacks.

There was almost constant movement, the living flag of the Freed campaign headquarters seeming to constantly wave as its individual components would gesture animatedly during the phone solicitations, or hop up eagerly from a seat to consult another staffer, often one of those with a computer, one per banquet table. Girls and boys with faces full of no experience, as pretty and handsome as a collection of Barbie and Ken dolls come to life, they were enough to make you wake up screaming from the American dream.

By the front window, in the small, eye-of-the-hurricane

reception area, were two tables of Democratic Action party literature, one of which bore a communal coffee urn, Styrofoam cups and a plate of cookies. I nibbled a cookie, a Lorna Doone, and thumbed through some of the campaign literature—much of it railing against the "Drug Conspiracy"—and overheard a phone solicitation by a pretty, bright-eyed blonde, of perhaps twenty.

"Your savings will be *safer* with us," she was saying, with the utter conviction of the very young. "You mustn't trust the banks—their collapse is *imminent* . . . I understand your concern . . . yes, unless Preston Freed is elected President, you can rest assured that your Social Security checks will stop within eighteen months. Your contribution is much appreciated, but I must stress that we can protect your *savings* as well."

I felt fingers tap my shoulder and I turned. A willowy redhead with a faint trail of freckles across her nose and dark blue eyes and red full lips was extending a hand for me to shake. She was in a red blouse and a blue skirt.

"Becky Shay," she said. "Volunteer for Democratic Action."

"Jack Ryan," I said, shaking her hand. "Holdout for Creative Skepticism."

Her smile glazed and so did her puppy-dog eager eyes, as she tried to sort that out.

I let go of her hand and said, "I'm just giving you a bit of a hard time. I'll tell you frankly—I picked up some literature on your party, at O'Hare, and read it on the plane coming here. I'm interested. I want to hear more."

The glaze melted away. "Where shall I start?"

"Anywhere you like."

She gestured toward the table of literature. "I'd suggest you pick up some of Mr. Freed's position papers. They are far more eloquent than I. And no contribution is necessary—though it is appreciated."

"What's the 'Drug Conspiracy?' "

"A complex alliance between the banks, certain governments and the crime syndicate."

"Oh. What are they conspiring to do, exactly?"

"To fatten themselves off the masses."

Everything this kid said sounded prerecorded; it was like hearing the robot Lincoln at Disneyland give the Gettysburg address: patriotic and hollow.

I leafed through a booklet. "This wouldn't happen to have anything to do with 'international Zionists,' by any chance?"

"Certainly. You've heard of the Illuminati?"

"Sure. I have all their records."

She ignored that; trying to kid her was like kidding a nun about the virgin birth.

She went on with the catechism: "The forces of evil are gathering. Only Preston Freed can lead this country out of the darkness."

"We're talking your basic good versus evil here."

"Precisely," she said. "The future of humanity is at stake."

I gestured with the booklet, nodded over at the two tables piled with them. "I see a lot here about what's wrong about America. And let's grant that there is a lot wrong. But what does your party intend to replace all of that with?"

"Common sense," she said, with a smug little smile.

Yeah, that oughta do it.

"Well," I said, smiling back, "you've given me a lot of food for thought. Suppose I wanted to make a contribution?"

Her smile widened, the smugness evaporated. "Why,

that would be wonderful . . ."

"I mean a sizeable contribution. Of a thousand dollars or more."

She touched my arm. "You'd immediately become a member."

"A member?"

In a hushed, pious voice she intoned: "Of the Democratic Action Policy Committee."

"I never dreamed," I said.

She just smiled.

"But I'd like to know how my money would be used," I said. "Where it would go."

She frowned a little, as if that were a concept that had never dawned on her.

I pressed on. "I'd like to talk to Mr. Freed's campaign manager. If I'm going to make a contribution of this size, I want to go straight to the top."

She thought about that.

"It's only common sense," I said.

She nodded, and went down the aisle between the rows of tables. I followed, but when we reached a closed door at the rear, she turned and raised a forefinger and narrowed her dark blues to tell me not to follow her into the office. She wasn't in there long, however.

Smiling, she ushered me in, and shut the door behind her, leaving me in a conference room where the walls were covered by a huge, much marked-up calendar, several arcane charts and various large maps—one of the United States, another of Iowa, another of New Hampshire, another of various Iowa counties and communities. Sticking pins of various colors in the Davenport map, as if it were a flat voodoo doll that controlled the city, was a man in his late forties in shirtsleeves and loosened tie. He did not wear the glee club apparel of his young staff, however; his pants were gray, and went with the gray suitcoat slung over a chair at the conference table. He had salt-and-pepper hair, longish but receding, and was well-fed but not fat, with a fleshy, intelligent face.

He put one more color-coded pin into the map, and turned a steel-gray gaze on me, as well as a practiced smile, a sly smile unlike those of the Night of Living Conservatives bunch in the outer room.

"You're Mr. Ryan," he said, and shook my hand. "I'm Frank Neely, campaign manager."

"A pleasure, Mr. Neely," I said. I gave him one of my business cards. "I'm doing some business in the Quad Cities and wanted to stop by. I knew Preston Freed's national HQ was located here, and I was anxious to get a first-hand look."

His smile remained, but his eyes turned wary. "Becky indicated you were a . . . *fresh* convert to our cause."

"Frankly no," I said, smiling back, taking the liberty of sitting at the conference table. "I've followed Preston Freed for some time. I only pretended to be a novice, so I could test the mettle of your staff. I can't say I was much impressed."

"Really," he said with concern, remaining wary and on his feet.

"Becky, if that's the name of the young woman who greeted me, is a good-looking kid. But her line of patter is strictly rote. She's like a damn tour guide."

He laughed, and finally sat, crossed his legs, ankle on knee.

"It's a problem," he said. "These kids are very enthusiastic, and very hard workers. They come into the party alert and questioning, but they get so indoctrinated, after a while, that they become, well, rather single-minded."

"They should be able to discuss the issues, not just parrot the party line."

"I couldn't agree more. What's your interest in the Democratic Action party, Mr. Ryan?"

"I just like what Preston Freed stands for. I represent a loose, informal group of businessmen from my community. We want to contribute several thousand dollars to the party—perhaps as much as ten."

He raised his eyebrows.

I raised one of mine. "But I want to make sure we wouldn't be pissing our money away."

He gestured around his little war room. "Do you think we'd make this effort if we didn't think it would amount to something?"

"Well, frankly, you yourself are probably well paid. Most professional campaign managers are. And your staff is obviously fresh out of college, looking for meaningful work, taking on a low-paying position for the experience and out of belief in a cause. Kids right out of college who haven't figured out, yet, that you can't deposit a cause in the bank."

He nodded, smiled wryly.

"And I would imagine some of your staff are college kids, drawing on the various campuses in the area . . . Augustana, St. Ambrose, Palmer . . ."

"Yes," he admitted. "Most of the area colleges allow political science students to work on campaigns for academic credit."

"So," I said, "I see that it's extremely possible for me to be pissing my and my associates' money away by donating to your party's election efforts. We might be better off supporting conservatives within the Republican party. Candidates who actually have a chance of winning."

"You're underestimating us, Mr. Ryan," he said, shaking his head. "We've been at this for a long, long time. This will be our third Presidential race. In our first attempt, we gathered less than eighty thousand votes in the national primaries. But last time around, we racked up a quarter of a million. And this year? Anything is possible."

"Except victory."

"You're not a fool, Mr. Ryan, nor am I, and certainly Preston Freed is anything *but* a fool. Victory is a practical impossibility." He raised a forefinger in a lecturing gesture. "However, we're undoubtedly going to be putting on the strongest third-party candidacy since George Wallace in 1968."

"You're anticipating that Preston Freed will become a kingmaker, at the Democratic Convention."

"We do anticipate that. Who can say what victories will come from that? And we can look forward to the *next* election. If our rate of growth continues, the next time around Preston Freed will be a viable candidate, and the Democratic Action party will be a third, vital, major party."

"All of this from a storefront in Davenport, Iowa."

"Don't be deceived, Mr. Ryan. This is only the first stop on the primary trail. We're getting an early start. The Iowa precinct caucuses January twenty-first sound the opening gun of the presidential race. But we're running *now*. Our candidate will begin making public appearances next week. Our volunteers, our staffers, will cover every county in Iowa, door-to-door and by telephone."

"And then on to New Hampshire."

"On to New Hampshire. And at least a dozen more primaries after that, and we'll be purchasing radio and TV spots in each of those states. Beyond that, we've already purchased four half-hour national television broadcasts."

"I'm starting to feel encouraged."

"You should feel encouraged. And the presidency is only the most visible aspect of our strategy. I don't have to tell you that where the Democratic Action party has made strides is in local and state government—we'll field thousands of candidates in those races, and we'll win a good share. We've done it before."

"You sure made a mess out of Illinois state politics not so long ago."

That made him grin. "Thank you. I had a certain small hand in that. We've had similar successes in California, Texas, Maryland and Oregon."

I stood and offered him my hand. "I won't take up any more of your time, Mr. Neely. I'll be talking to my fellow business people, back in Milwaukee. My report will be favorable."

His grin went ear to ear as he shook my hand. "I'm very glad to hear that. You will not, I assure you, be pissing any money away. All of you gentlemen will be welcome members of the Democratic Action Policy Committee."

I looked forward to getting the secret decoder ring.

"I had hoped," I said, "considering this is the national headquarters and all, to get to meet the candidate himself. Have a little one-on-one discussion, however briefly."

Neely shook his head and his smile turned regretful. "I wish that were possible. Mr. Freed doesn't drop by here often. In fact, not at all. And these headquarters, despite the 'national' designation, are strictly for the Iowa effort. We have a suite of offices upstairs, in the hotel, for our executive staff; and the actual command center is at the Freed estate."

"Not far from here," I said.

"Not far from here," he said, "but I'm afraid Mr. Freed

doesn't meet with individuals often . . . although once we know the exact size of your contribution, well. . . . But do keep in mind, Preston Freed is a political genius, and like all geniuses, he has his eccentricities. He's a bit of a recluse."

"Isn't that unusual for a political candidate?"

"Frankly, it is, and I've had to work on Preston to get him to come out and 'press the flesh' in these primary campaigns. You must understand that there are many people who would like to see Preston Freed dead."

"Such as?"

"The Soviets."

I managed not to laugh, and merely nodded with concern. "I can see that."

"And of course, the Mafia."

"The *Mafia?*"

"Certainly. You've read the Freed position paper on the Drug Conspiracy?"

"Oh yes. The alliance between the banking community and the crime syndicate."

He shook his head somberly. "It's all around us. Infiltrated like a spreading cancer. Did you see the papers today?"

"Actually, no."

"A local businessman was murdered just last night—by a syndicate assassin, it's thought."

"That's shocking."

"I know it is. Apparently this man—who I thought was a respectable member of the community, hell, we belonged to the same country club!—had a long history of 'mob ties,' as the QC *Times* put it."

"Disgraceful."

"Well, then you can understand why a man with the strong views and the bitter enemies of a Preston Freed would choose to fight from within a fortress, so to speak. In the last campaign, Preston made no public appearances, restricting himself to radio and TV speeches." Disgust twisted his mouth. "The Reagan administration ruled that we do not qualify for Secret Service protection, which shows you that our enemies are not restricted to Russians and Sicilians."

"But now Freed plans to get out among the voters."

Neely nodded. "Yes—at the insistence of myself and his top advisors. If we're to make our move into the political mainstream, to become the viable third party that we are already starting to become, to leave the stigma of the so-called 'lunatic fringe' behind, Preston Freed must emerge from his fortress and do battle in the corrupt outside world."

Arch as that sounded, Neely was right: there was no place in the scheme of things for an armchair politician. And, of course, as I well knew, the threat to Freed's life was a real one, even if it didn't have anything to do with the Soviet Union, even if the mob connection was only tangential.

"Does Freed have any enemies in the business community?"

"Certainly," Neely said.

"Anyone specifically?"

He paused. Then, rather reluctantly, he said, "One does come to mind. You have to understand that the Democratic Action party's policies represent neither the left nor the right, as conventionally defined. Some of what we stand for is thought of as conservative, and yet Preston Freed was first thought of as a leftist, and in fact led a splinter group out of the old SDS, during the sixties."

"Meaning?"

"One of Preston's best friends, closest advisors, who'd

been with him since those early days, became . . . frankly . . . disenchanted with some of the party policies, as we have become more aligned with what are seen as 'right-wing' ideologies." His voice seemed weary. "It's a loss to us all, that one of the movers and shakers of our party should go over to the other side."

"The other side?"

He nodded. "The Democrats. Of course, it would be no better if it were the Republicans. But in George's case, it was the Democrats . . . he's made sizable donations, been active in fund-raising and so on."

"You don't mean George Ridge, the real-estate guy?"

"Well, yes I do . . . let's say nothing more about it. All great causes suffer setbacks. But with Preston going high profile for this primary push, we can overcome anything."

He walked me to the door. Put a hand on my shoulder. "The thing of it is, Jack—if I may call you Jack—Preston is a charismatic public speaker. His personal magnetism is, frankly, our secret weapon. It's worked before."

"Germany, for example," I said, pleasantly.

And I smiled and patted him on the shoulder, and moved through noisy, bustling Zombie Central and out into the cold but real world.

TEN

The Embers restaurant was in Moline, just off 52nd Avenue, near South Park Shopping Center and not far from the airport. A two-story, brown-shingled, rambling affair in the midst of its own little park, the Embers was perched along the Rock River like just another rustic, if oversize, cottage. I left the black, "like-new" Sunbird in a nearly empty lot (it was late afternoon—before the supper hour) and briefly wandered the pine-scattered grounds, noting a teepee and a totem pole, a white pagoda bird bath, a statue or two of a Catholic saint, stone benches, wooden picnic tables, and a bright red sleigh awaiting snow. Along the gray river, with a well-traveled overpass bridge looming at left, was a cluster of gazebos with red-canvas roofs; there was even a band shell. Here and there plaster animals, deer mostly, were poised in plaster perfection, to make you feel close to nature.

This was just the sort of oddball, cobbled-together joint that went over well with tourists and locals alike. As the former owner of the Welcome Inn, I felt at home.

An awning covered the lengthy astro-turfed walkway up to the entrance, which was the back door of the place really, and a narrow wood-paneled hallway, decorated with ducks-in-flight prints and various signs ("Casual dress required," "Home of Aqua Ski Theater"), led to an unattended hat check area where I left my overcoat, with stairs to the right and a bar to the left.

I went into the bar, which opened out onto a dining room with a river view. The Embers' interior was just as studiedly rustic and quaint as the grounds. The ceiling was low and open-beamed with slowly churning fans, and there were plants and ferns here and there, though a Yuppie joint this was not. The barroom walls were populated with stuffed animals—small ones, birds and fish mostly. If the Bates Motel had had a restaurant, this would have been it.

A youngish blonde guy with glasses and a white shirt was working behind the bar. "We'll be serving dinner in about half an hour," he said.

"Fine. I'll wait."

"You can sit at the bar, or the hostess will be here in a moment and seat you."

"Fine," I said, noncommittally.

A couple of businessmen were sitting at the bar having drinks, munching peanuts. I noted several ashtrays cradling Embers matchbooks like those I'd found in the dark blue Buick.

I sat at a small round table near the big brick fireplace; a fire was going, and the warmth was all right with me. The afternoon had grown colder.

On the hearth was an aquarium, about two feet tall and four-and-a-half feet wide. In the tank swam a fish, silver, and a foot and a half long. He had a very sour expression. He would glide slowly to one end of his tank, make a swishing turn and glide to the other end of the tank, make a swishing turn and you get the idea. I supposed his life was no more meaningless than anybody else's.

"He's from the Amazon River," somebody said.

I looked up. It was the blonde bartender; he'd come over out of boredom or to take my order or something. He was perhaps twenty-five years old. The fish tank's lights reflected in his glasses.

"Amazon River, huh," I said.

"Notice the little goldfish down toward the bottom of the tank? They're his supper."

This fish tank sort of summed up everything anybody needed to know about life.

"I guess that makes him King Shit," I said.

"Guess so," the bartender said. "Till we come in some morning and he's belly up. Can I get you anything?"

"Well, it won't be fish."

"I mean, from the bar. We aren't serving dinner . . ."

"Till five, right. Just a Coke. Diet, with a twist of lemon."

He nodded and went briskly back behind the bar. I got

up and went and took the glass of Coke from him, to save him another trip. I sat two stools down from the businessmen and sipped my soda and said to the bartender, "This place been here a while?"

"Thirty-five years," he said. "Original owners are still associated with the place."

"Associated with it? You mean they don't own it anymore?"

"No. They just manage it. Some flood damage a few years ago hit 'em hard, and a local businessman bought 'em out." He made a clicking sound in his cheek and shook his head.

"Something wrong?"

"Well, I don't know what's going to happen now."

"What do you mean?"

"You're not from around here, obviously, but d'you see the papers today?"

"Sure."

"That fella that was shot? Ja read about that?"

"I'm vaguely familiar with the story."

"He owned this place."

I fingered a book of matches in the ashtray. "No kidding. What sort of guy was he?"

"Okay," he shrugged. "He wasn't around all that much. This was just another investment, I'd guess. One of many."

I lit a match, studied the flame.

"You want some cigarettes?" the bartender said.

I smiled, waved the match out. "No. I don't smoke. It's bad for you."

"Here's the hostess. She can seat you. We'll be serving in about fifteen minutes."

I turned and watched the hostess approach.

She was a very attractive blonde with dark blue eyes, in a

light blue, wide white-belted turtleneck dress, menus tucked under her arm. She filled the dress out nicely, if not spectacularly, but what was most impressive was the white dazzling smile. That, and the fact that I knew her.

She recognized me immediately, too. "Why, Mr. Ryan. Hello again."

I climbed off the bar stool. "How many jobs do you *have*, Ms. Jordan?"

"Make it Angela and I'll make it Jack. Deal?"

"Deal."

"And it's two jobs. Full-time at Best Buy, and weekends here. I'm a single, working parent."

"How many kids?"

"Two. Both girls. One in second grade, another in sixth. Where would you like to sit? The upstairs dining room doesn't open till six, but you can eat out here in the bar, by the fire, if you like, or . . ."

"Out where I can have a river view."

"Fine."

And I followed her through the dining room proper, past prints of riverboats and your occasional cigar store Indian, out onto a sort of sun porch, a glassed-in greenhouse-like area with plenty of plants and more rustic knickknacks.

I sat down and said, "Why don't you join me for a few minutes? Nobody's here yet."

She smiled, glanced behind her. "I shouldn't."

"Have a seat. After all, the boss is dead."

She tipped her head, viewed me through narrowed eyes. "How do you know that?"

"I read the papers. Sit down, please."

"That wasn't a very nice thing to say."

"If the fella was a friend of yours, I apologize. I was just trying to get your attention."

She smirked wryly. "Well, you got it." And she sat across from me, on the edge of her chair, ready to get up at a moment's notice, casting an occasional eye through the dining room into the bar area, watching for customers. A few waitresses, in black skirts and white blouses, were milling around.

"Really, that was a thoughtless thing to say," I said, and shook my head.

"That's okay." She leaned forward. "He was a son-of-a-bitch, anyway."

I smiled. "Really?"

She raised a hand and squeezed the air, palm up. "Handsy. You know."

"That's illegal. Sexual harassment."

"Tell me about it."

"How's your other boss in that department?"

"Lonny? He's very sweet to me. We're just friends."

"You say that like maybe he wishes you were more."

"Well . . ." She smiled a little, a modest smile, showing just a touch of dazzling white. "Maybe he does. Frankly, I got *both* these jobs because of who I am."

"Who are you?"

"Maybe I should say who I *was*. This is embarrassing. I hardly know you."

"I'm the guy who bought a car from you today."

"And don't think I don't appreciate it. The commission will help pay Jenny's orthodontics bill. Her father sure won't."

"No alimony? No child support?"

"He's way behind. The courts are slow. What can I say? But I have him to thank for my two jobs, in a way. That's what I started to say. Lonny Best is a good friend of Bob's, my husband, ex-husband. I think he . . . Lonny always . . . well, a woman knows."

117

"When one of her husband's friends has the hots for her, you mean."

She laughed shortly and shook her head. "Do you always say exactly what's on your mind?"

"No. The world isn't ready for that just yet."

Her smile turned arch. "Is that right?"

"That's right. So Lonny Best feels sorry for the sorry financial condition his pal Bob has put you in."

"Something like that. We have something else in common, too." She glanced out at the bar; no customers yet.

"What's that?"

"Well . . . boy, this is a little much to get into. Why do you want to know this?"

"I like you."

Wry little smirk. "Oh, yeah?"

"I bought a car from you, didn't I?"

"You're milkin' that for all it's worth, aren't you?"

"Wringing it dry. But I like to get to know a woman, if I'm attracted to her."

"You seem to say most of what's on your mind."

"What else do you and Lonny Best have in common? It's not stamp collecting."

"It's not stamp collecting," she admitted. "Lonny and Bob and I met . . . this sounds stupid. At a political rally."

"A political rally."

"Yes, I was there because this actor from a soap opera . . . this sounds really stupid . . . this actor was speaking. On behalf of the candidate. I just wanted to see this actor, get his autograph. I didn't care two cents about politics either way."

"When was this?"

"Roughly ten years ago. Anyway, I met Bob and was,

well, attracted to him right off the bat; thought he was real interesting. He was kind of a . . . well, a man's man. He'd been to Vietnam, he was in something called Air America, too."

A mercenary.

"He didn't *look* all that rugged, but he had a way about him. He seemed . . . dangerous. He was working for Victor Werner, on his 'personal staff,' at the time. What that amounted to was, well, he was a bodyguard. Carried a gun. I found that exciting. It sounds stupid, and immature, but I'm older and wiser now."

"What was *he* doing at this political rally? And don't tell me he was there to get the soap opera star's autograph, too."

"He'd been hired as security, another bodyguard stint really, but was told to blend in with the crowd. Only he ended up getting caught up in it, too."

"Caught up in it?"

She nodded, sighed, smiled sadly. "Preston Freed. He put both Bob and me under his spell. Bob's still under it. That's the problem."

"Preston Freed," I said, reflectively. "He's supposed to be a lunatic-fringe right-winger, isn't he?"

"He most certainly is," she said, and now her smile was tinged with self-disgust. "But you're talking to a real sucker for a persuasive line—or at least somebody who *used* to be a sucker for that kind of thing. I used to be a 'born-again' Christian—got saved over the TV when I was still in high school. I was into that heavy, which is how I met my *first* husband—a wimp and a weasel who ran off with a born-again *bitch*—and . . ." She shook her head again, not smiling. "Never again. Never again."

"Never again what?"

"Will I fall for some guy just because we belong to the same goddamn club. That's what these things are, you know."

"These things?"

"Ah, born-again anything. Preston Freed, his Democratic Action party, it's a club. No—it's a *cult*. Freed is a *great* speaker . . . hypnotic. He's got these light blue eyes, this terrific smile."

She said this smiling her own terrific smile. She could, under different circumstances, a lifetime or two ago, have made me join her cult, no questions asked.

"But Freed hasn't appeared in public much," I said.

"Not in recent years," she said. She laughed humorlessly. "He thinks the Russians want to kill him, and the Mafia . . . I think he's as self-deluded as his followers."

"If he's such a recluse, how does he control these followers?"

"Well, he goes on retreats with party members and staffers and such. And he's got that weekly cable TV show."

"TV show? I don't know anything about that."

"Oh, sure—it's a weekly half-hour show that he buys time for on all these cable channels. It's a 'news' show— only it's his version of the news—like pointing out which members of the President's cabinet are Soviet agents. He sells 'subscriptions' to his monthly magazine, *Freedom News*, and memberships to the party."

"Expensive?"

"The subscriptions are five hundred dollars a year. Party memberships are a thousand."

"Jesus. And people send in money?"

"Every day. I used to work for him; part of his secretarial staff at first, then helped produce the TV show. I was privy to this stuff—saw the envelopes with the cash."

"He's pocketing it?"

"Oh, sure, but he *does* plow a lot of it back into his campaign. He means it when he says he wants to be president. It's just . . . well . . . look, I've said enough. We've got way off the track here."

"No, I find this interesting. What soured you on Freed?"

Matter-of-fact facial shrug. "He's a hypocrite. He preaches against drugs, but he has a cocaine habit that puts Hollywood to shame. He rants and raves about the 'permissive society' and then sleeps with every female follower he can lay his paws on. And that's plenty of 'em."

I looked at her hard. "He tried to lay paws on you, too."

"Yes, he did. And I don't mean he was just 'handsy,' either. It was . . . much more serious than that. And when I told Bob . . ." She swallowed, shook her head. "This . . . this is too personal."

"Bob didn't care."

Eyebrow shrug. "Bob didn't believe me. I walked out. On Bob, and on that fucker Freed."

She stared at the tablecloth.

"Where does Lonny Best fit in?"

"He was a loyal Freed supporter, too, once upon a time. But he got disgusted about a year ago and dropped out. Freed's excesses, personal and political, finally got to Lonny."

"So he sympathized with your situation and gave you a job."

She nodded. "That about sums it up, I guess."

"Is the same true of Werner?"

"Pretty much. He stopped by Best Buy one day—just a few months ago—to talk to Lonny about something. Then he came out on the lot and talked to me, asked how I was doing. I said making ends meet, and he asked me if I was interested in moonlighting here, on the weekends. I said sure."

"Nice of him."

"He had his hand on my hip when he asked, so I knew what I might be up against. But he wasn't around here much. Actually, tonight was his night. Saturday night, I mean. He and his wife would have dinner. Even with her along, though, he'd manage to cop a feel."

"At least you don't have to put up with that anymore."

"Hey. Please. I didn't wish the guy dead."

"Just because he's dead doesn't mean you have to start thinking nice thoughts about him."

"Yeah," she said, indignantly. "What do I have to feel guilty about? I didn't kill him."

"Me either," I said, and smiled.

That made her laugh.

"You're a character. Whoops, I finally got customers."

"How late do you work tonight?"

She stood. "We serve till ten."

"Can I stop by for you?"

"I have my own car."

"I'm sure you do."

"Excuse me," she said, and went and tended to her customers.

A waitress came by and I ordered the barbecued ribs.

I was just finishing up when Angela stopped by the table and dropped a cocktail napkin before me.

"See you at ten," she'd written.

It was just a little after five now. That should give me time to do what I needed to do.

ELEVEN

I'd been down this road before. But it had been years ago, and the road had been dark then and was darker now. The moon, just a faint blur in an overcast sky, was no help; only my headlights lit the world, which is to say the stretch of concrete immediately before me.

This was the River Road, the road in question being narrow two-lane Highway 22, the river the Mississippi, although its presence over at my left—not at all far away— couldn't be proved by me. A blackness of trees, beyond the railroad tracks, obscured any river view.

Soon—not far from Davenport, really—the quarry began, or signs of it anyway: dunes of crushed rock rose at my right like monstrous anthills; my headlights caught swirls of powder, which built into a modest but steady dust storm. Then, at left, skeletal steel buildings and machinery mingled with silo-like structures, awash in a greenish-gray glow, amber lights winking here and there, white billowing smokestacks lathering the dark sky, tempting God's razor.

And now on my right was the vast quarry, acres of emptiness, beautiful in its barrenness, a natural wonder enduring this ongoing invasion stoically. An enclosed conveyor mechanism slashed across the sky diagonally, from the plant to the quarry, going again and again to this limestone well to make little bags of cement, and bigger bags of money.

Beyond the mile-long quarry was Buffalo, a village whose small business section—a few unpretentious restaurants, antique shop, gas station—was scattered along the right, with railroad tracks and, finally, the visible Mississippi at left, its surface reflecting the gray filtering of moonlight.

And beyond Buffalo was another quarry, an abandoned

one, filled with water now, put there by man or nature or somebody, so that it was, in effect, a lake. And on that lake, above its shimmering surface, above the ledges of limestone, was a house. It was not small; its lines were modern in the Frank Lloyd Wright sense, with the central part of the house a story taller than the rest. A few lights were on, glowing yellowy behind sheer curtains. From the highway, looking across the expanse of what for lack of a better term I'll call Lake Quarry, it seemed not just distant, but abstract.

Behind the house, the bluff rose, thick with trees; those trees were bare, but no matter—tonight they were an ebony blot against the charcoal sky. The home—the estate—of Preston Freed was seemingly impregnable. Fuck it; I was going calling, anyway.

Half a mile or so down, there was a road—two narrow lanes of gravel—that seemed the most likely access to the Freed estate. My Sunbird stirred up dust, climbing the bluff until it leveled out, and dipped and farmland began appearing on my left; but on my right was forest, and barbed wire with Signs that said, PRIVATE PROPERTY—TRESPASSERS WILL BE SHOT. Added to one of the signs, by somebody unimpressed by these cornfield threats, was: AND EATEN.

Soon, off to my right, a paved driveway materialized, blocked by a heavy, unpainted steel gate—nothing fancy, just formidable. A car, a brown Ford, was parked on the other side of the gate, on the grass, and somebody was in it; the orange glow of a cigarette showed on the driver's side.

I'd gotten a good look, going by, and without attracting undue attention, either. On gravel like this, you had to move slow; and on a night this dark, the watchdog in the parked Ford couldn't see whether I was looking his way or not. And what the hell, with that massive, unpleasant-

looking gate, anybody driving by for the first time was
bound to gawk a little.

About a mile down I found a little access inlet to a
cornfield, and I left the Sunbird there. I was wearing a black
windbreaker over a black turtleneck sweater with
black slacks and . . . let's just say I was wearing your basic
black and leave it at that. I wasn't nervous, but I wasn't not
nervous. Home invasions are not, as I believe I said, my
style. And a home invasion where an estate is involved—an
estate inhabited by a wealthy paranoid political crackpot
who thinks the Soviets are after him—was like nothing I'd
ever attempted.

I had a nine-millimeter in the shoulder holster, under
the windbreaker, which was unzipped. I did not have the
noise suppressor attached. If this little endeavor came apart
on me, I could need to do a lot of shooting, fast, considering the number of bodyguards and security types this guy
would likely employ. And a silenced gun can't be used rapid
fire; you have to work the action by hand, each round, because the gas you're suppressing, to keep the gun quiet, is
the very thing that makes the automatic automatic.

What I had instead—and what was in my hand this very
moment as I moved across the gravel road to the barbed
wire fence and its warning signs—was a so-called stun gun.
I'd picked it up at a pawnshop in Davenport this afternoon.
I'd never used one before, though I was plenty familiar with
the principle, as I'd carried its bulkier relative, the Taser,
on some jobs right before I quit the business.

The Nova XR-5000 Stun Gun was pocket size, not
much bigger than a doctor's beeper, which it somewhat re-
sembled; its two brass studs would send not a beep, but a
47,000-volt message. I gave it a test burst, and an arc
snapped and sizzled whitely between the two test elec-

trodes. Just like in an old Frankenstein movie.

This toy had its drawbacks: you had to be in direct contact with your man, and the jolt of the thing would probably make your man scream; it took three to five seconds of contact to make the subject lose muscle control. The Taser, on the other hand, shot darts, and at a good distance. But then the Taser needed reloading every two darts, and this puppy carried around thirty hits, if properly recharged.

Tonight, you see, I had to be careful not to kill anybody. It was a pain in the ass, but it was necessary.

The barbed wire fence was only waist high; it could be stepped over without much difficulty, if you were careful, and I was. For all the threatening NO TRESPASSING signs, and the heavy gate, Freed's security wasn't anything to write home about. State of the art it wasn't. There were no television cameras down by that gate, nor was the gate anything that couldn't be ducked under or over. Killing the watchdog in the Ford would be no real challenge to anybody who even vaguely knew what he was doing.

I moved slowly, breath visible in the chill air, easing through the trees, most of which were bare of leaves, though there were occasional pines, so I had both leaves and needles under my sneakered feet, which made for some crunching no matter how hard I tried not. I wasn't any fucking commando, after all, though I'd done some jungle fighting. But you didn't run into many pine cones or beds of leaves where I had my on-the-job training.

Finally I came to the edge of the trees and the house was perched on a gently rolling, landscaped lawn, like a tiny toy house on top of a great big cake. Only it wasn't a tiny house: it sprawled, an angular, many-windowed affair, dark natural wood and sandstone giving it the feel of a cabin or lodge.

My vantage point was to the right rear of the place; in back there was a big garage—big enough for a small fleet of cars—which connected to that paved driveway, which I now could see traveled along the edge of the quarry drop-off. I was up high enough to see the view: Lake Quarry; the narrow highway; some trees and the Mississippi beyond. Even on this dreary night, it was some view. A man who lived in a house like that—who owned a house like that— who looked out on a view like that—could come to think of himself as pretty all fucking powerful.

I almost didn't see the guard. He walked right by me, not five feet away. The trees hid me, and he was lazy, not directing his flashlight into the trees; in fact, his flashlight wasn't even on.

But he was a burly guy, in a heavy brown leather bomber jacket with a .357 mag on his hip; he looked like a sheriff's deputy but without the insignia. He didn't hear me come up behind him, slip the stun gun under his coat and against the small of his back. My hand was over his mouth, stifling his scream, slapping the wide slash of adhesive tape in place and his body shook from the shock of it. Nice part is, the shock doesn't transfer from his body to yours. You just hold on, pressing the button while counting One Mississippi, Two Mississippi, Three Mississippi, Four Mississippi, Five Mississippi, and he just does this pathetic jitterbug in your arms, wetting his pants.

I lowered him to the ground and brought his hands behind him, using flex-cuffs to bind him. I bought a gross of these "throw-away handcuffs" years ago—they're like garbage bag ties, little lightweight pieces of plastic with a serrated tip that draws up tight through an eye. I put another one of them around his ankles—the only way these things could be removed was by cutting the fuckers off—

and dragged him by the feet into the forest. He smelled bad. Full bladder.

There wasn't piss on his jacket, however, and he was enough bigger than me that it fit over my own; his keys were in the jacket pocket. He was out of it. It would be fifteen minutes before his brain resumed control. I removed his black western-styled holster and slung on his .357 mag. I picked up his flashlight, which he had dropped (understandably) and carried it in my left hand—the stun gun in my right, twenty-nine or so more pops to go—and moved with casual authority across the rolling golf-course of a lawn, toward the house.

It was a walk that took probably three minutes and only seemed an eternity. I walked across the paved area to the back of the house, where a stone stairway with wood banister rose to a landing flush with what was probably the kitchen, and was about to go up when the door opened and another sentry came out and said to somebody within, "It's quiet tonight, too quiet," archly ominous. And then he laughed. He was another big man, wearing jeans and plaid shirt with a big revolver on his hip. Probably another .357.

He was standing on the landing, lighting up a cigarette when I joined him and put the stun gun in his belly, slapping tape across his open mouth, his eyes so wide the white showing overwhelmed iris and pupil. He struggled, and I pushed against him, maintaining the contact, and he danced with the jolt, and peed, and broke the railing behind him and landed on his back about a story down. I pondered going down and cuffing him, but figured the sound of wood breaking and flesh-and-bone thumping might have roused people within the house, and I couldn't fuck around with it.

So I went inside, and it was a kitchen, a big, white, gleaming kitchen you could feed an army out of, though, incongruously, there was but a tiny table in its midst, where a paperback adventure novel was folded open, a cup of steaming coffee nearby, another empty cup before another chair, which was pulled out. No one sat at this table; apparently my most recent dancing partner had been sitting there. But so had somebody else, and where was the guy? Or was he the one who was sleeping in the forest, at the moment?

I moved into the house; the floor was slate—a stone waterfall, lit from below with amber lights, gurgled under a winding, open staircase. Off to the right was an office area, a secretarial post apparently, several photocopy machines, three desks with small computers, counters and cupboards for storage and work areas, the wall space decorated with framed posters from Freed's various campaigns, all of them showing his white-haired, tanned, blue-eyed, boyishly smiling countenance. As much as ten years separated some of the posters, yet he seemed the same in them all; plastic surgery, or a portrait aging in the attic, maybe.

The secretarial room opened doorless onto what was apparently a conference room, although it had a fireplace (unlit) over which reigned a framed oil painting of Freed, dressed as a riverboat captain, and a small but well-stocked bar was in one corner. This room was hung with wildlife paintings and prints and glassed-in displays of frontier weaponry, rifles, bowie knives, the like. Attached to this warm, open-beamed room, with no doorway separating it, was a small office/study, with a desk and many phones and a wall of photos of Freed with celebrities (including Angela Jordan's soap opera star), and two walls of books—political ones exclusively, authors ranging from Adolf Hitler to Robert F. Kennedy, from Karl Marx to Eugene McCarthy.

"Have you seen Dick?" somebody behind me asked.

I picked up a paperweight from the desk—a heavy brass replica of the Presidential seal, about as big around as a glazed doughnut—and turned and hurled it into the stomach of the approaching bodyguard, another brute, the missing link from the kitchen table, this one with thinning blonde hair and a light blue workshirt and jeans and, on his hip, the ever-present .357 mag.

Which he was going for, incidentally, when I reached out and shoved the stun gun in his belly and pressed the button; he let a yelp out, but not much of one, because the paperweight I had tossed into him, like a discus, had knocked the wind out of him and he hadn't recovered. And now he was busy doing the electrical dance. I kept my hand over his mouth till he was under, and eased him down. He didn't pee. Maybe that's where he'd been: the john.

I did take the time to flex-cuff this guy, hands and ankles both, and slap some tape on his mouth, and went back the way I'd come—past the winding staircase and waterfall, past the front entryway, and into a living room with the breathtaking picture-window view I'd expected. There was another fireplace, also unlit; over it was another oil portrait of Freed—this time dressed in buckskins, like a frontier hero. The furnishings were modern and expensive but looked comfortable; modular stuff, earth tones. A big twenty-seven-inch console TV was perched in one corner. Glass sliding doors opened onto a patio, or did in nicer weather, anyway.

I back-tracked again, and went up the winding staircase. I found myself in a round room, a circular bar with more political posters and Freed memorabilia on display, a few more antique frontier weapons hanging, and windows on the world. Chairs were gathered around the edges of the circle, as if someone (gee, I wonder who) might have occasion to stand center stage and pontificate in the round.

Off to the right, I could hear muffled sound; then laughter, also muffled. I moved closer to it. From behind a door, to the left of a well-stocked, leather-fronted bar. Talking, laughter, very muffled.

Sitcom.

Somebody was watching TV in there. But who, and how many of them were there? Well, sometimes one is reduced to the obvious. I looked through the keyhole.

Another large bodyguard type was sitting in a chair, and he was smiling; the chair was comfortable, he had a can of beer in one hand, and Bill Cosby was on the TV screen. What more could a man ask for?

I was on top of him putting the stun gun in his belly as he slouched there before he could do anything but try to scream into my hand and the adhesive strip, and pee his pants. Beer'll do it to you.

I cuffed him, hands in back, and secured his ankles, too, then looked around what seemed to be the quarters for the security staff. Though not much more than a cubicle, there was a TV, a small refrigerator, a couple of couches, several stacks of men's magazines and paperbacks and a private bathroom. Then I explored the room beyond: a simple guest room, double bed, empty dresser.

Moving back into the circular bar, I tried another doorway, found myself in a hallway; past a closed side door, at the end of the hall, was light. Muted light, but light, like the first glow of dawn over the horizon. If you get up that early.

I rounded the corner and there, on a waterbed the size of New Jersey, on black silk sheets, a mirror overhead, was the Democratic Action party's candidate, with his dick in the mouth of an attractive young woman. Or at least what I could see of her was attractive: her ass was to me.

That's where I hit her with the stun gun.

Right above the crack of it, actually, and fortunately for Freed, she opened her mouth wide, rather than clamp down, and I slipped the tape over her mouth and gave her a three-second jolt, which did the trick. Freed recoiled, his icy blue eyes damn near as shocked as the unconscious girl, who I noticed with certain amusement was the redhead from his campaign headquarters. He'd been feeding her the party line, but now he plastered his naked self against the fancy western-carved headboard of the waterbed, withering.

"W-What do you w-want?" he said. Even stuttering, his voice was melodious, like a radio announcer's.

"Sorry about your silk sheets," I said, making a tch-tch sound, noting the dampness the girl had caused.

"If you're going to kill me," he said, suddenly brave, "then get it over with."

"If I'd have agreed to kill you," I said, "my life wouldn't be so fucked up now. And you'd already be dead."

The blue eyes narrowed. "The Soviets?" he asked.

"Put some clothes on," I sighed. "I don't talk business with naked politicians."

TWELVE

He slipped into a dark blue silk robe while I cuffed the girl's hands and ankles. I moved her off the area of the bed she'd made wet—it was the least I could do—carrying her in my arms like a big baby. She was a nice looking woman, despite the circumstances.

He stood nearby, while I did that, nervous but hiding it pretty well. He was taller than me, and had considerable bearing, the mane of white hair, the china-blue eyes, the dark tan, a striking human being; feeling no humiliation at all, it would seem, despite being caught with his pants down.

"Are you going to tell me what this is about?" His baritone, melodious or not, did have an edge of irritation. Not that I blamed him. Nobody likes to get interrupted in the middle of a blow job.

"We have to get a couple things straight first," I said, and the nine-millimeter was in my gloved right hand now, the stun gun tucked away in a jacket pocket, his sentry's .357 on my hip.

"Such as?" he said. He had winced, just slightly, upon sight of the automatic; otherwise he maintained an admirable cool.

"Do we have it understood," I said, "that if I were here to kill you, you'd be dead by now? That if I were here to steal from you, you'd be trussed up and we wouldn't be talking at all? That if this were a kidnapping, I'd have hauled your ass out of here already? Do we understand all that?"

He nodded very slowly. The light blue eyes bored into me like soothing lasers. Their color reminded me of Linda's eyes. I tried not to think about that.

"I came in here the way I did for a couple of reasons," I said, "all of them good. First, you're not an easy man to see. I tried finding you at your campaign headquarters, and heard all about how reclusive you are. Second, I wanted to show you that if somebody *did* want to see you bad enough, they could get it done, reclusive or not."

His mouth twitched in a half-smile. "I thought I had excellent security."

"Your security is pretty half-assed. But even if it were

great, you could be gotten to. Anybody can be gotten to."

"If you're not here to kill me or steal from me or kidnap me," he said, "why *are* you here?"

"To make you a business offer, for one thing. For another, to save your life."

An eyebrow arched. "Why don't we go out in the bar and talk."

"Fine. But if any of your staff should show up—somebody I don't know about, or the one guy I didn't take time to bind up, or anybody else with a gun or something—you're going to make 'em back off. Otherwise, people are going to get hurt. And I can just about guarantee you, you'll be one of them."

He nodded, as if to say, *fair enough.*

"Could I use the bathroom first?" he asked.

There was one off the bedroom.

"Sure," I said. "Leave the door open."

He frowned at that, but said nothing. He went in there but didn't use the john. He ran water, washed his hands. Then he bent over the counter, like he was almost kissing it. I didn't know what he was up to, until he turned and was wiping a little white powder off his nose. The small mirror on the bathroom counter reflected the overhead light.

Then I followed him out into the circular bar.

"Would you care for something to drink?" he asked.

"No. But help yourself."

He went to the bar and poured himself several fingers of Scotch. Not one to deny himself anything, he withdrew a long fat cigar from a box on the bar and lit it with a wooden match; then he sat in a captain's chair, which he had dragged to the center of the circle, and motioned for me to sit nearby. I chose instead to take a chair that put my back to the wall and gave me a view of several doors and the open stairway. I kept the gun in my hand and in my lap.

"And what do I call you?" he asked. Half the room between us.

"You can call me Quarry. It's not my name, exactly, but it'll do."

"All right, Mr. Quarry. Perhaps you can explain why you've invaded my home—and, apparently, put my entire security staff out of commission."

"Let me ask you something first. If someone, this afternoon, had told you that one man would enter your compound and put you in the position you're in right now, what would you have said?"

"I would have found it impossible. Unbelievable."

"Fine. Keep that in mind when you consider the story I'm about to tell."

And I told Preston Freed, self-styled presidential candidate, the story. That I was a retired professional assassin who had been offered a million-dollar contract; that he was the target of said contract; that I had refused the contract; that an attempt on my life had subsequently been made. I did not mention the loss of my wife, my life at Paradise Lake. That was none of his fucking business.

Freed listened to this with rapt attention, eyebrows arching, nostrils flaring, eyes narrowing, widening, as one might expect. But disbelief was something I did not sense. Perhaps in a way I was making a dream come true for him: his paranoia was finally being substantiated, even if the Soviets weren't involved.

"Now," I said, "it would seem to me we have some mutual interests in this matter. For my part, I'd like to respond in kind to those who tried to have me killed."

"Understandable," Freed said, nodding.

"And you, I would think, would like to identify those

who're trying to have *you* killed."

"Frankly," he said, drawing on the thick cigar, "I'd like to do more than just identify them."

"I thought you might. You need to consider exactly what this situation is: I turned the contract down. That made me a loose end—in a political assassination, involving a national figure, a presidential candidate, one does not leave loose ends. But that speaks only to *my* situation. What about yours?"

"Mine?"

"Someone else—someone else like me—was approached with that million-dollar contract. Someone who *accepted* it."

"Is this a conclusion you've drawn, or . . . ?"

"It's more. It's direct knowledge. I understand you fear retaliation from what you describe as the 'Drug Conspiracy'—the banks and the mob."

"The Sicilian/Hebrew Connection," he said, nodding.

"Spare me. But I will give you this much: somebody with mob connections who died recently gave me that information."

The icy blue eyes narrowed to slits in the tanned face. "Victor Werner? You killed Victor Werner?"

"I didn't say that. Did you know him?"

"I never met the man, but I knew of him." Then, with contempt: "Knew of his 'family' ties. He told you of a *second* assassin?"

"Yes, Werner gave me a name. It's a name I'm familiar with. Which is one reason why I think I can head this thing off."

"Head it off?"

"I can stop the hit from going down. Because I know who it was that came to see me, the upstanding citizen who tried to hire me. And I know who he hired in my place."

"I have to do something about this!"

"No kidding. Look, we can go about this a couple of ways. I can just tell you who these people are, and fade away. You have men on your staff; you might be able to deal with this in-house."

I knew he wouldn't want that; but saying this gave me leverage.

"What's the other way?" he asked, sitting forward.

"I could handle it all. I can take out the other hitter. I can take out those who hired it done, as well."

"There . . . there might be more than *one* person behind this?"

"The man who tried to hire me said he was representing a group of patriotic private citizens."

He laughed mirthlessly at that. "And you said, this individual spoke of me as a 'spoiler'—meaning this threat might have come from the right *or* the left?"

I nodded.

"If I . . . were to turn you *loose* on this, to handle it as you wish . . . what would be in it for *you,* besides a certain satisfaction?"

I shrugged. "Well, the revenge factor is going to work in your favor. That 'certain satisfaction' you mentioned is going to make a hell of a perk. So all I need is ten grand. And you don't owe me anything unless I deliver."

Those spooky blues studied me suspiciously. "You said you were offered a million dollars."

"Ten grand for the assassin. Ten more for whoever hired him."

"That's still only twenty thousand dollars."

"Feel free to tip."

"Will they . . . look like accidents?"

"Not necessarily. No frills. Dead is dead."

He blew out a stream of smoke and raised his eyebrows and considered the ceiling's open beams.

"You know the name of the man who came to see you," he said.

"That's right. I did some snooping today."

"Are you a detective, or an assassin, Mr. Quarry?"

"Necessity has turned me into a little of both, Mr. Freed. Now do you want my help? Or do you want to handle this yourself, in which case I'll have to ask a finder's fee of five grand, if you want the names I know."

He was thinking.

"Or," I said, "I can just walk out of here, fade into the forest and out of your life. You can choose to not believe me. Or try to deal with this yourself, without the names."

He was shaking his head no. "I would like, Mr. Quarry, for you to handle this. But I wish to know none of the . . . messier details."

"That's best for all concerned."

"I would, however, like to know the name of the man who came to see you. Who tried to hire you?"

"You agree to my terms? Ten grand with a ten grand bonus?"

"Yes."

I drew my upper lip back across my teeth; it was my very worst smile. "Guess what I do if somebody reneges on me."

"I think I can guess that quite easily, Mr. Quarry."

"His name is George Ridge."

He sat up. Turned ashen.

"George Ridge," he intoned. "George . . ."

"You were friends once."

"Yes . . . yes, we were. He was one of my staunchest supporters . . ."

"And something went wrong."

He stood, began slowly to wander amidst the framed political posters and memorabilia. "How much do you know about me—that is, about my party?"

"I'm not political, Mr. Freed. I just don't care."

He ignored that. "You must understand—I am thought of, in most quarters, these days, as right-wing. That is a gross simplification. It is an attempt by the powers-that-be, of both major political camps, in league with the media, to defuse my efforts; the Illuminati understand that a third political party, not beholden to the bankers and the mobsters, with a *real* candidate, not some rehearsed synthetic one, threatens their stranglehold on America, on the world."

"Mr. Freed . . ."

"I have a ten-year plan, Mr. Quarry," he said, and his voice, his presence, added up to something persuasive, despite the Looney Tunes text. "I must keep it, or humanity is doomed. It is unlikely—though not impossible—that I will secure the Presidency this year; but in the following election, I *can and must* win—and global alliances are but a step away."

"Yeah, right. Look . . ."

"I'm keeping this simple, Mr. Quarry, because you say you are not political. But you live in a world, a society, controlled by politics. What is politics but human relationships? Make love not war, we once said; but *both* are politics!"

"Right. What about George Ridge?"

He looked out the window into darkness. "We were great friends. You must understand that my political adventure began in the sixties—in Far Left groups; you may recall the SDS, where both George and I were quite active, where George and I met, in fact. But the SDS seemed to us not to be accomplishing its stated goals, and we broke away. This was at Berkeley, where we formed Strikeforce Freedom, to weed out the leftist groups who were only paying lip service to the cause."

"How did you weed them out exactly?"

"We armed ourselves," he said matter-of-factly. "Not with guns: nothing more lethal than a length of pipe or a chain. It was an important moment, because our people understood that rhetoric wasn't enough. You had to stand and fight."

"Is that your idea of politics? Violent overthrow of the government?"

"It was then, in those more innocent days," he said, smiling, as if discussing a childish phase he'd once gone through. "My roots were in Communism, socialism . . . but I moved on to embrace larger, wider ideals."

Such as bilking old people out of their savings, I supposed, thinking of the phone scam I'd witnessed in progress at his campaign HQ. Well, that was his business.

I said, "So what are you saying? Ridge maintained his left-wing leanings, while you moved to the right?"

"I am neither right nor left. The Democratic Action party embraces disaffected Republicans and Democrats alike; we have a goodly number of former Ku Klux Klan in our ranks, standing shoulder to shoulder with former SDS. I favor a free-energy economy, and an end to reactionary oligarchs and financiers . . ."

"That's just peachy keen. But getting back to Ridge— you seem more disappointed than surprised that he's behind this."

"I suppose you're right," he said, with a world-weary smile that quickly disappeared. "And I doubt he represents any group. I think this is personal. He feels I've betrayed him—and he has obviously betrayed me."

I put my hand up in a stop gesture. "I don't think we can operate from the assumption he's alone. He may well represent a group—and if he does, you need to know."

"What about this assassin? Your replacement?"

"I know him. How he works, how he thinks. He won't, I don't think, hit you here at home—although you need to expand and improve your security, obviously. But this guy, he'll do it when you're out and about. Out among the public."

"During my primary campaign," he said, tensing, stopping in front of me. "I make my first public appearance this Tuesday morning. I've set up a press conference at the Blackhawk Hotel—which will be well attended by the national media . . ."

"When Ridge came to see me," I said, "he specifically mentioned that press conference. If that's when the hit's going down, we don't have much time."

"What should we do? What can we do?"

I was a little out of my element; a political hit differed drastically from the work I had done, which invariably involved a two-man team, staking out the victim well before the hit, a methodical approach that went out the window when dealing with a sheltered national figure who would present himself as a target only at public events like the coming press conference.

"We'll start with Ridge," I said. "I'll deal with him myself."

"You sound sure of yourself."

"I am. I'll need some details about the man before I go; where he lives, anything about his habits—I already know where his office is. But anything that might be useful."

"I can certainly help you on that score. Could Ridge lead you to the assassin?"

"Possibly. Probably. But Ridge doesn't get back in the country till Monday night. So—if Tuesday's press conference is really it, we'll have to alert your security staff, just in case I haven't been able to shut this thing down by then."

"But you intend to try?"

"Of course. Like I said, I know the man who took the contract. He's a pro—very good at what he does; stopping him will not be easy—once put in motion, well . . . but I know him. I worked with him. That's to our advantage. And I may be able to use what I know about him to find him beforehand; if we're right about Tuesday morning, he's probably already in town."

He sat in the chair next to me and thought. He smelled of musky cologne. The big house was silent. Well, a clock was ticking someplace, but that was about it.

"Let me suggest something," Freed said, finally, with a sly smile, a fairly demented twinkle in the blue eyes.

"Yeah?"

He lifted a gently lecturing forefinger. "Don't attempt to deal with this assassin until he tries something . . ."

"What?"

"Let him be shot down in the *attempt* on my life."

"Are you crazy?" Stupid question.

"It would have excellent publicity value," he said. "I would be taken seriously, immediately. The current administration's failure to provide me with Secret Service bodyguards would create a scandal. The eyes of America, the world, would be tightly focused on Preston Freed."

I hate it when people talk about themselves in the third person.

"That would be a very dangerous game," I said.

"Would it? But if we knew he were coming . . ."

"We could half-bake a cake. No, I won't play that game,

Freed. It's too dangerous. For all concerned."

He shrugged. "All right. It's just a suggestion. But I'll say this: if you feel you could arrange it in that fashion, I could see my way clear to offering a second bonus. Twenty-five thousand dollars."

That was impressive. Not as impressive as a million dollars, but impressive enough for me to say, "I'll think it over."

He extended his hand. "Good. I must say you're a very brave man, Mr. Quarry, storming my citadel as you've done."

I shook the hand; it was firm, not sweating at all. He had his share of stones, too, willing to go on the firing line just to get some publicity. Or maybe it was the coke and the booze making him brave.

"I'll give you my private phone number," he said, and went to the bar and scribbled it on a pad. He tore off the sheet and handed it to me, saying, "Day or night. If we need to meet . . ."

"We will. I may want to brief your security people—just those involved with press conference security. You'll have to introduce me as a security expert or something. We'll work that out. Oh, and I made contact with your campaign manager. He'll be mentioning me to you—Jack Ryan, the name will be—he'll say I want a private meeting, in return for a sizable contribution. But one way or another, I want immediate acceptance as an insider with the campaign."

"Done," he said. "How do I contact you?"

"You don't. I contact you. And I don't want to be followed. If any of your people follow me, I'll just disappear and you'll be on your own. And you wouldn't want that."

"No I wouldn't." He sighed, shook his head. Even for a man like Preston Freed, this had been a lot to absorb. "What now?"

"Fill me in a little more on Ridge. Then you're going to pick out one of your bodyguards for me to uncuff, to have drive me back to my car."

"Christ, I hadn't thought about them! How do I explain you to 'em?"

"I'm a security expert, remember?"

"Ah, yes . . ."

"Tonight, I was just a little test you were giving 'em," I said. "To see how secure your 'citadel' really was."

"A test," he said, smiling, liking it.

"Yeah," I said. "And they flunked."

THIRTEEN

I was running a little late; it was ten thirty-five and I hadn't had time to change my clothes and was still wearing the black windbreaker, turtleneck and slacks. The holstered nine-millimeter and the stun gun and such were in the Sunbird's trunk. I might have smelled a little raunchy, too—I'm not particularly nervous by nature, but I do sweat, particularly when I storm citadels.

But storming that citadel and briefing its potentate had taken all evening, and when I picked her up at the Embers, where she was sitting at the bar with an empty martini glass in front of her, pretty legs crossed, now all in white, Angela Jordan was a little irritated and marginally pie-eyed. She lifted an eyebrow at the young blonde bartender and played with her martini glass, then looked at me and smirked and said, "What's this? A ninja?"

The bar was still doing some business and people out in the dining area were lingering over meals. The fish from the Amazon was still traveling back and forth in his little kingdom, nibbling goldfish.

"Sorry I'm late," I said. "Fell asleep back at the hotel."

And that was all the explanation it took.

"Aw, no problem," she said, and smiled without smirkiness. "Sorry I greeted ya with a smartass remark." She was a good-natured kid. She slid off the stool and I gave her my arm. She needed a little steadying. She wasn't sloshed, but just the same I said, "Why don't we take my car?"

"Good idea. Let's see how she runs."

"She runs fine," I said, as we strolled out into the brisk night air. "You wouldn't sell me a lemon, would you?"

She hugged my arm. "Not to you," she said, like we were old pals. Lovers, even.

I didn't know if I was game for that. I hadn't made this little rendezvous because I was looking to get laid. I supposed someday sex would interest me again, but with Linda gone, the thought of it seemed pretty abstract right now.

But I needed to get close to this lovely, lonely divorcee. She knew all the principals: Best, Freed, and (having worked for Freed) presumably Ridge, even the late Mr. Werner. I might get some information. I might get some insights. It was my best option right now.

"Sorry I look so informal," I said, behind the wheel, exiting the Embers' lot.

"I don't mind," she said, settled comfortably in the bucket seat.

"Would you like to get a bite to eat?"

"No, I don't think so."

"Something to drink?"

"That'd be nice. How 'bout my place?"

"Your place?"

"My house. The girls are with my mom. She takes 'em

on the weekend, Friday and Saturday nights, that is. Between the restaurant and the car lot, I work most of the weekend. It's better for the girls."

"That'd be nice. If I'm not imposing."

"Don't be silly," she said.

"You'll have to guide me. I don't know my way around the Cities all that well."

"Head over to Davenport and go up Brady Street. It's a housing addition way out past the shopping malls and everything."

"Okay," I said, and pretty soon I looked over and she was slumped against the door, sleeping. Snoring a bit.

I didn't figure it was that she'd had all that much to drink. More that she was just bone tired, working two jobs to support her little family. It sort of pissed me off that her husband wasn't paying his share. There's a lot of lowlifes in this world.

We'd just glided past a shopping center called Brady Eighty, with signs signaling Interstate 80 up ahead, when I nudged her awake.

She sat up with a start and was immediately embarrassed. "Oh, Jack, I'm sorry . . . really . . ."

"Don't worry about it. You work hard. You get tired. You're entitled."

She rubbed one eye with the heel of a hand, smiled in a crinkly fashion. "You're really very nice."

"Yeah, I hear that all the time."

"It's right up here."

"What?"

"The Hastings addition. Where I live. Just to your right."

I made a turn into well-lit, well-tended, split-level suburbia. The houses were good size, but fairly close together.

It took money to live in this neighborhood, but these people weren't wealthy. Not, say, in the Victor Werner sense. Of course these people were alive, which is something they had over Werner.

She directed me into the driveway of a two-tone green split-level and I parked, got out, opened her door, gave her my arm and walked her up the curving sidewalk with its occasional steps. She wasn't drunk by any means; but she was tired, and she'd had a few. She fumbled for her keys and then we were inside.

The entryway was a landing between floors; the lower floor, from what I could see of it, seemed to be a family room. I followed her up the open stairs half a flight into the plush living room. This was definitely the home of somebody who grew up lower middle-class and came into a little money. It had that would-be-classy look of an above-average motel. Lots of massive Mediterranean furniture, drapes gathered with tassels, sofas and chairs of green and red with crushed velvet cushions, sculptured green carpet. Coats of arms and reproductions of Rembrandts and such on the walls. It was the home of somebody who used to bowl but now golfs.

I followed her through the living room into a smaller, stone-and-brick room; it had a warm look, lots of rusts and golds and browns.

"You know how to make a fire?" she asked, getting behind the bar.

I looked over at the stone fireplace. "Sure. You don't have any wood, though."

"You'll have to go outside and get some."

"Uh, chop it or . . ."

"No, silly," she said, stirring a pitcher of martinis, "it's piled just outside on the patio. Through those glass doors."

I went outside into the chilly night. I breathed deep. Closed my eyes. Swallowed. Then I picked up an armload of firewood and went in and made a fire.

"What would you like?" she asked, as she poured herself a martini.

"Do you have a Coke? Diet, preferably."

"Do I have to drink alone?"

"I don't drink."

That seemed to disappoint her. "Oh?"

"I got nothing against it. It's just not a habit I picked up. You have whatever you want, however much you want. You're a hardworking girl. You got it coming."

"Thanks," she said. "You're a sweetie."

Actually, if she got a little drunker, I might get more information out of her.

She came over, in her nyloned stocking feet, the belt of the white dress gone now, and handed me a tall, icy glass of Coke.

"It's Diet," she said.

"Good," I said, sipping it. "I'm trying to take some weight off."

"That why you wear black?"

"It is slimming, isn't it?"

"You don't look heavy to me. Your face looks . . . well, actually it looks a little drawn."

"I haven't had much of an appetite the last few days."

"Oh, I see," she said, as if she did. "You make a nice fire."

"I've had some experience."

"Want to sit in front of it?"

I said nothing.

"I said, want to . . ."

"Sure," I said.

She tossed some cushions on the floor—it was a shag carpet in here, very homey—and we lay on them and watched the fire.

"You must think I'm terrible," she said.

"Why would I think that? Which I don't."

"Inviting a strange man to my home."

"I'm not a strange man. I'm a good customer."

She almost did a spit-take with her martini. "Geez, that sounds even *worse* . . ."

I smiled at her. "I didn't mean it to. I like you. I like being around you."

It wasn't a lie. It wasn't the reason I was here, but it wasn't a lie.

"I've had kind of a . . . rough time of it lately," she said. "I wanted some company tonight."

"Glad to oblige. Why a rough time?"

"My boss . . . Lonny . . ." Shook her head. "He's making things tough . . ."

"How so?"

"I like Lonny. We were friends for years, or anyway he and Bob and Laureen—that's Lonny's wife, ex-wife now—well, we were all friends. Socially, and involved with the party."

"Democratic Action party, you mean?"

"Right. And, anyway, Lonny's been really sweet, giving me this job and all. But he's been, well, pressuring me."

"He getting 'handsy,' too?"

"I wish it were that simple. He's asked me out. We've *been* out. I've . . . let him kiss me a few times." She made a face. "Damn, this sounds so, so *high* school. I've never slept with him. I just don't . . . don't feel that way about him."

She sipped her martini.

"But he's serious about you," I said.

She nodded. "I know now that he only gave me that job to be close to me."

"Afraid if you tell him you're not interested in him you'll lose your job?"

"That's not it, exactly. I'm good at what I do. I sell a lot of cars. I could go elsewhere, I really could. I was a good student, you know—or I was till my senior year, when dad died. I got pregnant in junior college, and was already involved with that Born Again bull, and my life sort of got away from me. Then working for Preston Freed I realized I *still* had brains, that I could go out in the business world and *make* something of myself, without Bob's help, screw him if he doesn't want to help his own kids . . . well, one of 'em's his, anyway."

"Then what's the big deal with telling Lonny how you feel? You're not afraid for your job, after all."

"I know," she said, rim of the martini glass near her lower lip, "but I *like* him. He's been sweet. I just don't want to hurt him."

"You afraid of hurting your ex-husband, too?"

"Bob? Why, what do you mean?"

"If he isn't paying his child support and alimony, throw his butt in jail."

She shook her head wearily. "It isn't that simple. Bob . . . that's something else that's been a little rough on me lately. Sorry if I sound like I'm feeling sorry for myself . . ."

"It's okay. Bob."

"Bob," she said. "You see, he wants me back. He says he's not going to run around anymore. Learned his lesson and all that garbage. He apologized for that time he didn't buy what I said about, you know, Freed getting 'friendly.' He . . . he wants his family back."

"Do you want *him* back?"

"No. I loved him once, but he's too smothering. He'd never let me work; this house was my world. And since the split I found out I *like* to work. Anyway, he's been coming around a lot . . . it's hard, it really is. See, he's holding back on what he's supposed to pay, knowing that for me to do anything about it I have to take him to court."

"Have you done that?"

"Yes. I saw an attorney six months ago. And faced with that, Bob paid up, four months' worth. Now he's pulled the same thing—three months behind. I'll have to go through the same damn rigmarole."

"Unless you take him back."

"Unless I take him back."

"Which is in the no-way-in-hell category, I'd guess."

"Sure is. Even though he's trying to work on me through the girls."

She stopped, something catching in her throat; she had tears in her eyes. She finished the martini and got up and got herself another one. I sat up and poked at the fire while she did that.

Then she settled herself on the cushion again, on her stomach, ankles crossed behind her, white dress hiked up, and said, "Why do you ask so many questions?"

"I'm interested in you."

"Why?"

"You got a nice smile."

"Is that all?"

"You got nice just about everything."

She gave me a kiss; even the alcohol on her breath didn't take anything away from it. Slow, kind of wet, very sweet. I liked it.

"You don't know me," I warned her, wondering why I was warning her.

"I don't want to know anybody right now," she said, smiled and sipped her martini. "Just want some company. Okay? Just be company."

"Fine."

We listened to the fire crackle.

Then I said, "Somehow I can't picture you getting caught up with this Freed character."

"Then you've never heard him speak. He's something. Those eyes really hold you. Charmed the pants off many a girl."

"You said as much earlier. He really fools around with a lot of those pretty young things on his staff?"

"He sure does. I was almost one of 'em, remember? But you know what I heard?"

"What did you hear?"

Giggled, sipped her martini. "I heard the damnedest rumor. Thing of it is, I think I believe it."

"Which is?"

"Well, you know he has this TV 'news' show, I told you about. In fact, I used to be sort of involved with it—if you call carting-the-tape-every-Monday-night-to-the-little-cable-outfit-that-does-his-uplinks being involved. He has a small but pretty elaborate studio at his house. Actually it's more than a house, it's kind of a mansion. Anyway, he tapes his weekly show right there."

"Yeah. So?"

"They say that's not *all* he tapes there. They say he's got a video-tape library, of all his 'conquests.' "

"You mean, his *sexual* conquests?"

"Yeah, yeah. There's this mirror over his bed, they say, and there's a camera behind it. He tapes himself doing it with these girls."

"You're kidding."

"I heard it on good authority. From a girl who found out and was pissed off, man, really pissed."

"So he doesn't tell them, then?"

"Hell, no! He just takes 'em into his bedroom and has his way with 'em and watches the replays to his heart's content."

There *was* a mirror over Freed's bed. And the bedroom *had* been well lit. And the candidate *was* a narcissistic son-of-a-bitch. It made a perverse sort of sense.

"And none of these girls knew, at the time at least, they were on camera. Can you imagine?"

If the Democrat Action party's presidential candidate had been taping tonight, I'd been on camera, too. Stunning the stunning behind of Freed's latest conquest. I didn't like the thought of that. Leaving my image on tape, no, that I couldn't allow. I'd have to check this out.

"Angela, what's the deal with Best and Freed? Why did Best drop out of the party? Did he get fed up with Freed's excesses—political and/or sexual?"

"Hey, this home porno-movie deal isn't well known, not at all. I don't think Lonny or anybody knows. I shouldn't have told you. If I wasn't who-knows-how-many-sheets-to-the-wind, I wouldn't't've."

"So it was a political rift, then?"

"What?"

"That split up Best and Freed."

"I don't think so. Frankly, I think Lonny still believes in what Freed stands for. But as a businessman, visible in the community, Lonny doesn't want to be associated with somebody controversial like Freed."

"Well, is Lonny active with any other political group?"

"He's a Republican. He gives 'em some money."

"But he's never been really active in politics since splitting with Freed."

"No. Not nearly. Why are you so interested in this?"

I'd gone too far with my questions. Time for a strategy shift.

I leaned close to her. "Well, frankly . . . can you keep a secret?"

She grinned, very crinkly. "Judging by the way I've been spilling things tonight, no. But I'm willing to try to learn."

"Good. I'm not really in the auto parts business. I'm in security work."

"You mean you're a detective?"

"No. Security. I was approached by Preston Freed to help him train and prepare his security team for the upcoming primary campaign."

That perked her up. "Oh, yeah?"

"I haven't taken the job yet. I knew Freed was something of a nut, and I didn't know if I wanted to get involved with him, professionally speaking. So I needed to check him and some of his friends out."

"Is that why you hit on me?"

There was no expression in her face. Her eyes, deep blue, were unreadable as they fixed upon me.

"Yes," I said.

She smiled sadly, looked into her martini.

"That," I said, "and your smile, and I wasn't lying about liking you."

"You came to the car lot looking for me, then?"

"No! That was a coincidence."

"A coincidence?"

"Well, I was there to check Best out. I didn't know anything about you. Just that you were a pretty woman in red, white, and blue—and I'm as patriotic as the next guy."

She smiled one-sidedly and touched my cheek. "I guess I don't take it back. That you're a nice guy."

"I didn't mean to take advantage of your good nature."

"Frankly," she said, "I wish you would."

She kissed me again; another slow, sweet, sticky kiss. She rolled over on top of me and my arms slipped around her, my hand settling on her ass, dress hiked up over pantyhose and panties; nice shape to her ass, soft yet firm. Something stirred in me, below the belt. She kept kissing and I kissed back. The fire was warm on us. I rolled over on top of her, felt her breasts through her dress; she reached behind and unzipped it and brought it down over her breasts in a wispy bra that she slipped down and my hands went onto her cool flesh, warming to my touch and the glow of the fire. Her nipples were hard under my fingertips and I put my mouth on her breasts, suckled, and she moved my hand to her pantyhose, inside her panties, in front, and I pulled away, like my fingers had touched fire, not soft curly hair.

I was breathing hard. Blinking. Something was wrong.

"Jack . . . Jack, what's wrong?"

She was sitting next to me, looking lovely if disheveled in the fire's glow, and I tried to say something but my tongue was thick. My dick wasn't.

"Jack, what is it? You're . . ."

"What?" I managed to say.

"You're crying."

I touched my face. I'll be damned if I wasn't.

"What is it, Jack?"

"I . . . I'm sorry, Angela. I just can't."

She smiled wryly, but sympathetically, her arm around my shoulder. "You were doing fine. Just fine."

"Can't."

She dabbed my face with the cloth of her dress. "What is it, Jack?"

"I lost my wife not long ago."

"Oh, Jack . . ."

"I . . . haven't been with a woman since."

She swallowed. Patted my shoulder. "How long has it been?"

"A year."

It seemed like a year. And it seemed like a moment ago.

"I guess I'm just not ready," I said.

"Oh, Jack, I understand."

"I feel funny."

"What is it?"

"The oddest feeling."

"Are you sick?"

"I don't know."

"You . . . you want some aspirin or something?"

"No. It'll be all right. Let me catch my breath."

What was this feeling?

"It's natural to feel a little guilty," she said.

Was *that* it? *Guilt?* Of all things.

"Why don't you stay here tonight," she said. "You can sleep out on the couch, if you like. We can just be there for each other. I think maybe we can both use some company tonight."

I nodded.

We walked back through the living room and down a hallway. Several family photographs in frames lined the wall. I stopped at one.

"Your girls?" I asked.

"Yes. Taken a few years ago."

"They look like you. They're going to be beauties."

She hugged my arm.

I envied her a little; even without a partner, she had something here. Kids and a house and a life. Mediterranean furniture or not, I could almost see myself here. In this house with this woman and her family and her life.

We moved to the next picture, a larger family portrait, and I stopped short.

"Your, uh, ex?" I asked.

"I should take it down, I know," she said. "But to the girls he's still dad."

"What's Bob doing for a living these days?" I asked her, studying the portrait.

"Are you okay, Jack?"

"What's he doing for a living?"

"He works for George Ridge now. Real estate counseling, I guess you'd call it."

I said nothing.

"Yeah," she went on, "he's making good money, too, flitting around. In Canada this weekend, some fancy deal."

"Is that right?" I said. "I . . . I don't think I can stay tonight, Angela."

The dark blue eyes were very wide as she searched my face. "Why not?"

"I'd like to. But I just can't."

"The guilt," she said, nodding sympathetically, eyes narrowing.

I said nothing. I just kissed her, briefly, and let her walk me out to my car.

And I drove away from there, from that house, from the family picture that included the round, pasty face, several facial moles and all, of the man who had come into my house and killed my wife, and my wife's brother, and who had in turn been killed by me.

FOURTEEN

Around ten the next morning, Sunday, I went down to the lobby of the hotel and had a word with the man at the desk.

"I'm working for the Freed campaign," I told him.

He nodded, smiled noncommittally. He was in his mid-twenties and blandly handsome; crisply dressed in a navy blazer and red and blue striped tie, he would be a manager here someday. The two women back behind the counter, doing the real work, wouldn't have a chance.

"With the press conference tomorrow," I said, "we have to be careful."

"Certainly," he said, the smile gone, very serious now, as if what I'd said was something he well knew, when actually it had never occurred to him.

"Our sources have informed us," I said, "that one of the major parties has hired a political dirty trickster to disrupt the press conference."

I was careful not to say which party. That way, if he were a Democrat he could assume Republican, and vice versa.

Whatever, he nodded, narrowed his eyes, leaned forward, pretended to be concerned.

"The agent provocateur in question," I said, "makes G. Gordon Liddy look like Mother Teresa."

He smiled at that, but a serious smile.

"We would like your help in keeping an eye out for him," I said. "We'd like no one but yourself—and your night relief—to be aware of this request."

"Do you have a photograph?"

"No. But I can give you a detailed physical description, and I know several of the names he frequently travels under."

"That's helpful."

"He's a slender man a few years shy of fifty. Six-one, pockmarked. Cleft chin. Eyes have kind of an oriental cast. Dark hair, widow's peak, pale complexion." I could tell, from his black expression, he wasn't visualizing anything yet, despite that laundry list of facial features. I tried again: "You know the guy in 'Star Trek'?"

"William Shatner?"

"No, the other one—but without the pointed ears."

He smiled, nodded.

"He looks something like that guy," I said. "He sometimes uses the name Stone. He sometimes uses the name Brackett. Sometimes Pond. Sometimes Green."

That was all the names I knew.

"Let me check the registry," he said, and he began flipping the little cards, looking up each name. "Nothing," he said.

"What about the description? Did it ring a bell?"

"Well, yes it did."

I leaned against the counter. "What room number?"

"No, I just meant I knew which guy on 'Star Trek' you meant."

Maybe he wouldn't be a manager someday.

"How long are you on?"

"Till five."

"Two other shifts, then, after you?"

"Yes."

"When does the graveyard shift start?"

"One A.M."

"Good." I handed him two twenties, folded once, lengthwise. "I'll talk to the two night men personally. You just keep this to yourself."

"That isn't necessary, sir," he said, meaning the money, which he was trying not to look at.

159

"Sure it is." I let go of the bills and they made a little tent on the counter. "Now, I'm going to have to look things over for security purposes. Where is the press conference going to be held?"

He pointed across the lobby to some stairs going down. "The Bix Beiderbecke Room," he said. "At nine o'clock Tuesday morning."

"Thanks. By the way, my status with the Freed campaign is known only by the top-level people. So don't go throwing my name around."

"Oh, what *is* your name, sir?"

"Ryan. Jack."

"Of course," he said, smiling, as if the name had just momentarily slipped his mind.

I gave him a smile and a little forefinger salute and left him and the money behind.

The Blackhawk was an older, recently refurbished hotel; the lobby's black and white marble floor gave it an Art Deco feel, though the extensive mahogany woodwork and whorehouse-red-trimmed-gold ceiling harked back to frontier days. The lobby wasn't small, but a low ceiling and comfortable furnishings made it seem intimate, as did the way the thick pillars separated it off into areas. A row of shops and offices—one of them the rear end of the Freed campaign headquarters—was just around the corner from the check-in desk.

I went down marble stairs, following a sign that said ARCADE, and found an arcade in the earlier, pre-Pac Man sense: a row of shops and businesses, about a half a block long, beneath the hotel lobby. The walls were light plaster and decorated with amateurish murals depicting New Orleans street scenes, in honor of Davenport's legendary Dixieland jazzman, Bix Beiderbecke, who died young. Frightened by the mural, possibly, with its grotesque Mardi Gras figures and frozen Basin Street musicians.

The shops were closed today, although from the looks of things, several stalls were shuttered no matter what day it was. Among those currently in business were a barber shop, a beauty shop, a shoeshine stand and an architect's office. A ghost town on Sunday; I was alone down here, despite the crowd brunching it upstairs at the hotel's Sundance Restaurant.

The arcade walkway was really just a hall—perhaps eight feet wide—with a fairly low ceiling made lower by chandelier-style light fixtures. At the end of the hallway were carpeted steps moving up into a newer, beige-brick section of the hotel.

But just prior to that was the entry to the Bix Beiderbecke Room, a short hallway with a short flight of steps that led down to an open area outside the room itself: a medium-size meeting hall with a door at right and another down at its other end, at left. I peeked in the door at right.

A podium was set up facing a room full of chairs, arranged in rows with a central aisle. Seating for probably a hundred or so. Standing in that doorway, I was within twenty feet of the podium.

I looked at my watch, waited for the second hand to point straight up. Then quickly ran from the doorway, down the short hall out to the arcade and up the carpeted steps. Checked the second hand.

Ten seconds.

I looked up from my watch and saw that I was indeed in the new part of the hotel, a high-ceilinged add-on that connected the Blackhawk with its parking. I was a few steps away from a door to the street, where there was plenty of parking at the curb on both sides of the wide one-way; and a few steps away from the parking garage itself, where if I had a car parked on the bottom floor nearby I was within seconds of wheeling out of here. A few more steps to my right, down a gentle Oriental-carpeted ramp-like walkway, were hotel elevators.

Back up the ramp, still in the beige-brick modern addendum, which was overseen by a huge, old-fashioned wall clock, I was facing the glass wall of the indoor swimming pool/sauna area. A few families were in there splashing around. I'd have a swim later. The door was kept locked— but your room key would open it.

The upper lobby's arcade connected nearby and I wandered back in, thinking over what I'd seen. A row of telephone booths, set in the mahogany walls, was at my right. I used one of the phones to call the number Freed had given me.

After several rings, Freed himself answered.

"Yes?" he said, thickly, obviously awakened by the call.

"This is Quarry."

"Quarry!"

"That's Jack Ryan to you."

"Yes, certainly—what is it?"

"I've had a look around here at the Blackhawk Hotel. We better have that security briefing we talked about. Gather the key people who are going to be covering your butt at the press conference. I need to talk to them."

"I can do that. When?"

"Is this afternoon too soon?"

"One o'clock?"

So I went in the front way this time, a hunting-jacketed sentry in the brown Ford climbing out to open the unpainted metal gate, and I drove down the paved drive, forest on either side of me, until I was driving along the edge of the quarry drop-off, the lake below shimmering with what little sunlight was filtering through today's overcast.

I parked in back and was met by an armed guard in a brown leather bomber jacket and tan slacks; he had that same deputy sheriff look as some of those I'd stun-gunned last night, but I didn't recognize this one, a round-faced man with rosy cheeks and thinning hair.

Me, I wasn't in ninja black today, but spiffed up in a suit and tie and brown leather overcoat.

Freed came down the wooden stairway in back, off the kitchen, its railing freshly repaired, and greeted me with a smile and an extended hand. I shook it, smiled back. He was wearing a blue suede jacket and a light blue shirt with a string tie; his mane of white hair brushed neatly back, and the light blue eyes in the tanned face, made him seem almost otherworldly.

"Jack," he said, "it's good to see you again."

And he slipped his arm around my shoulder.

"Been a long time," I said.

Soon we were in the open-beamed conference room, where the oil portrait of Freed as a riverboat captain held sway; at a large table sat four men, two of whom I recognized. All four stood as Freed introduced me, and one by one shook hands with me.

One of them was campaign manager Frank Neely, he of the steel-gray gaze and fleshy, intelligent face. He was wearing a sweatshirt that said WHY NOT A *REAL* PRESIDENT? VOTE FREED, with the last word given extra prominence by a somewhat protruding belly.

"Mr. Ryan," he said, smiling warily, "please excuse my informality—this was a last-minute meeting . . ."

The other one that I recognized was a thirtyish, somewhat heavy-set, balding blond guy, who I'd met in this very

163

room last night, introducing myself by way of a brass Presidential seal in the belly. He was dressed much the same as the night before: blue workshirt and jeans. When we shook hands he kept his grip insolently limp, dark eyes drilling into me, his smile a scowl. His name, Freed said, was Larry.

"You can stuff the apology," Larry said, sneering.

"What apology?" I said.

"Larry," Freed said. "Just sit down."

Larry sat down and did a slow burn. Nobody's favorite stooge.

The other two men were named Blake and Simmons; one had brown hair and the other blond, but they were pretty much interchangeable, a pair of oversize WASP ex-cops who had probably been football players in college or anyway high school. Linebackers, I'd say. They were, Freed had informed me last night, his security chiefs on the primary swing.

Both had firm grips; both smiled without revealing any warmth—or teeth, for that matter.

We all sat, except Freed, who stood at the head of the table, his back to the fireplace, which was going, his own portrait looking over his shoulder.

"Jack Ryan is an old friend of mine," Freed said, beaming at me, so convincing a liar I almost had memories of our friendship, "who also happens to be one of the best security men around. Yesterday he handed Frank here a line, and Frank was ready to set up a meeting between Jack and myself, without running any kind of security check first. I think we've learned something, haven't we, Frank?"

Freed said this gently, and Neely seemed to take it well, smiling a little, though the smile was tight at its corners.

The candidate continued, in his mellifluous baritone:

"Last night—as Larry can tell you first hand—Jack ran a little test on my security team here at the house. We came up a little short, didn't we, Larry?"

"Yes, Mr. Freed."

"We're going to be making some changes. Adding some staff. Changing some procedures. But that's not why Mr. Ryan is here today. Jack, would you like to take over?"

Freed sat and I stood.

"As the candidate probably has told you," I said, "we have reason to believe an assassination attempt may be made at the press conference Tuesday morning."

Blake—or was it Simmons?—chimed in. "With all due respect, Mr. Ryan," he said in a gravelly voice (maybe he'd been a tackle), "we got that covered." He opened his coat and revealed the holstered revolver there.

"Ah, a .38," I said.

He nodded.

"Must help you remember your I.Q."

Simmons—or was it Blake?—glowered at me, but I got over it.

"First suggestion," I said, looking at Freed, "is you change the site of the press conference. But don't announce the change till the last minute."

"That's impossible," Neely said, shaking his head. "It would be a logistical nightmare, and make for very bad relations with the media."

I looked at Simmons and Blake. "Have you people scoped out the Bix Beiderbecke Room?" I looked at Freed. "Appropriately named, 'cause you could die before your time there."

Freed was watching me intently. "Why do you say that, Jack?"

"If I were doing this thing," I said, "I could shoot you

and be on my way, in my car, *moving*, in under thirty seconds."

Simmons and Blake smirked at each other, eyes rolling.

But Freed said, "Explain."

"An assassin staying in the hotel could take the elevator from his room down to the parking garage entry area, walk down the steps to the Bix Beiderbecke Room, block the meeting room door at left—with a table or whatever—open the door at right, getting a direct shot at the speaker at the podium, take that shot, quickly block that door, run up the steps, walk to his car—either in the garage or on the street—and be gone before anybody's figured out whether the candidate's dead or not."

Neely said, "It would be difficult to change locations. Not impossible perhaps, but . . ."

Freed said, "The location stays. What can we do to secure *that* location, Jack?"

I sighed. "Well. Post several men outside the conference room. They need detailed descriptions of the man we believe will be attempting the hit—which I'll provide—but they just generally will need to play heads-up ball. For what's at stake, our man could easily shoot more people than just the candidate. How big is your security force?"

Blake—or was it Simmons?—said, "Half a dozen."

"Armed, of course," the other one said.

"Add a couple men," I said. "You have the advantage of knowing that he's coming."

"Are you convinced of that now?" Freed said.

"After seeing the set-up for the press conference," I said, "I tend to be. Anybody wanting a crack at you would be crazy not to take advantage of this. Will there be any cops on hand?"

Neely said, "We requested police support, but were denied. We're not popular at City Hall."

Freed said, "Should I wear a bullet-proof vest?"

"Soft body armor might be worth the trouble," I said, "but, frankly, he's going to go for a head shot."

"And he could do it from the doorway, there?"

"At that range, he could throw a glass ashtray and get the job done."

Simmons and Blake, no longer rolling their eyes or smirking, seemed to be convinced. Larry didn't like me, but I could tell he was taking me seriously, too. Neely looked ashen, sick. The thought of his campaign starting off with this kind of bang didn't seem to agree with him.

"And for God's sake," I said, "tighten up security at the hotel itself. I went to the desk and told the guy I was with the Freed campaign and without even asking my name, let alone to see credentials, he went along with everything I asked him and pointed to where the press conference was going to be held and you name it. Put a lid on this thing, boys. You've got a controversial candidate with a lot of enemies. Get on the defensive."

Simmons and Blake swallowed, glanced at each other embarrassedly. Neely remained ashen, and Freed looked glazed. Larry was picking his nose.

"Now, gentleman," I said, "if you'll excuse me, I need to use the facilities. Talk this over amongst yourselves, and we'll get into some of the specifics of revising your security plan when I get back. And I'll give you a detailed description of the man we *believe* will be the assassin."

"Let's make that *would-be* assassin," Freed said, with a nervous smile.

"That's up to your friends here," I said pleasantly, and left the room.

I walked out through the adjacent secretarial room and

out where the waterfall gurgled by the winding staircase. I went up those stairs, and crossed the circular bar to the door that opened onto the hallway that led to Freed's bedroom.

About half-way down that hallway, at my left, was a closed door. A closet door, one might assume. I hadn't paid it much notice the night before, when the glow at the end of the hall had beckoned. But right now I was more interested in what was behind this door, to which I put my ear—and heard nothing. Gently, I tried the knob; locked.

But not very locked: a credit card opened it. This was a fairly quiet operation, though not a silent one, so I paused and listened for the sounds of anybody else who might be up here—a bodyguard in that room across the bar, for example—but heard nothing.

I opened the door and entered a room that wasn't a closet, though it wasn't much bigger than one. At right was a window; a video camera on a tripod was aimed at the window, and on a table nearby a big bulky video tape machine squatted, not a home VCR, but an industrial model. I glanced out the window and saw Freed's bedroom. The camera was pointed directly at the waterbed with its elaborate western headboard and its black silk sheets. I didn't remember a mirror on the wall, but there must've been one. The mirrors overhead must've been strictly for fun, not two-way video windows.

Otherwise the rumor that Angela Jordan had heard would seem to be no rumor.

Because at my left was a library of video tapes, shelves of the black plastic boxes; on the spine of each black box was a woman's name written in bold white letters: Sheila, Jane, Sally, Heather, Clarice, thirty-some women in all.

And one tape box had the name "Angela" on its spine.

I removed it from the shelf, took the tape from the box, and put the empty box back on the shelf. Then I went to the video tape machine near the camera and pressed the eject button. I removed the tape; on the counter nearby was what I presumed was the tape's black plastic box, which had the name "Becky" on the spine, and Becky was (if memory served) the name of the eager staffer I'd encountered at Freed campaign HQ and whose butt I'd electrically prodded last night.

I slipped the "Angela" tape in one of my suitcoat pockets, and the "Becky" tape in the other. I was surprised that Angela had actually made it onto a tape—she'd said several times that Freed had come on to her but that she'd rebuffed him—but it was an understandable lie. I don't always tell the truth myself.

The tapes, somewhat larger than the home-machine variety, were bulky in my pockets, so I went to the kitchen where I'd left my brown leather overcoat and transferred the tapes to those deeper pockets.

Then I went back into the conference room and joined in on the discussion about how to keep candidate (and home-video buff) Preston Freed from getting blown away (as opposed to just blown) on the first day of his primary campaign.

FIFTEEN

Pennants flapped lazily overhead as the last few Sunday afternoon browsers strolled around the BEST BUY lot, peering in windows, perusing price stickers, kicking the tires. The day was too cloudy, too cold, to attract much business; and the sales personnel, Angela Jordan among them, had finally made a concession to the undeniable reality of winter by wearing heavy coats of various sorts over their identical red blazers. It was almost five. Quitting time.

I waited for Angela to deal with the young couple looking droolingly at a shiny silver Firebird, and when they left in a boxy little brown AMC something-or-other, talking animatedly, I figured she had another sale in the bag.

"Next trip in," I said, "and you'll sell 'em."

"I think so," she smiled. "Just hope they can afford it. I'm trying to steer them toward something a little smaller."

"Better not let your boss hear you talk like that."

"You don't understand the car business," she said. "If I treat those two right, they'll be my customers for the next thirty years."

We walked toward the showroom.

I said, "I'm sorry about last night."

"No need to apologize. I understand. It's tough enough adjusting to the single life, after divorcing somebody you *don't* love anymore, let alone after . . . losing somebody you still *do* love."

"I was hoping I could take you out for a bite of supper."

"That'd be nice. I don't have any plans."

"Maybe we could take your girls along."

She smiled; teeth didn't come much whiter, smiles didn't come any better. "Wish you *could* meet them. And you will one of these days. But my mom drove the girls into Chicago for the day for a big shopping spree. They won't be back till nine or ten tonight."

"How much longer are you here?"

She checked her watch. "It is five, isn't it? I'm off as of now. Let me go back in my office and change clothes. I'm going to be pretty casual . . ."

I was still in the suit and brown leather overcoat. "Well,

I could always change into my ninja threads," I said.

She laughed and said I looked just fine.

I followed her into the showroom and the smell of new cars. "You got any place special you'd like to eat?" I asked her.

"Any place but the Embers," she said, and flashed her smile and disappeared into a small office. The other sales people had either gone or were going. But sitting in his office, staring out at me, was chunky little Lonny Best in his shirtsleeves and red-white-and-blue tie. He had a filtered cigarette going. He was frowning at me.

He stood and crooked his finger, like I was a kid he was summoning.

What the hell.

I went into his office and closed the door behind me.

"What the fuck's the idea?" he said.

"Could you be a little more specific?"

He came out from behind the desk, apple cheeks blazing, eyes hard and small and glittering. He thrust a hard fore-finger into my chest.

"You lied to me," he said. "What was that shit about auto parts?"

"Come again?"

"You're in the security game. Working for Freed. I know all about it."

I had hoped Angela would be more discreet.

"Maybe I was checking up on you," I said.

He thumped my chest again. "Well I don't fuckin' *appre-ciate* it! And stay away from Angela; I don't want you havin' anything to do with her."

"Don't touch me again."

He shoved me hard. "I'll touch you. I'll fuckin' kill you."

I opened my coat and reached under my arm and took out the nine-millimeter.

His eyes got very large, considering how small they were, and he backed up. "Jesus—what's the idea . . ."

I slapped him alongside his head with the barrel and he went down like a kid's tower of blocks.

I sat on top of him and put the gun's nose against his. His ear was bloody from where the gun slapped him. His eyes looked back and up at me, frantic and afraid. "Jesus, Jesus . . . I didn't mean . . ."

"Don't threaten to kill people," I said. "It isn't nice, unless you mean it. It isn't nice if you mean it, either, but in that case, what's the difference?"

He was sweating. "What . . . what do you want?"

"Like you said, I'm in the security game. And I'm working for Preston Freed."

"What . . . what's that to me?"

"That Buick that was stolen off your lot."

His eyes tensed. That told me something.

"The men who took it," I said, "did not have Preston Freed's best interests at heart. Only I don't think they 'took' it. I think you gave it to them."

"You're . . . you're fuckin' nuts."

I twisted the bleeding ear and he howled.

"You used to be a Freed supporter," I said. "What turned you against him? Why do you want him dead?"

"I don't want *anybody* dead!"

"You can be dead yourself, if you don't come clean." I twisted the ear again. "Talk to me Lonny," I said, above his howl.

A knocking at the office door interrupted us. "What's going on in there?" Angela's voice cried. "Lonny? Is *Jack* in there? Lonny, are you all right?"

I climbed off him, helped him up. He was shaking and shaken.

"Not a word about this," I said, putting the gun away. "Find something to wipe off your ear."

"You're crazy," he said, breathlessly; it was not an accusation, or an insult—more a surprised statement of assumed fact. He stumbled into a small washroom off his office and used a damp cloth on his ear.

I cleaned his blood off my hand with a handkerchief and opened the door and a wide-eyed, worried Angela was standing there, poised to knock again. I slid past her and pulled her along.

"Come on," I said. "Let's get something to eat."

"What was going on in there?"

"Your car or mine?"

"Let's take both this time, I'll follow you; but what . . ."

"I'll tell you when we get there."

The Sundance Restaurant in the Blackhawk Hotel was a yuppie's notion of the old west—pottery and Indian-blanket carpeting, sepia photos of Wild Bill Hickok and Sitting Bull, mingling with the usual hanging plants. Rather large, the open-beamed place was sectioned off and made to seem cozy, its unfinished pine walls cluttered with wagon wheels and mounted buffalo heads and lamps made from antlers. We sat by ourselves in a nook below a blue-and-orange stained-glass skylight.

"What was going on in Lonny's office?" she asked, leaning forward. The ride over had not dimmed her interest or her concern. She was nervously toying with the gold chain around her neck; she was wearing a white blouse and blue jeans.

"Don't worry about it," I said. I would have liked to take off my coat and tie and unbutton my top button; but I still wore my nine-millimeter in its shoulder holster. So I remained less than casual.

"You'd said you'd tell me," she said with brittle, barely controlled anger. "It sounded like you were *fighting* in there."

"It was just a scuffle."

"A scuffle! What about?"

"You. He told me to stay away from you, and took a swing at me. I decked him, then sat on him a while till he was cooled down. That's all."

Exasperated, she shook her head, eyes large, said, "Does this sort of thing happen to you often?"

"It used to. I been leading a pretty quiet life lately."

"Well, you're certainly getting back into the swing of things, aren't you?"

"Yes. But I wish I wasn't."

"What do you mean, Jack?" Her anger was fading already.

"Nothing. Let's forget about this and just have a nice meal, okay?"

"Oh-kay," she sighed, smirking with frustration, and we ordered drinks—her a martini (again) and me a Diet Coke (again), and I got her talking about her kids for awhile. The older one was a cheerleader, but not such a great student; the younger girl was shy, though her marks were excellent. Angela's eyes lit up when she talked about them. The sadness that I'd noticed in her last night was absent this evening, at least when her kids were the topic of discussion.

I hadn't eaten anything today, so I had a full dinner, the main course wiener schnitzel (the Sundance menu wasn't particularly frontier-oriented); Angela, who probably weighed one hundred twenty, had the diet plate.

She was having a second martini, an after dinner one, when I got back into it.

"I need to ask you something about your husband," I said.

"Bob? What about him?"

"You said he's working for George Ridge now."

"Yes. He's an . . . executive assistant, I think is the title."

"But Ridge and Preston Freed had a bitter falling out. Are you aware of that?"

"Yes," she said, nodding.

"Yet you indicated your husband is still under Freed's 'spell.' "

"Yes, Bob's still a member of the Democratic Action party. I don't think he's as active as he used to be, but . . . I don't get your point."

"Well, the point is, how can he work for Ridge, and still be involved with Freed?"

"I don't know. Lots of people who work together, who're in business together, disagree politically. Is that so unusual?"

I let some air out. Shrugged. "I just figured the rift between Ridge and Freed was so acrimonious, it'd spill over into other things . . ."

"Maybe so. I really don't know anything about it. Why don't you ask George Ridge about it? Or Freed? Or Bob, for that matter?"

She didn't know it, of course, but nobody was going to be talking to Bob again, not unless it was with a Ouija board. And the same would be true of George Ridge, before long, once I'd met him and his plane Monday night. Freed I could, and would, ask.

"Something else we need to talk about," I said.

"Yes?" Her smile was eager; she was assuming, wrongly, this would be pleasant.

"Don't ask me how I know this. Don't ask me how I did this exactly."

"Know what? Did what?"

"That rumor about Preston Freed's video-tape library."

She smiled, laughed softly. "His triple-X home movies, you mean. What about it?"

"It's no rumor."

She shrugged. "I'm not really surprised. But how'd you verify it? Oh, sorry—you said not to ask . . ."

She wasn't as impressed as she should be.

I reached over to the chair next to me where my brown leather coat was draped. I got the black plastic box out of one pocket and showed it to her. "This is from his private library."

She smiled one-sidedly, a little amazed. "You're kidding!"

"No. Check out the spine."

She looked at it. " 'Angela,' " she said. "Well, this isn't me, if that's what you're thinking."

"Hey, he's got a camera pointing right at his bed. He's got a shelf of over thirty tapes with the names of women on every one of them. There's no reason to kid me."

"Jack. Read my lips. This isn't me. I never slept with Freed. Or did anything with him. Have you screened this?"

"No," I said. "I don't know where to find a machine that'll play it. It won't play in a home VCR—I need the kind they use at TV stations."

"Three-quarter inch, not half-inch," she said, nodding. "You know, I think I know where I can find us a screening room."

We took her car. It was dark now, as we headed up Brady through its neon franchise canyon, gliding along by BEST BUY, heading on out past the shopping malls and even her own housing addition. Well past the city limits, as Iowa farmland began to kick in, a cluster of small buildings appeared at our left, a garden of big metal mushrooms—satellite dishes—along its one side.

We got out of the car and she looped her arm in mine, saying, "If Chuck still works here, and I think he does, we'll be in business. I used to drop Preston Freed's weekly 'news' show off to 'im."

There were no lights on in the front office part of the small building complex, but a few windows glowed toward the rear. The side door, marked "Cable Vision Employees Only," just this side of the mesh fence that enclosed the satellite-dish garden, was unlocked. I followed her in and down a narrow hall.

An open door to the right revealed a small studio, lights unlit, cameras unattended; she knocked at the next door and, shortly, a shaggy-haired mustached guy in a dark green sweater and blue jeans answered, Styrofoam coffee cup in hand. He was about thirty-five and sleepy-eyed; dope was in his past and maybe his present. Behind him was a small but elaborate control booth, video tape machines and monitors and banks of switches, with a big window looking out on that empty studio.

"Well! How ya doin', beautiful," he said, brightening at seeing her. "Don't tell me you're workin' for the Great White Father again."

She laughed. "No, I had enough of that windbag to last a lifetime. You're still running on caffeine, I see."

He sipped his coffee. "It's legal. What's the occasion?"

"Need a favor, Chuck."

"Hey, anything for a pretty face. You still selling cars?"

"Yes, and that's why I'm here. We had this hotshot advertising firm out of Cedar Rapids do some commercials for us, but when the tape arrived, it was on three-quarter. All we have at the showroom is a VHS."

"And you wanna screen the sucker. Well, no problem, babe. There's a machine and a monitor in the office next door." He pointed with his thumb to a door that said STATION MANAGER. "It's not locked."

"Thanks, Chuck."

"No problem-o, babe. Gotta get back to work. Let me know when you're leavin' . . ."

He toasted her with his coffee and shut himself back in his booth.

"They run a pretty tight ship around here," I said.

"It's a small operation," she said, leading me into the station manager's office, a cluttered cubbyhole with a desk and several files but also a stand on which sat a TV monitor and, under it, a big VCR. "They serve several small communities. And they're making some dough uplinking Freed's show for him every week."

I handed her the tape and she inserted it in the machine and we stood and watched.

Watched, thanks to a sharply focused if stationary camera, Preston Freed in spirited action with a lovely blonde girl of about twenty. I fast-forwarded it through several sexual positions and practices and some mutual coke use and, while it was hardly a testimonial to the conservative values Preston Freed extolled, the tape had nothing to do with Angela Jordan.

Almost immediately she said, "That's Angela Huseby."

"So it isn't you."

"No, of course not. See for yourself. I'm not the only Angela in the world."

"Who is this girl?"

"She was only with the party for a few months. She's dead."

I looked at her sharply. "Dead?"

"She had a nervous breakdown. Suicide."

"When was this?"

"At least two years ago."

I shut the tape off. "I'm sorry. I should've believed you."

She smiled at me, touched my arm. "You were trying to do me a favor, weren't you? You saw the name on that tape, and assumed it was me, and took it. To give to me."

"Yeah, or to destroy," I said. Like I had already done with the other tape, the one that had the name "Becky" on the spine, co-starring me and my stun gun.

"You're sweet," she said. "But that tape isn't me. It *is*, however, political dynamite. If you're working for Freed, you'd better get rid of it."

"Maybe I'm a blackmailer."

She smiled wide. "I don't think so. You're just not the type. And I'm a pretty good judge of character."

If she were a good judge of character, she wouldn't be a divorcee twice over. But I didn't point that out to her.

I tucked the tape back in my pocket and we exited the cubbyhole. Out in the silent hall, she stuck her head in the studio and waved at Chuck through the glass of his booth; he looked up from inserting a tape in a machine and smiled and waved.

Soon we were on the road again, heading back to Davenport.

"Would you mind stopping by my house for a few minutes?" she asked. "We'll be going right by. It's getting late and I'd like to check and see if Mom and the girls are back yet."

"That's fine. I'd like to meet your family."

But when she pulled into the driveway of the green split-level, next to a shiny white Pontiac Bonneville, she said "Damn! They're not home . . ."

"Then whose car is that?"

She paused. Made a face. "Lonny's."

"I'll handle the little jerk," I said.

She touched my arm. "Don't let things get out of hand."

"I'll just send him on his way."

I got out of the car and opened her door for her and escorted her up the sidewalk. He was sitting up on the front stoop, the tip of his cigarette an amber eye in the darkness; he stood as we approached, still in his BEST BUY blue blazer, no topcoat.

She got between us. "Now, I don't want any trouble . . ."

But I could already see from Lonny's haunted expression that this was about something else.

"Angela," he said. "Please. We have to talk."

"We can talk at work on Monday."

He paused. "I'm afraid I have some bad news. It's Bob."

"What *about* Bob?"

"Bob . . ." He sighed. "He's apparently drowned. Him and Jim Crawford both."

She clutched my arm. "Oh, my God. How . . . how did it happen?"

"A boating accident," he said.

"A boating accident?" she asked, incredulous.

"I know it sounds crazy, this time of year. But Bob and Jim Crawford were apparently takin' a small cabin cruiser, this morning, to this island on Lake Superior. I guess some business associates of their boss, Ridge, lived on this island and, well, a storm blew in out of nowhere and . . . a wind like that can dump a vessel a lot larger, they said . . ."

"Oh, my God. What will I tell the girls? What will I tell the girls?"

"The boat was found, capsized. Nobody aboard."

"What about Ridge?" I asked.

"He never was aboard," Best said. "They were going to that island to meet him." To her, he said: "There's . . . I'm sorry, honey, but they said there's really not much chance of recovering the bodies."

She was weeping now, into my arm. "Jack . . . Jack . . . what can I do?"

I patted her back.

Best, looking stunned himself, shook his head, touched her shoulder; said, "Sorry, hon. I'm very sorry."

"Why'd they call *you?*" I asked him.

"Authorities been trying to reach Angela all day," he said, refusing to get defensive about it. "Somebody finally led 'em to the car lot. When they called, it was just after you left, and I was the only one still around."

I looked at him hard, looking for complicity in his reddish round face; but I couldn't find any. He seemed genuinely concerned, upset, himself.

"You want me to hang around?" he asked her.

She shook her head no.

He swallowed again, nodded, said he was very sorry, to let him know if there was anything he could do, and, head lowered, ear scabbed over some from where I tagged him, he shuffled down the curving walk to his shiny new car and drove away.

I guided her into the house and we sat on a sofa. I let her cry into my shoulder for a while. She was having a rough time of it. So was her ex-husband, poor old Bob Jordan: first I shoot him and burn his body, and now he up and drowns.

Perhaps fifteen minutes later, she stood. "The girls will be home before long."

I stood.

She hugged me.

"Oh, Jack. You've been so kind." She swallowed. Looked up at me with those dark blue eyes, shining with tears. "Part of me still loved the bastard, I guess. It's hard . . . so hard. But then you know all about that."

I touched the tears on her cheek.

"You know all about losing somebody you love," she said.

I said nothing.

"I think I'd like to be alone now," she said. "Try to collect my thoughts before the girls get here."

I thought that was a good idea. I called a taxi and sat with her till it arrived.

SIXTEEN

There were half a dozen flights from Chicago to monitor. It was Monday evening, and George Ridge, routed through O'Hare on one of three shuttle airlines, would be on one of them. I could not go down to the gate where he'd be coming in. Doing that would mean crossing the concourse, through security, and the nine-millimeter under my arm—in the shoulder holster, the noise suppressor in my suitcoat pocket to attach if need be—would win me the grand prize if I tried to walk through the metal detector.

I didn't want to kill him here, anyway. I wanted to talk to him before I sent him on his way. He knew things that I wanted to know.

In the small gift shop I bought a Snickers bar (supper) and a late edition of the Quad City *Times*. I wasn't in the mood to read it or anything, but I needed something to hide behind, and I'm just not the sunglasses and fake mustache type. George Ridge and I had, after all, met—back on the deck of my A-frame, when he first approached me to kill Preston Freed. Not only could he easily recognize me, he might even be on the lookout for me; he obviously knew I wasn't dead: the cover-up he'd arranged for the deaths of Bob Jordan and Jim Crawford indicated he knew just how badly his attempt to kill me had gone awry.

Both Jordan and Crawford had their pictures on the front page of the very *Times* I held in my hands. I'd seen the pictures in the morning edition, so it came as no surprise to me (nor had it this morning) that Crawford, who had accompanied George Ridge and Angela's ex-husband on that ill-fated expedition up north, was a certain thin, blonde, cadaverous guy. It did come as a surprise to me to learn he'd died in a boating accident. I seemed to remember putting an axe in the back of his fucking head.

I planted myself in a seat in the wide, open area near baggage claim; the airport had a single conveyor belt affair that handled baggage from all flights. Ridge would just about have to come here. And even if he sent some flunky after his luggage, from where I was sitting I could see where the concourse emptied out all returning passengers. He wouldn't escape me.

My intention, unless he made me, was to follow him. I could have waited at his fancy house—I knew where it was, I'd cased the outside of the place earlier today—but I thought there was a possibility he might make a stop somewhere on his way home to confer with some fellow conspirator. After all, me and the shit had hit the fan while he was (conveniently) out of the country, and tomorrow morning was the press conference-cum-shooting gallery. So tonight, it stood to reason, would be a lively night for George Ridge. Lively for a while, anyway.

In the parking lot I had found the chocolate-brown

BMW he had driven to my place; mud no longer coated the license plate, which was Scott County. I touched the car, my hand trembling. I wanted this fucker. I wanted this fucker.

Ridge was large in my thoughts, but he wasn't alone.

He shared them with the man he'd hired to do the job I turned down.

I had, in fact, spent the day trying to track that man— Stone—without much luck. I felt he had to be in town—I almost *sensed* he was here, if I believed in that shit—but he had apparently not checked into the Blackhawk. I was dealing with desk clerks on all three shifts and none of them seemed to have seen him.

Having worked with him, I knew he liked to roost close to the site of a hit. It was something we argued about, one of the reasons, really, why I had asked the Broker for somebody else to work with. I'd learned a lot from Stone, he was a good teacher, but he had a serious flaw: I felt he left a trail. He would go so far as to stay in the same hotel as his target and that, I knew, was stupid.

But either he had gotten smart in the intervening years, or he just hadn't checked in yet. I laid twenties on desk clerks in three other, nearby downtown Davenport hotels, but my description of Stone, and his aliases, rang no bells there, either.

Stone had two other quirks. First, he liked arcade games, was your classic pinball wizard, and he particularly, predictably, enjoyed shooting games. Surveillance over a period of days, even weeks, is tiring, intense work, and I could understand him taking a breather with the mindless challenges presented by an arcade full of games. But he was excessive. In a bar, Stone could park himself at pinball or an electronic Ping-Pong game for hours.

When I was teamed with Stone, it was before the video-game craze came (and, largely, went). But I had a hunch Stone would have flipped out over *PacMan* and *Donkey Kong* and *Galaga* and the like. So I spent the afternoon doing what I thought was a clever piece of detective work, checking out several video arcades in Davenport, thinking Stone might be killing time within. But he hadn't been. So much for my investigative abilities.

Stone's other quirk? He liked to swim. He would invariably stay at a hotel or motel with a pool, an indoor one this time of year; the relaxation, the soothing, meditative qualities of it were something Stone craved. I had, in fact, picked up the same habit. It wasn't the only thing Stone had taught me, but in a way it was the most important. Swimming was a constant in my life: in Lake Paradise in the summer months, at the Y in Lake Geneva other months. And like Stone, I would tend to seek out an indoor pool wherever I was staying on a job.

I had swum last night, and today, at the Blackhawk's pool, relaxing and staking the place out at the same time, my nine-millimeter wrapped in a towel, poolside.

No Stone.

I had also spent some of my time hanging around the non-video arcade below the lobby of the Blackhawk; a shoe shine stand with four seats was unattended and I plopped myself down and watched the world go by. It was a world Stone wasn't part of.

And I wasn't surprised, really. Not much by way of recon was necessary on this gig. It would take Stone about five minutes to map it all out, the Bix Beiderbecke Room right next to the steps up to the parking garage, Christ. It was too easy.

By now it was eight-thirty and George Ridge had not

been on any of the four flights that arrived so far. The next one would be in at nine-fifteen. I stood and stretched, bones popping in my back. I folded the paper under my arm and walked a bit.

Speaking of video arcades, the airport had its own small one next to the gift shop. I peeked in, and Stone wasn't there, either. I let out a short laugh at my own expense. As a detective, I made a good hitter. I fed some quarters into several of the machines; there was a *Ms. PacMan* that I did pretty well on, but couldn't make the Scoreboard. I checked my watch. Not quite nine. I put some quarters into a game based on the cartoon character Popeye. It was pretty good—Bluto and Olive Oyl were on hand, behaving in character, namely Olive Oyl was a whiney bitch and Bluto was a brutal cheat. I got the hang of it quickly, and on my third quarter made it to the hardest level, a pirate ship. On my fourth quarter I made the Scoreboard.

Hot damn, I said to myself, as I punched in three letters (all you were allowed): RYN, for Ryan. I was number two on the Scoreboard.

Number one was STO.

I stared at it, wondering if it were some guy's initials or . . . no, it couldn't be Stone . . . could it?

I went back to my seat and hid behind the *Times,* waiting, the gun rubbing under my shoulder. People came and went. So did the nine-fifteen flight, which did not get in till nine-thirty. No Ridge.

Shortly before ten something disturbing happened: reporters began showing up. Print guys and TV teams from three stations, with minicams in tow. I began wondering what they were here for, and when the ten o'clock flight arrived, Ridge was on it, and they were on him.

My mouth went dry, seeing him again. The same handsome if slightly heavy-set man who'd come calling at my A-frame, every salt-and-pepper hair in place, though he looked tired, drained, even though he was moving quickly.

He had to. The press was swarming him. Ridge was accompanied by two men, who (like him) were dressed in London Fog raincoats over business suits; nonetheless, they had the rough-around-the-edges look of bodyguards, in other words cut from the same cloth as Jordan and Crawford. The bodyguards went to get the luggage while Ridge cut quickly through the reporters, smiling somberly, answering a few questions but not lingering.

He hadn't noticed me, which was one small blessing. I hadn't figured on the reporters. If I'd been thinking I would have known that the Quad Cities was just small enough an area, and Ridge large enough a local celebrity, for the "boating accident" of the day before to have attracted regional media attention. It had already gotten big play in the local papers, after all.

I followed on the heels of the reporters through automatic doors out into the chilly night and watched, with a sick sinking feeling, as Ridge climbed into a chauffeured limo, a sleek black stretch Lincoln. The bastard wasn't even waiting for his luggage!

Weaving between cars and taxis, I ran across the several lanes that separated the airport from its vast parking lot, hurtled a low cement fence and was soon in the Sunbird, behind several cars in line, waiting to pay the parking fee. I kept an eye on that limo, saw it caught behind some traffic in the exit lane nearby. Another small favor.

I was able to slide in behind the limo at the stoplight, planning to keep at least one car between us for the ride to wherever we were going. Then, oddly, the limo turned almost immediately, wheeling into the airport Howard Johnson's.

We weren't going far at all. George Ridge lived in a big, Frank Lloyd Wrightish home on the so-called Heights in Davenport, up above where Werner had lived, with a magnificent view of the Mississippi. He had not been home for several days, but rather than retire to his modernistic castle, he was being dropped off at a room at a Howard Johnson's.

Interesting.

I moved along by, while Ridge got out of the limo, shooing it on its way. He stood there in his London Fog, on the sidewalk by the first-floor rooms on the west side of the motel. He withdrew something from an inside pocket; light glinted off it. Soon he was smoking. Then he put the flat silver cigarette case away. He was watching and waiting. Possibly he was watching to see if any of the media people had followed him.

I had pulled into one of the motel stalls and sat in darkness with the nine-millimeter in my lap. I was down a ways from him, but I could see him. I felt myself tightening like a fist, and made myself relax. It was hard to do. I've killed people before, as you may have gathered; and usually with utter dispassion. But George Ridge was someone I would enjoy killing. I was sorry only that I was limited to killing him once.

He was nervous. I hoped that was because he knew I was out here somewhere. He just didn't know how close. That made me smile. He checked his watch. Then, quickly, he slid open one of the glass doors of the room just behind him and stepped in and slid it shut again.

I thought about that. I knew he wasn't meeting a woman for an affair in there, at least it was unlikely; he was divorced, although I supposed a married woman might be meeting him here. More likely—much more likely—he was meeting with someone about tomorrow's press conference. Where he'd cast his vote by way of a bullet delivered by a surrogate, putting an end to the candidacy of Preston Freed. Isn't democracy grand?

The question was, when to go in? If he was meeting with, say, Stone, and I went in, the shooting could start before any questions got asked and answered. And in the motel setting, I'd have to use the suppressor, and that meant the relative slowness of working the gun's action by hand after every shot. Well, I'd have to make the best of it.

I was about to get out of the car when a figure walked quickly by, in front of my parked Sunbird, heading in the direction of the room Ridge had slipped into. The man was heavy-set and balding but moved with an athlete's grace. He was about six feet one and was wearing a long black leather topcoat and black slacks. He looked like something out of an Italian western.

He was Stone.

Older. Less hair, and what there was of it grayed, the widow's peak a casualty of time; and heavier. Why hadn't I thought of that? I was heavier myself, although not *that* much heavier. I had given the hotel desk clerks descriptions of Stone as I had known him perhaps a dozen years ago. I had not allowed for—and, in fairness to myself, could not foresee the exact nature of—the effect of time.

Stone's hands slid open one sliding door. That meant he was expected: otherwise those doors would be locked. He ducked in there.

I crouched between two cars, nine-millimeter in hand, watching the glass doors, draped, shut, possibly locked now, perhaps ten feet away. I was trying to decide how to go in—the room number was no problem, it was posted above the glass doors, 114—when Stone came back out, moving quickly.

His face was white. Stone was naturally pale, but not *that* pale; and his eyes were round and wild.

He ran back the way he came, not past where I was now crouching, not seeing me, and moments later I heard a car start up and tires squealed and I glanced back and saw a sporty little cinnamon car—a Dodge, maybe—flash by, and he was gone.

The glass doors were not only unlocked, one remained open, the cold breeze making the blue drape flap like a ghost.

I stepped in quickly, fanning the nine-millimeter around, easing the door shut behind me with a gloved hand. Other than Ridge, the room was empty, but I checked the bathroom, including shower stall, and closet. Nobody there.

Just Ridge.

Ridge, who was on the floor next to the bed on his back, still in his London Fog raincoat, which was appropriate, because his throat was raining blood. He'd been cut from ear to ear, an obscene scarlet grin below the sorrowful frown and empty open eyes of the late George Ridge. The only real estate in his future would be a cemetery plot.

And there'd be no talking to him now; no questions, no answers.

Shit!

I wouldn't even get to kill the fucker once.

SEVENTEEN

I dove into the pool, into the deep; no diving board, just off the edge. Sign said NO DIVING but another said NO LIFEGUARD ON DUTY, and I'd broken rules before. A nice clean dive, and I stayed under, swam the length of the pool that way and came up in the shallow.

The pool room was steamy, the lighting subdued, the blues and grays of the tile floor and the brown of the brick walls as soothing as the heated pool itself. Skylights above revealed the night; this was a small rectangular room, taken up mostly by the small rectangular pool. It was after eleven now, midnight approached, and I had the place to myself. The glass wall, separating the pool room from the beige-brick parking-garage entry area, was steamed up; but the occasional shapes of people, going to and from their cars, to and from the hotel, could be made barely out, smudgy apparitions haunting the hall.

I swam laps for a while. Very easily. I don't push myself when I swim. Exercise is not the point for me. Relaxation is. It helps me not to think, when that's what I want; and it helps me to think, when that's what I want—the way they used to claim a sensory deprivation tank would bring you in closer touch with yourself. I was in close touch with myself already, thanks, but I did like the way the water and the warmth slowed my thoughts and at the same time brought them clarity.

I had told no one about finding Ridge's body, having left as quickly as I arrived, apparently unseen. I considered calling Freed, and I would tell him, but now was not the time.

But I had called Angela Jordan, albeit not to tell her about Ridge. I'd apologized for calling so late—ten-thirty is late to make a phone call, anyway in the Midwest it is—and asked her how she was doing.

"Just fair," she said. "The girls . . . especially Kristie . . . are just devastated. Mom's staying here with me. With us. Thank God for her. It's been just awful."

"Have there been arrangements to make?"

"No, not really. Bob's parents are taking care of everything—there's a memorial service Wednesday."

"I didn't know if I'd catch you at home," I said. "I kind
of thought you might be at the funeral home or something."

"No. There's no . . . body, remember?"

Actually, there was a body—partially cremated in my
A-frame; by now, no doubt, it was buried in a grave with
one of my names on it.

"It'll be a church service," she was saying. "I . . . don't
get along with Bob's folks very well. I mean, I'm not the
wife, I'm the ex-wife. But the girls aren't his ex-daughters,
so . . . aw, jeez. This has just been a horrible day."

I was about to make it even worse.

"What if I said I thought your husband's death was not
an accident."

A stunned silence followed, briefly.

Then, in a somewhat accusatory tone: "What do you
mean?"

"What if I said I thought it was murder."

"Murder? Murder? I know Bob was involved in some . . .
rough things sometimes, but . . ."

"And what if I said I thought I knew who was responsible."

"Jack, what are you saying?"

"What if I said I couldn't prove it, and that there was no
way we could go to the police about it."

There was firmness in her voice now: "Jack, if you know
something, we're going to the police. Right now—no discussion."

"Forget I mentioned it."

"Forget you . . . Jack, I'm coming there to talk to you."

That's what I wanted anyway.

"Okay," I said. "Make it midnight in the lobby of the

Blackhawk. I'll spell things out."

She'd agreed to that. I'd called her from my room. Now I needed that swim. To relax. To think.

And for another reason.

I sat in the shallow section, my head out of water, rest of me under, and waited. Played a hunch. I was starting to feel foolish, not to mention wrinkled, when I was suddenly not alone.

Another guest of the hotel invaded my dank, until-then solitary chamber. As I had hoped he might. He was six-foot or so, a pale, potbellied, balding man wearing a dark blue knee-length terrycloth robe and black thong sandals. Something heavy was in one pocket of his robe; the right. His face was pockmarked, his chin cleft.

He was the man I'd known as (among other things) Stone.

He took off the robe and draped it carefully across a yellow deck chair. Stepped out of his sandals and, ignoring the sign just as had I, dove into the water. Graceful as an Olympic diver, if considerably fatter.

He ignored me entirely, started doing laps, arms cutting the surface; he didn't take it as easy as I did, rather made the water churn. I sat there in the waves he made, watching.

Finally, he came up for air in the shallow, came up gulping air, actually, like a heavy, getting-older man would do, and glanced over at me.

The glance turned into a fixed expression, as his slate-gray, oriental-cast eyes locked onto me. The skin around them tensed.

"Quarry?" he asked.

"Stone," I said and nodded.

He smiled briefly, as if about to say "Small world," but the smile and the thought didn't survive long.

"What are you doing here?" he asked. Flatly.

"Having a swim."

"Besides that."

"It's a long story. How about a sauna?"

He looked at me through slits. "Ever drown anybody, Quarry?"

"I threw a TV in a bathtub once. A soap opera was playing."

"Somebody in the tub at the time?"

"What would've been the point if there wasn't?"

He twitched a smile, shrugged. Said, "I could stand to sweat off some flab."

We left the pool area and entered the small sauna that was off the short hall to the showers, johns, and lockers. He was in his robe again. I was in my trunks, carrying my rolled-up towel under my arm; tightly under my arm. In the towel was the nine-millimeter. No suppressor. The towel, and a contact wound, would make it unnecessary.

We had the redwood cubicle to ourselves—just me and Stone and the heating stones; we selected the higher of two shelves, sat side by side on the slatted wood. I sat on the right, he on the left; that put my rolled-up gun-in-towel under my right hand.

He left the robe on. The heat was dry, and thick enough to slice—if you had a knife.

He sat hunched, looked up at me, his strange eyes placid. "You still in the business, Quarry?"

"Not exactly."

"What does that mean?"

"It means I was in retirement, but somebody tried to get me to make a comeback. To do one special job."

"Really. Isn't that flattering."

"Hope to shout. Million-dollar contract."

His eyes flickered.

"I'll tell you about it," I said.

And did.

There were parts I left out: I didn't tell him I'd contacted Freed and was working for the candidate; and I didn't tell him anything about Angela Jordan. I also didn't mention trailing George Ridge from the airport tonight (and all that entailed). But the rest I gave him.

He sat and sweated and considered what I'd said. It had taken almost five minutes, and he hadn't interrupted once.

Now he said, "I'm sorry about your wife. But it doesn't have anything to do with me."

"It has everything to do with you."

He shook his head no. Moisture beads flew off his forehead. "Like you said: you were a loose end. They tried to tie you off."

"You don't think you'll be an immediate loose end yourself? You really think you'll survive this, to spend your dough?"

"They've already put up half the dough. Up front."

"Half a million bucks?"

"That's right. In a numbered Swiss account."

I'd only been offered a paltry hundred grand—but in cash.

"How are they supposed to pay the balance?"

"A deposit to that account."

"They'll find you," I said, "and have you killed."

"I don't think so."

"You think you're smarter than they are?"

"Yeah. And you."

"Where I failed, you'll succeed, you think."

"You didn't fail, Quarry. They didn't kill you. You killed them."

"Like you killed Ridge tonight?"

That threw him. And this was a Stone not easily thrown.

"I didn't kill him," he said, sitting back, resting his hands on his knees; that put his right hand near the right, somewhat weighted-down pocket of the robe.

"I saw Ridge go in, and I saw you go in, and—I went in after you took off."

"You get around."

"But you know, I never knew you to kill with a knife. How'd you manage that? You didn't even get blood on you."

"That's because he was dead when I went in there," he said.

"Well, then who killed him?"

"How should I know?"

We sat and listened to each other sweat.

Then I said: "Ridge was the man who contacted you about the hit?"

He nodded.

"And you were supposed to meet with him tonight?"

He shook his head no. "I didn't know it would be him. There was a message at the hotel. There were going to be some . . . 'last minute changes.' "

"So then everybody's presumption is correct? Tomorrow's press conference *is* where, and when, the hit's going down?"

He just looked at me. Then he nodded again. Paused. Arched one eyebrow. He did look like a sinister Mr. Spock, gone bald and slightly to seed. "But when I got there, Ridge was dead on the floor, throat cut. I just got the fuck out."

"Why are you still here? Why haven't you split? Isn't somebody icing Ridge enough to queer the deal for you?"

He slipped out of the robe; it made a slight clunk as he put it beside him. Beside his right hand.

He said, "Yes it was. I was planning to blow. To just get

the fuck out." He shook his head, smiled faintly. "Even though this hit is a piece of cake . . . brother. You check out the lay of the land?"

I nodded. "It looks like the easiest million this side of the lottery."

"Yeah, well I don't gamble."

"Then why are you still hanging around here?"

"I'm deciding whether to stay or not. Whether to go through with it or not."

"Why in hell would you still want to go through with it?"

He thought for a moment, not sure if he wanted to tell me something.

Then, casually: "Because there was an envelope waiting for me at my room. Somebody slid it under the door. It had ten one-thousand dollar bills in it. Crisp as fuckin' lettuce."

"And all I got was a mint on my pillow."

"There was a typewritten note."

"Which said?"

He shrugged. " 'Tomorrow as planned.' "

"Well, surely you don't intend to *take* that advice."

"I intend to take the ten grand. But I got to think the other through . . ."

"Stone, there's nothing to think through. Ridge was another loose end that got tied off. You're next in line."

"But I'm already a loose end. Why not at least take a shot at the other half mil?"

"Who are you going to collect from? Did you deal with anybody besides Ridge?"

"No. But that just means I'm no danger to anybody. I can't finger anybody. They might just as well pay me off."

"You told me, way back when, never do a political kill. You said if you want to commit suicide, jump off a bridge."

His slightly yellow smile was spooky yet oddly gentle.

"That was a long time ago, Quarry. You take *all* the advice I gave you back then?"

"Some of it. Let's not get all mushy, now. You're no father figure."

"I remember you bitching about the 'trail' I leave."

"I found you, didn't I? Without hardly trying. By the way, I beat you at *Popeye* earlier this evening."

That also threw him a little, but he laughed. "I bet you didn't."

"You must want to quit pretty bad."

He looked at me sharply. "What?"

"You been at this a long time. You were a mob guy, right? Where, Cleveland? Then you broke away and went freelance. That's a lot of contracts. You must be tired. You certainly look old."

"You're older, too."

"I'm older. You're old. Like I'm heavier, where you're fat. You're going to die, Stone. You go through with this, they'll kill you."

"Or maybe you will."

"Why should I?"

"To get back at 'em." His lip curled up in a faint, sardonic smile. "Whoever it is that put this contract in motion, whoever it is that's responsible for what happened to your wife. For fucking up your life. If you can get in the way of tomorrow's plans, you'll screw things up for them."

"You might be right," I said, my hand in the towel.

He *was* older, and fatter: before he could even slip his hand in the robe pocket, for his gun, the nose of mine was against his sweaty temple.

I met her in the lobby just after midnight. I'd been up to my room to change; I was casually dressed—jeans and a sweatshirt and running shoes. I felt refreshed. The swim had done me good.

She was in jeans, too, and a blue blouse, hastily thrown on; her hair was messed-up, looking greasy, obviously unwashed, her eyes were red and circled, she wore no make-up. But she still looked good to me.

We sat on a sofa, in the otherwise deserted lobby, a couple of ferns eavesdropping nearby. I told her that the man responsible for her husband's death could not be touched by the police; I explained why—and I explained how he *could* be otherwise touched, done terrible damage—without violence.

We talked for forty-five minutes. She was alternately upset and angry but, finally, when I revealed what I had in mind, she was laughing. A little hysteria was in it, but it *was* laughter.

"Here," I said, and handed her the black plastic box.

She smiled and nodded.

"And don't forget these."

I handed her the small bottle of Seconal.

"Think you can handle this?" I asked.

"I know I can," she said.

"And put on some make-up before you go in."

She smirked. "Thanks for the beauty tip."

"No problem."

She got up and I walked her down the stairs out onto the street and to her red Sunbird. It was cold and our breath showed.

"Angela," I said.

"I know," she smiled. " 'Be careful.' I will."

"It's not that."

I took her in my arms and I kissed her.

"What's that for?" she asked, smiling, confused.

"Luck," I said.

And it was goodbye. I wouldn't be seeing her again.

EIGHTEEN

I was not expected at the Freed estate, but the gate man—that same guy in the hunting jacket sitting in the brown Ford—recognized me. I got out of the Sunbird, and we talked across the metal gate, at first. I told him I needed to see the candidate. He said he'd check and see if the "chief would see me." "Tell him it's urgent," I said, as the beefy, sandy-haired sentry returned to his car to call in on something.

He wasn't gone long; he unlocked and swung the gate open. "You can go on up to the house," he said, jerking a thumb over his shoulder, his other hand resting on the butt of his holstered revolver. "But no cars in the compound tonight."

"Security's pretty tight."

"Yeah. And I hear you're the guy that's responsible." He grinned. "Some of the guys are pissed at you."

"Some of the guys pissed, period, last time I saw 'em."

He laughed. "Why don't I drive you up?"

"That's okay. It's a nice night. I'll walk."

The guy shrugged, said, "Suit yourself," and climbed back in the Ford, where he lit up a cigarette and went back to work.

It really was a nice night, more cool than cold, though I was glad for the sweatshirt under the black windbreaker. I had the nine-millimeter stuffed in my waistband, in back; still not bothering with the suppressor. This was an armed camp. If shooting started, noise would be the least of my problems.

Hands in the windbreaker pockets, I walked slowly up the paved drive, which cut through the forest, the smell of the pines reminding me of Wisconsin and Paradise Lake. Above me the sky was clear tonight: stars, moon. I felt relaxed. I wasn't happy—I wasn't about to fall into *that* trap again. But I felt peaceful.

The trees came to an abrupt stop as the rolling landscaped area began, the modern yet rustic-looking house far enough away to look small. The drive was near the edge of the quarry, and I wandered off the pavement to stand on the ledge of earth and look down at the water that filled the old pit, watched its surface reflect the stars and the moon. For just an instant, it seemed to call to me.

I got back on the pavement, followed it around behind the house. One of Freed's deputy-like watchdogs was waiting in back. It was the heavy-set, balding blonde one called Larry.

He turned his mouth sideways, at sight of me, doing his best to look as disgusted as he could, nodding toward the stairs that led up to the rear of the house, into the kitchen.

"He's waiting for you in the livin' room," Larry said.

"Thanks, Larry."

He snorted. Snot, not coke. "You're no big deal, Ryan."

"What, Larry?"

"You and me, we'll settle up one of these days."

"Larry," I said, standing close to him, smiling, "don't take a little security check so personal."

Larry's head bobbed back and he stuck his tiny chin out and looked down his nose at me. He smelled like lime aftershave.

"You just don't know who you're messin' with," Larry said.

"Yeah, right," I said, and took my hand out of the jacket

pocket and stuck the stun gun in his stomach and shocked him senseless. While he was down on the ground, shaking, pissing his pants, mouth already covered with tape, I flex-cuffed his hands behind him and his ankles. Then I dragged him under the steps where he wouldn't be easily seen.

"Add that to the bill, Larry," I said.

I went on in; nobody in the kitchen. Going on through, I could see past the open doors of the secretarial area into the outdoorsy conference room, where several security boys were playing cards, money on the table. The security wasn't all *that* tight since I'd come aboard.

I found my way past the stone waterfall and its amber lights and into the sprawling living room. The lights were out, but a fire was going in the stone fireplace, over which the oil portrait of the candidate-in-buckskins smiled like a frontier god. The subject of the painting was wearing his dark silk robe again. He was lounged back on a light brown sofa, the upholstery looking like burlap; his slippered feet were up on an ottoman. A glass of Scotch was in one hand. He looked comfortable, sitting staring out his big picture window, with its view of the quarry, the narrow highway, trees and the glistening Mississippi.

"Lovely view, Mr. Ryan, don't you think?"

"From up here. It's polluted though. Get close, you'll see that easy enough."

"If the people put the right man in office, we can take care of that kind of thing."

Somehow, despite all the trappings of the great outdoors that decorated this place, I didn't figure environmentalism would be a major priority in his platform.

He turned his spooky china-blue gaze on me, a smile tearing his leathery face. "Are you here for a last-minute, pre-game pep talk? Or is there really something urgent?"

I sat next to him. Not terribly close. But on the sofa. The nine-millimeter dug into my back. "We just need to talk, before tomorrow. What time is it?"

He checked his watch. "Quarter till two. Why do you ask?"

"Something I have to do at two. Why aren't you sacked out? Shouldn't you be getting in your beauty sleep, before the big day?"

"Ah, my friend, I only look calm. Inside, I'm a collection of frayed nerves. I'm just a man, after all. Don't let the accouterments of power fool you."

"Cut you, you bleed, you mean?"

His smile quivered, then broadened momentarily, then disappeared. "Something like that," he said, looking away from me, out his window, where the reflection of the fire flickered.

"You've got your security team in place for tomorrow morning?"

"I certainly do. And I *will* be wearing soft body armor, whether you find that practical or not."

"Won't hurt anything. Think there'll be a good media turnout?"

"Excellent. Representatives from all three major networks, plus CNN; coming in from their Chicago bureaus, for the most part. The newspaper world should be equally well represented."

"I saw something in the paper about you today."

"The 'GSA Today' poll? Yes, it said my recognition is up seventy percent since my previous campaign."

"Yeah, but sixty percent of those who recognize you think you're a loon."

His eyes narrowed in irritation. "I believe the question was, 'Do you take Preston Freed seriously as a candidate?'

Perhaps after tomorrow they will."

"That's one of the things we need to talk about. You can leave your bullet-proof underwear home and call off your security. Well, the extra security, anyway. A presidential candidate always ought be protected, don't you think?"

He was frowning now. "What are you talking about?"

"Stone is no longer a problem."

He looked at me sharply. "You . . . found him?"

"Yes, I did."

Eyes peered out through cuts in his face. "And you killed him?"

I nodded, then raised a finger gently. "You said you wanted no details, remember? Besides, it was nothing flashy. Bullet in the brain. You can read about it in the *Times* tomorrow."

He sighed, shook his head. "Damn."

He was visibly disappointed.

"You wanted him nailed at the Blackhawk tomorrow morning, didn't you?"

"Of course I did," he said irritably. "The attention an assassination attempt would focus upon me would make for invaluable publicity. I explained that. Well, you blew your bonus, didn't you, Quarry?"

"Nobody's perfect. Heck, I thought you'd be grateful that I took him out. He *was* hired to kill you, you know."

"Yes," he said, through white teeth, clenched wolf-like, "but we knew he was coming!"

I smiled. Whether it was wolf-like or not, I couldn't say.

What I did say was this: "That's what this was about from the beginning, wasn't it?"

He brushed back his white mane of hair. "What in hell are you babbling about?"

"*You* took the contract out."

His smile seemed one of amused amazement. "What, on myself?"

"On yourself."

He laughed, shook his head, sipped his Scotch. "Really, Mr. Ryan."

"You wanted to be a martyr. A *living* martyr. You wanted attention called to yourself. That was the intention from day one, to publicly avert an assassination attempt, which you figured was easy enough, when, as you say, you know it's coming."

He gestured with the glass in hand, dismissively. "This is all nonsense." He scowled at me. "I'd like you to leave my home, Mr. Ryan, or Quarry, or whatever. I don't think I have any further need for your services."

"I was sought out because I have vague mob connections. When the authorities dug that out—after I was shot down by your bodyguards, at your press conference—that'd seem to give credence to your pet theory, the 'Drug Conspiracy,' the mob and bankers, all that bullshit."

He looked at me with apparent pity. "The Drug Conspiracy is very real."

"Yeah, and where would your cocaine habit be without it? You can plug Stone into that same scenario, incidentally. In fact, he's a better choice than me—his mob ties weren't so vague as mine."

"This is insanity. We both know that George Ridge is the man who hired you."

"And now I'll tell you that George Ridge is dead, and you can act surprised."

His eyes and mouth opened wide; he dropped the glass of Scotch and it spilled on the wheat-colored carpet. "What? George? Dead?"

"That was very good. You're real smooth. Quite the

actor. Did you kill Ridge yourself, or use a flunky? I'd say yourself. It's an amateur's weapon, a knife, and you've got all this hunting shit around, western stuff, there's knives handy. You had the meeting set up at the motel, he came in, you did him, you went out through the motel. You don't know how close you came to bumping into first Stone, then me. That would've been cute."

He gave me his most earnest look, mixed in with some indignation. "George Ridge and I were bitter enemies!"

"Hardly. Oh, I was fed a convincing denunciation of you by Ridge, claiming to represent a 'concerned group of patriotic citizens' and such shit. That was just in case by some fluke I was not killed in the attempted hit, and fell into police and/or federal hands. That gave me a story to tell."

"George's break with me—"

"Was just more acting, mister candidate. Ridge was not the left-wing type. Sure, back in your salad days, you were both in that SDS fringe group; but that wasn't politics, that was college. That was make-believe. Before Ridge learned about the realities, the glories of capitalism and real estate and especially selling gullible assholes *tapes* about getting rich quick. Jesus, why didn't I think it through? George Ridge is about the least likely liberal I can think of. That was strictly for public consumption."

He rolled those blue eyes. "*Now* who's the conspiracy nut?"

"There were several people involved, beyond you and Ridge, but I don't think any of them know they were working for anyone *but* Ridge—like his hapless flunkies Jordan and Crawford, two prime fuck-ups who have managed to die twice in the last few days. And Ridge tapped into his friend Werner for the names and whereabouts of the 'mob hitmen.' And Lonny Best, I believe, was asked by

Jordan to provide a car for the Wisconsin run, reported 'stolen' after the fact. The only thing really stolen were the Rock Island county license plates; the new car would've had none, otherwise. Best, you see, despite his public posture, is also still a Freed man—he knew I was doing 'security' for you, he told me so today; I thought I knew who told him that, but I was wrong—it was either you or someone in your camp. My hunch, though, is Best at most only vaguely knows he was part of any criminal conspiracy. I wouldn't bother having him snuffed, if I were you."

"Your security advice is *always* appreciated, Mr. Ryan."

"But, all in all, at its root, it was a two-man conspiracy. That's why you killed Ridge yourself. And that's why I know I'm right about all this—how I finally put this together. Only *you* knew that *I* knew Ridge had taken that contract out. Only you knew that Ridge, too, was a loose end that now needed tying off."

"If all that's true, why didn't I have you killed?"

"Well, you'd have probably had to do it yourself, and I think you know you're not up to it. I didn't tell you where I was staying, and I warned you that if I were followed, there'd be hell to pay. No, I think you wanted me there, at the press conference; I think I'd have been shot down in the confusion, to provide even more proof that some mob conspiracy had attempted to snuff out your idealistic flame. Why not a *real* president? If the mob wants him dead, he can't be *all* bad!"

Finally he dropped the pretense and smiled with infinite smugness. His face took on an almost demonic cast, thanks to the glow and the shadows from the fire behind us. "It would work. It would've worked."

"I think it would've at that. It was foolish for a man as public as Ridge—whose business was public speaking, after all, even if most of it was on audio tapes—to show himself to me. He would risk that only to help contain the conspiracy, and with the knowledge that I'd be taken out, later, anyway. You planned the same for Stone, of course. And all it's really cost you is that ten grand you slipped under Stone's hotel room door tonight."

His smile now was one of almost gentle amusement. "What about all your talk of a 'million-dollar contract'?"

"Well, Stone told me about the numbered Swiss account. He just wasn't smart enough to know that the account was yours; that you no doubt have it set up for deposits *and* withdrawals. Pardon me if it comes as no surprise that a guy like you, bilking his supporters for every buck he can, would have dough stashed in a Swiss bank."

He turned his body on the sofa to pay me complete and apparently benign attention, his voice mellow, soothing, like the glow of the fire behind us. "Mr. Ryan. Let's suppose what you've said is substantially true. What is there left for you out of this? I can offer you money, if you're interested—and I won't play any tricks with numbered accounts. But you're a man who can stand exposure no more than I, in this. Perhaps we can agree to go our separate ways."

"My wife is dead. She was pregnant."

He licked his lips; lowered his gaze as if respectful. "That is most unfortunate." Then he lifted and trained the light blue eyes on me; persuasion radiated like heat over asphalt. "But I had nothing, nothing whatever, to do with that. Whether it was Ridge's doing, or simply those bunglers Jordan and Crawford, I can't say. But I never approved such a thing. Would never approve of such a thing."

"Yeah, well you got your hands bloody tonight, just to protect your own ass. But, what the hell? Whose ass *should* you be expected to protect? Oh, what time is it?"

He checked his watch. "A few minutes after two."

"You're missing yourself on TV. You're missing your show."

Quick half-smile. "I thought just this once I could."

"How does that work, anyway?"

"What do you mean?"

I gestured with one hand. "Something about a satellite feed."

He frowned impatiently. "Well, there's a small cable outfit that uplinks the show for me. Show goes out to approximately two-hundred stations across the U.S.—they air it two A.M., central time, on Monday night. Some of them tape and air it again. Why should that concern you, and at this particular moment?"

"Oh, it just seemed a curious time for a show to air."

He shrugged, annoyed by this digression. "It's less expensive to air at this time. We're not the Republicans, we're not the Democrats, we're not the goddamn 700 Club. There's a limit to our funds. Why are we talking about this?"

"Let's turn the TV on. Let's see this show of yours."

"Don't be ridiculous."

I reached behind my back, took the nine-millimeter out. "Let's take a look. And if you call for your watchdogs, I'll shoot up the fuckin' place. Remember that, if any of 'em interrupt us."

He nodded, more irritated than afraid.

A big twenty-seven-inch console straddled the far corner of the room. He rose slowly, smoothed put his silk robe, walked over to the set and turned it on. He pushed the buttons on the cable box on top until he found the correct station.

And what he saw was himself.

Naked.

Apparently engaging in what polite folks call anal intercourse, if polite folks call it anything at all.

"Is that just rear entry, or are you really stirring the fudge there?"

His mouth dropped open to the floor. "What . . . what . . ."

"That poor little girl's name is Angela. I don't know her last name, but I understand she had a nervous breakdown, committed suicide, not long after you cast your vote in her every bodily orifice."

"That tape . . . that tape . . . where . . ."

"Came from your collection upstairs. I don't know how much longer this'll air. Somebody'll probably run out to that cable station and shut it off. I'd imagine your phone'll start ringing pretty soon."

"Jesus . . . Jesus . . . what have you done?"

"Publicly embarrassed you. Pretty much ruined you personally and politically for all time, I'd say. Sunk you and your loopy 'cause,' whatever the fuck it is, forever." I pointed to the screen. "Oh, you don't just pork that poor kid, by the way—you engage in some chemical shenanigans, as well, after a-while. That freebasing is pretty dangerous, don't you think? Do you really think you ought to be doing that on TV, where you might influence young people adversely?"

His eyes were wide; he was moving his head slowly, side to side, the phosphorescence of the TV an aura on his face. "How . . . how did you . . ."

"Somebody must've switched tapes. Your weekly show got exchanged for 'Debbie Does Preston.' Probably just a clerical error. And the guy who works at the station, he's all alone, and no matter how much coffee he downs, he's got to fall asleep on the job sooner or later."

He finally looked away from the set to glare at me. "You son-of-a-bitch . . ."

"Hey, lighten up. I could kill you. But I decided to let the press and the public crucify you instead. I'll let you suffer the humiliation. Fate worse than death. That sort of thing."

He found a smile; it was ugly—the real him at last. "You really think this will work? I'll expose this for a fraud." He crouched before the TV, as if worshipping. "The camera's back far enough . . . I can insist it's a hoax . . . look-alike actors . . ."

"Hey, yeah, maybe that'd work. The Drug Conspiracy— the Latvian/Martian Connection. Whatever. Give it your best shot at the press conference tomorrow."

He stood; his smile was tight and not right. "You think I can't. But you're wrong. You're wrong."

"Who knows? You wanted an assassination attempt, but I guess you'll just have to settle for character assassination. At least you can call off some of your security tomorrow. Your problem isn't going to be Stone—who's no problem to anybody anymore, anyway; your problem's going to be ducking questions, not bullets. And you'll have a good press turnout, don't you worry."

"I'll pull it off," he said, mesmerized by his own fucking image. "I'll pull it off."

"Yeah, give it a shot."

And I turned to go, gun still in hand.

Behind me, he said, "That's it? You're just going?"

I turned back to him. "That's right. You know, my only mistake was not taking the goddamn job in the first place, and save us all a lot of trouble. Because the mistake *you* made was thinking that once I'd been set in motion, I could've been stopped."

I pointed the nine-millimeter at him.

His mouth fell open. The china-blue eyes were suddenly empty, his leathery face a mask.

It was tempting; but it wasn't how I wanted it.

"So long, mister candidate," I said.

And I walked out of there. When I went down the back steps, Larry was still under them; he was awake now, struggling like a fish, eyes bugged, mouth slashed with tape. I smiled and waved at him.

I stood at the edge of the quarry and looked in at the water. I couldn't see myself. Just the moon and stars, shimmering.

I headed down the paved path to my Sunbird. I would drive to a motel, somewhere well beyond the Cities, and sleep (I'd kept a few of Linda's Seconals for myself) and eventually wake up and head for Milwaukee. I had a name up there and a little money and maybe I didn't have a life, anymore, but I might be able to put something together. It wasn't like I didn't have a trade.

When I got to the motel, though, I'd have a phone call to make before hitting the sleeping pills and the sack.

I'd call Stone, back at the Blackhawk, and tell him that security tomorrow morning should be no problem, though he ought to be aware that media coverage of the press conference would be heavy. Stone understood that he might not get anything out of it beyond that ten grand that had been slipped under his door; but after I'd explained it all to him, earlier, much as I had just explained it to Freed, he was eager to honor the contract. It wasn't the money—it was the principle of the thing.

After all, once you set somebody like Stone in motion, it's a mistake to think he can be stopped.

Quarry's Luck

Once upon a time, I killed people for a living.

Now, as I sit in my living quarters looking out at Sylvan Lake, its gently rippling gray-blue surface alive with sunlight, the scent and sight of pines soothing me, I seldom think of those years. With the exception of the occasional memoirs I've penned, I have never been very reflective. What's done is done. What's over is over.

But occasionally someone or something I see stirs a memory. In the summer, when Sylvan Lodge (of which I've been manager for several years now) is hopping with guests, I now and then see a cute blue-eyed blonde college girl, and I think of Linda, my late wife. I'd retired from the contract murder profession, lounging on a cottage on a lake not unlike this one, when my past had come looking for me and Linda became a casualty.

What I'd learned from that was two things: the past is not something disconnected from the present—you can't write off old debts or old enemies (whereas, oddly, friends you can completely forget); and not to enter into long-term relationships.

Linda hadn't been a very smart human being, but she was pleasant company and she loved me, and I wouldn't want to cause somebody like her to die again. You know—an innocent.

After all, when I was taking contracts through the man I knew as the Broker, I was dispatching the guilty. I had no idea what these people were guilty of, but it stood to reason

213

that they were guilty of something, or somebody wouldn't have decided they should be dead.

A paid assassin isn't a killer, really. He's a weapon. Someone has already decided someone else is going to die, before the paid assassin is even in the picture, let alone on the scene. A paid assassin is no more a killer than a nine-millimeter automatic or a bludgeon. Somebody has to pick up a weapon, to use it.

Anyway, that was my rationalization back in the seventies, when I was a human weapon for hire. I never took pleasure from the job—just money. And when the time came, I got out of it.

So, a few years ago, after Linda's death, and after I killed the fuckers responsible, I did not allow myself to get pulled back into that profession. I was too old, too tired, my reflexes were not all that good. A friend I ran into, by chance, needed my only other expertise—I had operated a small resort in Wisconsin with Linda—and I now manage Sylvan Lodge.

Something I saw recently—something quite outrageous really, even considering that I have in my time witnessed human behavior of the vilest sort—stirred a distant memory.

The indoor swimming pool with hot tub is a short jog across the road from my two-room apartment in the central lodge building (don't feel sorry for me: it's a bedroom and spacious living room with kitchenette, plus two baths, with a deck looking out on my storybook view of the lake). We close the pool room at ten P.M., and sometimes I take the keys over and open the place up for a solitary midnight swim.

I was doing that—actually, I'd finished my swim and was letting the hot tub's jet streams have at my chronically sore lower back—when somebody came knocking at the glass doors.

It was a male figure—portly—and a female figure—slender, shapely, both wrapped in towels. That was all I could see of them through the glass; the lights were off outside.

Sighing, I climbed out of the hot tub, wrapped a towel around myself, and unlocked the glass door and slid it open just enough to deal with these two.

"We want a swim!" the man said. He was probably fifty-five, with a booze-mottled face and a brown toupee that squatted on his round head like a slumbering gopher.

Next to him, the blonde of twenty-something, with huge blue eyes and huge big boobs (her towel, thankfully, was tied around her waist), stood almost behind the man. She looked meek. Even embarrassed.

"Mr. Davis," I said, cordial enough, "it's after hours."

"Fuck that! *You're* in here, aren't you?"

"I'm the manager. I sneak a little time in for myself, after closing, after the guests have had their fun."

He put his hand on my bare chest. "Well, *we're* guests, and *we* want to have some fun, too!"

His breath was ninety proof.

I removed his hand. Bending the fingers back a little in the process.

He winced, and started to say something, but I said, "I'm sorry. It's the lodge policy. My apologies to you and your wife."

Bloodshot eyes widened in the face, and he began to say something, but stopped short. He tucked his tail between his legs (and his towel), and took the girl by the arm, roughly, saying, "Come on, baby. We don't need this horseshit."

The blonde looked back at me and gave me a crinkly little chagrined grin, and I smiled back at her, locked the glass door, and climbed back in the hot tub to cool off.

"Asshole," I said. It echoed in the high-ceilinged steamy room. "Fucking asshole!" I said louder, just because I could, and the echo was enjoyable.

He hadn't tucked towel 'tween his legs because I'd bent his fingers back: he'd done it because I mentioned his wife, who we both knew the little blonde bimbo wasn't.

That was because (and here's the outrageous part) he'd been here last month—to this very same resort—with another very attractive blonde, but one about forty, maybe forty-five, who was indeed, and in fact, his lawful wedded wife.

We had guys who came to Sylvan Lodge with their families, we had guys who came with just their wives, and we had guys who came with what used to be called in olden times their mistresses. But we seldom had a son of a bitch so fucking bold as to bring his wife one week, and his mistress the next, to the same goddamn motel, which is what Sylvan Lodge, after all, let's face it, is a glorified version of.

As I enjoyed the jet stream on my low back, I smiled and then frowned, as the memory stirred . . . Christ, I'd forgotten about that! You'd think that Sylvan Lodge itself would've jogged my memory. But it hadn't.

Even though the memory in question was of one of my earliest jobs, which took place at a resort not terribly unlike this one . . .

We met off Interstate 80, at a truck stop outside of the Quad Cities. It was late—almost midnight—a hot, muggy June night; my black T-shirt was sticking to me. My blue jeans, too.

The Broker had taken a booth in back; the restaurant wasn't particularly busy, except for an area designated for truckers. But it had the war-zone look of a rush hour just past; it was a blindingly white but not terribly clean-looking place and the jukebox—wailing "I Shot the Sheriff" at the moment—combated the clatter of dishes being bused.

Sitting with the Broker was an oval-faced, bright-eyed kid of about twenty-three (which at the time was about my age, too) who wore a Doobie Brothers T-shirt and had shoulder-length brown hair. Mine was cut short—not soldier-cut, but businessman short.

"Quarry," the Broker said, in his melodious baritone; he gestured with an open hand. "How good to see you. Sit down." His smile was faint under the wispy mustache, but there was a fatherly air to his manner.

He was trying to look casual in a yellow banlon shirt and golf slacks; he had white, styled hair and a long face that managed to look both fleshy and largely unlined. He was solid-looking man, fairly tall—he looked like a captain of industry, which he was in a way. I took him for fifty, but that was just a guess.

"This is Adam," the Broker said.

"How are you doin', man?" Adam said, and grinned, and half-rose; he seemed a little nervous, and in the process—before I'd even had a chance to decide whether to take the hand he offered or not—overturned a salt shaker, which sent him into a minor tizzy.

"Damn!" Adam said, forgetting about the handshake. "I hate fuckin' bad luck!" He tossed some salt over either shoulder, then grinned at me and said, "I'm afraid I'm one superstitious motherfucker."

"Well, you know what Stevie Wonder says," I said.

He squinted. "No, what?"

Sucker.

"Nothing," I said, sliding in.

A twentyish waitress with a nice shape, a hair net and two pounds of acne took my order, which was for a Coke; the Broker already had coffee and the kid a bottle of Mountain Dew and a glass.

When she went away, I said, "Well, Broker. Got some work for me? I drove hundreds of miles in a fucking gas shortage, so you sure as shit better have."

Adam seemed a little stunned to hear the Broker spoken to so disrespectfully, but the Broker was used to my attitude and merely smiled and patted the air with a benedictory palm.

"I wouldn't waste your time otherwise, Quarry. This will pay handsomely. Ten thousand for the two of you."

Five grand was good money; three was pretty standard. Money was worth more then. You could buy a Snickers bar for ten cents. Or was it fifteen? I forget.

But I was still a little irritated.

"The two of us?" I said. "Adam, here, isn't my better half on this one, is he?"

"Yes he is," the Broker said. He had his hands folded now, prayerfully. His baritone was calming. Or was meant to be.

Adam was frowning, playing nervously with a silver skull ring on the little finger of his left hand. "I don't like your fuckin' attitude, man . . ."

The way he tried to work menace into his voice would have been amusing if I'd given a shit.

"I don't like your fuckin' hippie hair," I said.

"What?" He leaned forward, furious, and knocked his water glass over; it spun on its side and fell off my edge of the booth and we heard it shatter. A few eyes looked our way.

Adam's tiny bright eyes were wide. "Fuck," he said.

"Seven years bad luck, dipshit," I said.

"That's just mirrors!"

"I think it's any kind of glass. Isn't that right, Broker?"

The Broker was frowning a little. "Quarry . . ." He sounded so disappointed in me.

"Hair like that attracts attention," I said. "You go in for a hit, you got to be the invisible man."

"These days everybody wears their hair like this," the kid said defensively.

"In Greenwich Village, maybe. But in America, if you want to disappear, you look like a businessman or a college student."

That made him laugh. "You ever see a college student lately, asshole?"

"I mean the kind who belongs to a fraternity. You want to go around killing people, you need to look clean-cut."

Adam's mouth had dropped open; he had crooked lower teeth. He pointed at me with a thumb and turned to look at Broker, indignant. "Is this guy for real?"

"Yes indeed," the Broker said. "He's also the best active agent I have."

By "active," Broker meant (in his own personal jargon) that I was the half of a hit team that took out the target; the "passive" half was the lookout person, the back-up.

"And he's right," the Broker said, "about your hair."

"Far as that's concerned," I said, "we look pretty god-damn conspicuous right here—me looking collegiate, you looking like the prez of a country club, and junior here like a roadshow Mick Jagger."

Adam looked half bewildered, half outraged.

"You may have a point," the Broker allowed me.

"On the other hand," I said, "people probably think

we're fags waiting for a fourth."

"You're unbelievable," Adam said, shaking his greasy Beatle mop. "I don't want to work with this son of a bitch."

"Stay calm," the Broker said. "I'm not proposing a partnership, not unless this should happen to work out beyond all of our wildest expectations."

"I tend to agree with Adam, here," I said. "We're not made for each other."

"The question is," the Broker said, "are you made for ten thousand dollars?"

Adam and I thought about that.

"I have a job that needs to go down, very soon," he said, "and very quickly. You're the only two men available right now. And I know neither of you wants to disappoint me."

Half of ten grand did sound good to me. I had a lakefront lot in Wisconsin where I could put up this nifty little A-frame prefab, if I could put a few more thousand together . . .

"I'm in," I said, "if he cuts his hair."

The Broker looked at Adam, who scowled and nodded.

"You're both going to like this," the Broker said, sitting forward, withdrawing a travel brochure from his back pocket.

"A resort?" I asked.

"Near Chicago. A wooded area. There's a man-made lake, two indoor swimming pools and one outdoor, an 'old town' gift shop area, several restaurants, bowling alley, tennis courts, horse-back riding . . ."

"If they have archery," I said, "maybe we could arrange a little accident."

That made the Broker chuckle. "You're not far off the mark. We need either an accident, or a robbery. It's an insurance situation."

Broker would tell us no more than that: part of his function was to shield the client from us, and us from the client, for that matter. He was sort of a combination agent and buffer; he could tell us only this much: the target was going down so that someone could collect insurance. The double indemnity kind that comes from accidental death, and of course getting killed by thieves counts in that regard.

"This is him," Broker said, carefully showing us a photograph of a thin, handsome, tanned man of possibly sixty with black hair that was probably dyed; he wore dark sunglasses and tennis togs and had an arm around a dark-haired woman of about forty, a tanned slim busty woman also in dark glasses and tennis togs.

"Who's the babe?" Adam said.

"The wife," the Broker said.

The client.

"The client?" Adam asked.

"I didn't say that," Broker said edgily, "and you mustn't ask stupid questions. Your target is this man—Baxter Bennedict."

"I hope his wife isn't named Bunny," I said.

The Broker chuckled again, but Adam didn't see the joke.

"Close. Her name is Bernice, actually."

I groaned. "One more 'B' and I'll kill 'em *both*—for free."

The Broker took out a silver cigarette case. "Actually, that's going to be one of the . . . delicate aspects of this job."

"How so?" I asked.

He offered me a cigarette from the case and I waved it off; he offered one to Adam, and he took it.

The Broker said, "They'll be on vacation. Together, at

221

the Wistful Wagon Lodge. She's not to be harmed. You must wait and watch until you can get him alone."

"And then make it look like an accident," I said.

"Or a robbery. Correct." The Broker struck a match, lighted his cigarette. He tried to light Adam's, but Adam gestured no, frantically.

"Two on match," he said. Then got a lighter out and lit himself up.

"Two on a match?" I asked.

"Haven't you ever heard that?" the kid asked, almost wild-eyed. "Two on a match. It's unlucky!"

"*Three* on a match is unlucky," I said.

Adam squinted at me. "Are you superstitious, too?"

I looked hard at Broker, who merely shrugged.

"I gotta pee," the kid said suddenly, and had the Broker let him slide out. Standing, he wasn't very big: probably five seven. Skinny. His jeans were tattered.

When we were alone, I said, "What are you doing, hooking me up with that dumb-ass jerk?"

"Give him a chance. He was in Vietnam. Like you. He's not completely inexperienced."

"Most of the guys I knew in Vietnam were stoned twenty-four hours a day. That's not what I'm looking for in a partner."

"He's just a little green. You'll season him."

"I'll ice him if he fucks up. Understood?"

The Broker shrugged. "Understood."

When Adam came back, Broker let him in and said, "The hardest part is, you have a window of only four days."

"That's bad," I said, frowning. "I like to maintain a sur-veillance, get a pattern down . . ."

Broker shrugged again. "It's a different situation. They're on vacation. They won't have much of a pattern."

"Great."

Now the Broker frowned. "Why in hell do you think it pays so well? Think of it as hazardous duty pay."

Adam sneered and said, "What's the matter, Quarry? Didn't you never take no fuckin' risks?"

"I think I'm about to," I said.

"It'll go well," the Broker said.

"Knock on wood," the kid said, and rapped on the table.

"That's Formica," I said.

The Wistful Wagon Lodge sprawled out over numerous wooded acres, just off the outskirts of Wistful Vista, Illinois. According to the Broker's brochure, back in the late forties, the hamlet had taken the name of Fibber McGee and Molly's fictional hometown, for purposes of attracting tourists; apparently one of the secondary stars of the radio show had been born nearby. This marketing ploy had been just in time for television making radio passé, and the little farm community's only remaining sign of having at all successfully tapped into the tourist trade was the Wistful Wagon Lodge itself.

A cobblestone drive wound through the scattering of log cabins, and several larger buildings—including the main lodge where the check-in and restaurants were—were similarly rustic structures, but of gray weathered wood. Trees clustered everywhere, turning warm sunlight into cool pools of shade; wood-burned signs showed the way to this building or that path, and decorative wagon wheels, often with flower beds in and around them, were scattered about as if some long-ago pioneer mishap had been beautified by nature and time. Of course that wasn't the case: this was the hokey hand of man.

We arrived separately, Adam and I, each having reserved

rooms in advance, each paying cash up front upon registration; no credit cards. We each had log-cabin cottages, not terribly close to one another.

As the backup and surveillance man, Adam went in early. The target and his wife were taking a long weekend—arriving Thursday, leaving Monday. I didn't arrive until Saturday morning.

I went to Adam's cabin and knocked, but got no answer. Which just meant he was trailing Mr. and Mrs. Target around the grounds. After I dropped my stuff off at my own cabin, I wandered, trying to get the general layout of the place, checking out the lodge itself, where about half of the rooms were, as well as two restaurants. Everything had a pine smell, which was partially the many trees, and partially Pine-Sol. Wistful Wagon was Hollywood rustic—there was a dated quality about it, from the cowboy/cowgirl attire of the waiters and waitresses in the Wistful Chuckwagon Cafe to the wood-and-leather furnishings to the barnwood-framed Remington prints.

I got myself some lunch and traded smiles with a giggly tableful of college girls who were on a weekend scouting expedition of their own. *Good,* I thought. *If I can connect with one of them tonight, that'll provide nice cover.*

As I was finishing up, my cowgirl waitress, a curly-haired blonde pushing thirty who was pretty cute herself, said, "Looks like you might get lucky tonight."

She was re-filling my coffee cup.

"With them or with you?" I asked.

She had big washed-out blue eyes and heavy eye make-up, more sixties than seventies. She was wearing a fifties-style cowboy hat cinched under her chin. "I'm not supposed to fraternize with the guests."

"How did you know I was a fraternity man?"

She laughed a little; her chin crinkled. Her face was kind of round and she was a little pudgy, nicely so in the bosom. "Wild stab," she said. "Anyway, there's an open dance in the ballroom. Off the Wagontrain Dining Room? Country swing band. You'll like it."

"You inviting me?"

"No," she said; she narrowed her eyes and cocked her head, her expression one of mild scolding. "Those little girls'll be there, and plenty of others. You won't have any trouble finding what you want."

"I bet I will."

"Why's that?"

"I was hoping for a girl wearing cowboy boots like yours."

"Oh, there'll be girls in cowboy boots there tonight."

"I meant, just cowboy boots."

She laughed at that, shook her head; under her Dale Evans hat, her blonde curls bounced off her shoulders.

She went away and let me finish my coffee, and I smiled at the college girls some more, but when I paid for my check, at the register, it was my plump little cowgirl again.

"I work late tonight," she said.

"How late?"

"I get off at midnight," she said.

"That's only the first time," I said.

"First time what?"

"That you'll get off tonight."

She liked that. Times were different, then. The only way you could die from fucking was if a husband or boyfriend caught you at it. She told me where to meet her, later.

I strolled back up a winding path to my cabin. A few groups of college girls and college guys, not paired off together yet, were buzzing around; some couples in their twenties up into their sixties were walking, often hand-in-hand, around the sun-dappled, lushly shaded grounds. The sound of a gentle breeze in the trees made a faint shimmering music. Getting laid here was no trick.

I got my swim trunks on and grabbed a towel and headed for the nearest pool, which was the outdoor one. That's where I found Adam.

He did look like a college frat rat, with his shorter hair; his skinny pale body reddening, he was sitting in a deck chair, sipping a Coke, in sunglasses and racing trunks, chatting with a couple of bikinied college cuties, also in sunglasses.

"Bill?" I said.

"Jim?" he said, taking off his sunglasses to get a better look at me. He grinned, extended his hand. I took it, shook it, as he stood. "I haven't seen you since spring break!"

We'd agreed to be old high-school buddies from Peoria who had gone to separate colleges; I was attending the University of Iowa, he was at Michigan. We avoided using Illinois schools because Illinois kids were who we'd most likely run into here.

Adam introduced me to the girls—I don't remember their names, but one was a busty brunette Veronica, the other a flat-chested blonde Betty. The sound of splashing and running, screaming kids—though this was a couples' hideaway, there was a share of families here, as well—kept the conversation to a blessed minimum. The girls were nursing majors. We were engineering majors. We all liked Credence Clearwater. We all hoped Nixon would get the book thrown at him. We were all going to the dance tonight.

Across the way, Baxter Bennedict was sitting in a deck chair under an umbrella reading *Jaws*. Every page or so, he'd sip his martini; every ten pages or so, he'd wave a waitress in cowgirl vest and white plastic hot pants over for another one. His wife was swimming, her dark arms cutting the water like knives. It seemed methodical, an exercise workout in the midst of a pool filled with water babies of various ages.

When she pulled herself out of the water, her suit a stark, startling white against her almost-burned-black skin, she revealed a slender, rather tall figure; tight ass, high, full breasts. Her rather lined leathery face was the only tip-off to her age, and that had the blessing of a model's beauty to get it by.

She pulled off a white swim cap and unfurled a mane of dark, blond-tipped hair. Toweling herself off, she bent to kiss her husband on the cheek, but he only scowled at her. She stretched out on her colorful beach towel beside him, to further blacken herself.

"Oooo," said Veronica. "What's that ring?"

"That's my lucky ring," Adam said.

That fucking skull ring of his! Had he been dumb enough to wear that? Yes.

"Bought that at a Grateful Dead concert, didn't you, Bill?" I asked.

"Uh, yeah," he said.

"Ick," said Betty. "I don't like the Dead. Their hair is greasy. They're so . . . druggie."

"Drugs aren't so bad," Veronica said boldly, thrusting out her admirably thrustworthy bosom.

"Bill and I had our wild days back in high school," I said. "You shoulda seen our hair—down to our asses, right Bill?"

"Right."

"But we don't do that anymore," I said. "Kinda put that behind us."

"Well I for one don't approve of drugs," Betty said.

"Don't blame you," I said.

"Except for grass, of course," she said.

"Of course."

"And coke. Scientific studies prove coke isn't bad for you."

"Well, you're in nursing," I said. "You'd know."

We made informal dates with the girls for the dance, and I wandered off with "Bill" to his cabin.

"The skull ring was a nice touch," I said.

He frowned at me. "Fuck you—it's my lucky ring!"

A black gardener on a rider mower rumbled by us.

"Now we're really in trouble," I said.

He looked genuinely concerned. "What do you mean?"

"A black cat crossed our path."

In Adam's cabin, I sat on the brown, fake-leather sofa while he sat on the nubby yellow bedspread and spread his hands.

"They actually do have a sorta pattern," he said, "vacation or not."

Adam had arrived on Wednesday; the Bennedicts had arrived Thursday around two P.M., which was check-in time.

"They drink and swim all afternoon," Adam said, "and they go dining and dancing—and drinking—in the evening."

"What about mornings?"

"Tennis. He doesn't start drinking till lunch."

"Doesn't she drink?"

"Not as much. He's an asshole. We're doing the world a favor, here."

"How do you mean?"

He shrugged; he looked very different in his short hair. "He's kind of abusive. He don't yell at her, but just looking at them, you can see him glaring at her all the time, real ugly. Saying things that hurt her."

"She doesn't stand up to him?"

He shook his head, no. "They're very one-sided arguments. He either sits there and ignores her or he's giving her foul looks and it looks like he's chewing her out or something."

"Sounds like a sweet guy."

"After the drinking and dining and dancing, they head to the bar. Both nights so far, she's gone off to bed around eleven and he's stayed and shut the joint down."

"Good. That means he's alone when he walks back to their cabin."

Adam nodded. "But this place is crawlin' with people."

"Not at two in the morning. Most of these people are sleeping or fucking by then."

"Maybe so. He's got a fancy watch, some heavy gold jewelry."

"Well that's very good. Now we got ourselves a motive."

"But *she's* the one with jewels." He whistled. "You should see the rocks hanging off that dame."

"Well, we aren't interested in those."

"What about the stuff you steal off him? Just toss it somewhere?"

"Hell no! Broker'll have it fenced for us. A little extra dough for our trouble."

He grinned. "Great. This is easy money. Vacation with pay."

"Don't ever think that . . . don't ever let your guard down."

"I know that," he said defensively.

"It's unlucky to think that way," I said, and knocked on wood. Real wood.

★ ★ ★ ★ ★

We met up with Betty and Veronica at the dance; I took Betty because Adam was into knockers and Veronica had them. Betty was pleasant company, but I wasn't listening to her babble. I was keeping an eye on the Bennedicts, who were seated at a corner table under a buffalo head.

He really was an asshole. You could tell, by the way he sneered at her and spit sentences out at her, that he'd spent a lifetime—or at least a marriage—making her miserable. His hatred for her was something you could see as well as sense, like steam over asphalt. She was taking it placidly. Cool as Cher while Sonny prattled on.

But I had a hunch she usually took it more personally. Right now she could be placid: she knew the son of a bitch was going to die this weekend.

"Did you ever do Lauderdale?" Betty was saying. "I got *so* drunk there . . ."

The band was playing "Crazy" and a decent girl singer was doing a respectable Patsy Cline. What a great song.

I said, "I won a chug-a-lug contest at Boonie's in '72."

Betty was impressed. "Were you even in college then?"

"No. I had a hell of a fake I.D., though."

"Bitchen!"

Around eleven, the band took a break and we walked the girls to their cabins, hand in hand, like high school sweethearts. Gas lanterns on poles scorched the night orange; a half-moon threw some silvery light on us, too. Adam disappeared around the side of the cabin with Veronica and I stood and watched Betty beam at me and rock girlishly on her heels. She smelled of perfume and beer, which mingled with the scent of pines; it was more pleasant than it sounds.

She was making with the dimples. "You're so nice."

"Well thanks."

"And I'm a good judge of character."

"I bet you are."

Then she put her arms around me and pressed her slim frame to me and put her tongue halfway down my throat.

She pulled herself away and smiled coquettishly and said, "That's all you get tonight. See you tomorrow."

As if on cue, Veronica appeared with her lipstick mussed up and her sweater askew.

"Good night, boys," Veronica said, and they slipped inside, giggling like the schoolgirls they were.

"Fuck," Adam said, scowling. "All I got was a little bare tit."

"Not so little."

"I thought I was gonna get laid."

I shrugged. "Instead you got screwed."

We walked. We passed a cabin that was getting some remodeling and repairs; I'd noticed it earlier. A ladder was leaned up against the side, for some re-roofing. Adam made a wide circle around the ladder. I walked under it just to watch him squirm.

When I fell back in step with him, he said, "You gonna do the hit tonight?"

"No."

"Bar closes at midnight on Sundays. Gonna do it then?"

"Yes."

He sighed. "Good."

We walked, and it was the place where one path went toward my cabin, and another toward his.

"Well," he said, "maybe I'll get lucky tomorrow night."

"No pick-ups the night of the hit. I need back-up more than either of us needs an alibi, or an easy fuck, either."

"Oh. Of course. You're right. Sorry. 'Night."

" 'Night, Bill."

Then I went back and picked up the waitress cowgirl and took her to my cabin; she had some dope in her purse, and I smoked a little with her, just to be nice, and apologized for not having a rubber, and she said, "Don't sweat it, pardner, I'm on the pill," and she rode me in her cowboy boots until my dick said yahoo.

The next morning I had breakfast in the cafe with Adam and he seemed preoccupied as I ate my scrambled eggs and bacon, and he poked at his French toast.

"Bill," I said. "What's wrong?"

"I'm worried."

"What about?"

We were seated in a rough-wood booth and had plenty of privacy; we kept our voices down. Our conversation, after all, wasn't really proper breakfast conversation.

"I don't think you should hit him like that."

"Like what?"

He frowned. "On his way back to his cabin after the bar closes."

"Oh? Why?"

"He might not be drunk enough. Bar closes early Sunday night, remember?"

"Jesus," I said. "The fucker starts drinking at noon. What more do you want?"

"But there could be people around."

"At midnight?"

"It's a resort. People get romantic at resorts. Moonlight strolls . . ."

"You got a better idea?"

He nodded. "Do it in his room. Take the wife's jewels and it's a robbery got out of hand. In and out. No fuss, no muss."

"Are you high? What about the wife?"

"She won't be there."

"What are you talking about?"

He started gesturing, earnestly. "She gets worried about him, see. It's midnight, and she goes looking for him. While she's gone, he gets back, flops on the bed, you come in, bing bang boom."

I just looked at him. "Are you psychic now? How do we know she'll do that?"

He swallowed; took a nibble at a forkful of syrup-dripping French toast. Smiled kind of nervously.

"She told me so," he said.

We were walking now. The sun was filtering through the trees and birds were chirping and the sounds of children laughing wafted through the air.

"Are you fucking nuts? Making contact with the client?"

"Quarry—she contacted me! I swear!"

"Then *she's* fucking nuts. Jesus!" I sat on a bench by a flower bed. "It's off. I'm calling the Broker. It's over."

"Listen to me! Listen. She was waiting for me at my cabin last night. After we struck out with the college girls? She was fuckin' waitin' for me! She told me she knew who I was."

"How did she know that?"

"She said she saw me watching them. She figured it out. She guessed."

"And, of course, you confirmed her suspicions."

He swallowed. "Yeah."

"You dumb-ass dickhead. Who said it first?"

"Who said what first?"

"Who mentioned 'killing'? Who mentioned 'murder'?"

His cheek twitched. "Well . . . me, I guess. She kept

saying she knew why I was here. And then she said, 'I'm why you're here. I hired you.' "

"And you copped to it. God. I'm on the next bus."

"Quarry! Listen . . . this is better this way. This is much better."

"What did she do, fuck you?"

He blanched; looked at his feet.

"Oh God," I said. "You did get lucky last night. Fuck. You fucked the client. Did you tell her there were two of us?"

"No."

"She's seen us together."

"I told her you're just a guy I latched onto here to look less conspicuous."

"Did she buy it?"

"Why shouldn't she? I say we scrap Plan A and move to Plan B. It's better."

"Plan B being . . . ?"

"Quarry, she's going to leave the door unlocked. She'll wait for him to get back from the bar, and when he's asleep, she'll unlock the door, go out and pretend to be looking for him, and come back and find him dead, and her jewels gone. Help-police-I-been-robbed-my-husband's-been-shot. You know."

"She's being pretty fucking helpful, you ask me."

His face clenched like a fist. "The bastard has beat her for years. And he's got a girl friend a third his age. He's been threatening to divorce her, and since they signed a pre-marital agreement, she gets jack shit, if they divorce. The bastard."

"Quite a sob story."

"I told you: we're doing the world a favor. And now she's doing us one. Why shoot him right out in the open, when we can walk in his room and do it? You got to stick this out, Quarry. Shit, man, it's five grand a piece, and change!"

I thought about it.

"Quarry?"

I'd been thinking a long time.

"Okay," I said. "Give her the high sign. We'll do it her way."

The Bar W Bar was a cozy rustic room decorated with framed photos of movie cowboys from Ken Maynard to John Wayne, from Audie Murphy to the Man with No Name. On a brown mock-leather stool up at the bar, Baxter Bennedict sat, a thin handsome drunk in a pale blue polyester sportcoat and pale yellow banlon sportshirt, gulping martinis and telling anyone who'd listen his sad story.

I didn't sit near enough to be part of the conversation, but I could hear him.

"Milking me fucking dry," he was saying. "You'd think with sixteen goddamn locations, I'd be sitting pretty. I was the first guy in the Chicago area to offer a paint job under thirty dollars—twenty-nine ninety-five! That's a good fucking deal—isn't it?"

The bartender—a young fellow in a buckskin vest, polishing a glass—nodded sympathetically.

"Now this competition. Killing me. What the fuck kind of paint job can you get for nineteen ninety-nine? Will you answer me that one? And now that bitch has the nerve . . ."

Now he was muttering. The bartender began to move away, but Baxter started in again.

"She wants me to sell! My life's work. Started from nothing. And she wants me to sell! Pitiful fucking money they offered. Pitiful . . ."

"Last call, Mr. Bennedict," the bartender said. Then he

repeated it, louder, without the "Mr. Bennedict." The place was only moderately busy. A few couples. A solitary drinker or two. The Wistful Wagon Lodge had emptied out, largely, this afternoon—even Betty and Veronica were gone. Sunday. People had to go to work tomorrow. Except, of course, for those who owned their own businesses, like Baxter here.

Or had unusual professions, like mine.

I waited until the slender figure had stumbled halfway home before I approached him. No one was around. The nearest cabin was dark.

"Mr. Bennedict," I said.

"Yeah?" He turned, trying to focus his bleary eyes.

"I couldn't help but hear what you said. I think I have a solution for your problems."

"Yeah?" He grinned. "And what the hell would that be?"

He walked, on the unsteadiest of legs, up to me.

I showed him the nine-millimeter with its bulky sound suppresser. It probably looked like a ray gun to him.

"Fuck! What is this, a fucking hold-up?"

"Yes. Keep your voice down or it'll turn into a fucking homicide. Got me?"

That turned him sober. "Got you. What do you want?"

"What do you think? Your watch and your rings."

He smirked disgustedly and removed them; handed them over.

"Now your sportcoat."

"My what?"

"Your sportcoat. I just can't get enough polyester."

He snorted a laugh. "You're out of your gourd, pal."

He slipped off the sportcoat and handed it out toward me with two fingers; he was weaving a little, smirking drunkenly.

I took the coat with my left hand, and the silenced nine-millimeter went *thup thup thup;* three small, brilliant blossoms of red appeared on his light yellow banlon. He was dead before he had time to think about it.

I dragged his body behind a clump of trees and left him there, his worries behind him.

I watched from behind a tree as Bernice Bennedict slipped out of their cabin; she was wearing a dark halter top and dark slacks that almost blended with her burnt-black skin, making a wraith of her. She had a big white handbag on a shoulder strap. She was so dark the white bag seemed to float in space as she headed toward the lodge.

Only she stopped and found her own tree to duck behind.

I smiled to myself.

Then, wearing the pale blue polyester sportcoat, I entered their cabin, through the door she'd left open. The room was completely dark, but for some minor filtering in of light through curtained windows. Quickly I arranged some pillows under sheets and covers, to create the impression of a person in the bed.

And I called Adam's cabin.

"Hey, Bill," I said. "It's Jim."

His voice was breathless. "Is it done?"

"No. I got cornered coming out of the bar by that waitress I was out with last night. She latched onto me—she's in my john."

"What, are you in your room?"

"Yeah. I saw Bennedict leave the bar at midnight, and his wife passed us, heading for the lodge, just minutes ago. You've got a clear shot at him."

"What? Me? I'm the fucking lookout!"

"Tonight's the night and we go to Plan C."

"I didn't know there *was* a Plan C."

"Listen, asshole—it was you who wanted to switch plans. You've got a piece, don't you?"

"Of course . . ."

"Well you're elected. Go!"

And I hung up.

I stood in the doorway of the bathroom, which faced the bed. I sure as hell didn't turn any lights on, although my left hand hovered by the switch. The nine-millimeter with the silencer was heavy in my right hand. But I didn't mind.

Adam came in quickly and didn't do too bad a job of it: four silenced slugs. He should have checked the body—it never occurred to him he'd just slaughtered a bunch of pillows—but if somebody had been in that bed, they'd have been dead.

He went to the dresser where he knew the jewels would be, and was picking up the jewelry box when the door opened and she came in, the little revolver already in her hand.

Before she could fire, I turned on the bathroom light and said, "If I don't hear the gun hit the floor immediately, you're fucking dead."

She was just a black shape, except for the white handbag; but I saw the flash of silver as the gun bounced to the carpeted floor.

"What . . . ?" Adam was saying. It was too dark to see any expression, but he was obviously as confused as he was spooked.

"Shut the door, lady," I said, "and turn on the lights."

She did.

She really was a beautiful woman, or had been, dark eyes and scarlet-painted mouth in that finely carved model's face, but it was just a leathery mask to me.

"What . . ." Adam said. He looked shocked as hell, which made sense; the gun was in his waistband, the jewelry box in his hands.

"You didn't know there were two of us, did you, Mrs. Bennedict?"

She was sneering faintly; she shook her head, no.

"You see, kid," I told Adam, "she wanted her husband hit, but she wanted the hit man dead, too. Cleaner. Tidier. Right?"

"Fuck you," she said.

"I'm not much for sloppy seconds, thanks. Bet you got a nice legal license for that little purse peashooter of yours, don't you? Perfect protection for when you stumble in on an intruder who's just killed your loving husband. Who *is* dead, by the way. Somebody'll run across him in the morning, probably."

"You bitch!" Adam said. He raised his own gun, which was a .380 Browning with a homemade suppressor.

"Don't you know it's bad luck to kill a woman?" I said.

She was frozen, one eye twitching.

Adam was trembling. He swallowed; nodded. "Okay," he said, lowering the gun. "Okay."

"Go," I told him.

She stepped aside as he slipped out the door, shutting it behind him.

"Thank you," she said, and I shot her twice in the chest.

I slipped the bulky silenced automatic in my waistband; grabbed the jewelry box off the dresser.

"I make my own luck," I told her, but she didn't hear me, as I stepped over her.

I never worked with Adam again. I think he was disturbed, when he read the papers and realized I'd iced the woman after all. Maybe he got out of the business. Or maybe he wound up dead in a ditch, his lucky skull ring still on his little finger. Broker never said, and I was never interested enough to ask.

Now, years later, lounging in the hot tub at Sylvan Lodge, I look back on my actions and wonder how I could have ever have been so young, and so rash.

Killing the woman was understandable. She'd double-crossed us; she would've killed us both without batting a false lash.

But sleeping with that cowgirl waitress, on the job. Smoking dope. Not using a rubber.

I was really pushing my luck that time.

Guest Services

An American flag flapped lazily on its silver pole against a sky so washed-out a blue the handful of clouds were barely discernible. The red, white and blue of it were garishly out of place against the brilliant greens and muted blues of the Minnesota landscape, pines shimmering vividly in late morning sunlight, the surface of gray-blue Sylvan Lake glistening with sun, rippling with gentle waves. The rails of the grayish brown deck beyond my quarters were like half-hearted prison bars that I peeked through, as I did my morning sit-ups on the other side of the triple glass doors of my well-appointed guest suite.

I was not a guest of Sylvan Lodge, however: I ran the place. Once upon a time I had owned a resort in Wisconsin not unlike this—not near the acreage, of course, and not near the occupancy; but I had *owned* the place, whereas here I was just the manager.

Not that I had anything to complain about. I was lucky to have the job. When I ran into Gary Petersen in Milwaukee, where he was attending a convention and I was making a one-night stopover to remove some emergency funds from several bank deposit boxes, I was at the loosest of loose ends. The name I'd lived under for over a decade was unusable; my past had caught up with me, back at the other place, and I'd lost everything in a near instant: my business yanked from under me, my wife (who'd had not a clue of my prior existence) murdered in her sleep.

Gary, however, had recognized me in the hotel bar and

used a name I hadn't used since the early seventies: my real name.

"Jack!" he said, only that wasn't the name he used. For the purposes of this narrative, however, we'll say my real name is Jack Keller.

"Gary," I said, surprised by the warmth creeping into my voice. "You son of a bitch . . . you're still alive."

Gary was a huge man—six-six, weighing in at somewhere between three hundred pounds and a ton; his face was masked in a bristly brown beard, his skull exposed by hair loss, his dark eyes bright, his smile friendly, in a goofy, almost child-like way.

"Thanks to you, asshole," he said.

We'd been in Vietnam together.

"What the hell have you been doing all these years, Jack?"

"Mostly killing people."

He boomed a laugh. "Yeah, right!"

"Don't believe me, then." I was, incidentally, pretty drunk. I don't drink often, but I'd been through the mill lately.

"Are you crying, Jack?"

"Fuck no," I said. But I was.

Gary slipped his arm around my shoulder; it was like getting cuddled by God. "Bro—what's the deal? What shit have you been through?"

"They killed my wife," I said, and cried drunkenly into his shoulder.

"Jesus, Jack—who . . . ?"

"Fucking assholes . . . fucking assholes . . ."

We went to his suite. He was supposed to play poker with some buddies but he called it off.

I was very drunk and very morose and Gary was, at one

time anyway, my closest friend, and during the most desperate of days.

I told him everything. I told him how after I got back from Nam, I found my wife—my first wife—shacked up with some guy, some fucking auto mechanic, who was working under a car when I found him and kicked the jack out. The jury let me off, but I was finished in my hometown, and I drifted until the Broker found me. The Broker, who gave me the name Quarry, was the conduit through whom the murder for hire contracts came, and, what? Ten years later the Broker was dead, by my hand, and I was out of the killing business and took my savings and went to Paradise Lake in Wisconsin, where eventually I met a pleasant, attractive, not terribly bright woman and she and I were in the lodge business until the past came looking for me, and suddenly she was dead, and I was without a life or even identity. I had managed to kill the fuckers responsible for my wife's killing, but otherwise I had nothing. Nothing left but some money stashed away, that I was now retrieving.

I told Gary all this, through the night, in considerably more detail though probably even less coherently, although coherently enough that when I woke up the next morning, where Gary had laid me out on the extra bed, I knew I'd told him too much.

He was asleep, too. Like me, he was in the same clothes we'd worn to that bar; like me, he smelled of booze, only he also reeked of cigarette smoke. I did a little, too, but it was Gary's smoke: I never picked up the habit. Bad for you.

He looked like a big dead animal, except for his barrel-like chest heaving with breath. I looked at this man—like me, he was somewhere between forty and fifty now, not the kids we'd been before the war made us worse than just men.

243

I still had liquor in me, but I was sober now. Too deadly fucking sober. I studied my best-friend-of-long-ago and wondered if I had to kill him.

I was standing over him, staring down at him, mulling that over, when his eyes opened suddenly, like a timer turning on the lights in a house to fend off burglars.

He smiled a little, then it faded, then his eyes narrowed, and he said, "Morning, Jack."

"Morning, Gary."

"You've got that look."

"What look is that?"

"The cold one. The one I first saw a long time ago."

I swallowed and looked away from him. Sat on the edge of the bed across from him and rubbed my eyes with the heels of my hands.

He sat across from me with his big hands on his big knees and said, "How the hell d'you manage it?"

"What?"

"Hauling my fat ass into that Medivac."

I grunted a laugh. "The same way a little mother lifts a Buick off her baby."

"In my case, you lifted the Buick onto the baby. Let me buy you breakfast."

"Okay."

In the hotel coffee shop, he said, "Funny . . . what you told me last night . . . about the business you used to be in?"

I sipped my coffee; I didn't look at him—didn't show him my eyes. "Yeah?"

"I'm in the same game."

Now I looked at him; I winced with disbelief. "What . . . ?"

He corrected my initial thought. "The tourist game, I mean. I run a lodge near Brainerd."

"No kidding."

"That's what this convention is. Northern Resort Owners' Association."

"I heard of it," I said, nodding. "Never bothered to join, myself."

"I'm a past president. Anyway, I run a place called Sylvan Lodge. My third and current, and I swear to God, everlasting wife, Ruth Ann, inherited it from her late parents, rest their hardworking souls." None of this came as a surprise to me. Grizzly bear Gary had always drawn women like a great big magnet—usually good-looking little women who wanted a father figure, Papa Bear variety. Even in Bangkok on R & R, Gary never had to pay for pussy, as we used to delicately phrase it.

"I'm happy for you. I always figured you'd manage to marry for money."

"My ass! I really love Ruth Ann. You should see the knockers on the child."

"A touching testimonial if ever I heard one. Listen . . . about that bullshit I was spouting last night . . ."

His dark eyes became slits, the smile in his brushy face disappeared. "We'll never speak of that again. Understood? Never."

He reached out and squeezed my forearm.

I sighed in relief and smiled tightly and nodded, relieved. Killing Gary would have been no fun at all.

He continued, though. "My sorry fat ass wouldn't even be on this planet, if it wasn't for you. I owe you big-time."

"Bullshit," I said, but not very convincingly.

"I've had a good life, at least the last ten years or so, since I met Ruthie. You've been swimming in Shit River long enough. Let me help you."

"Gary, I . . ."

"Actually, I want you to help me."

"Help *you?*"

Gary's business was such a thriving one that he had recently invested in a second lodge, one across the way from his Gull Lake resort. He couldn't run both places himself, at least not "without running my fat ass off." He offered me the job of managing Sylvan.

"We'll start you at 50K, with free housing. You can make a tidy buck with no overhead to speak of, and you can tap into at least one of your marketable skills, and at the same time be out of the way. Keep as low a profile as you like. You don't even have to deal with the tourists, to speak of—we have a social director for that. You just keep the boat afloat. Okay?"

"Okay," I said, and we shook hands. Goddamn I was glad I hadn't killed him . . .

Now, a little more than six months into the job, and a month into the first summer season, I was settled in and damn near happy. My quarters, despite the rustic trappings of the cabin-like exterior, were modern—pine paneling skirting the room with pale yellow pastel walls rising to a high pointed ceiling. It was just one room with bath and kitchenette, but it was a big room, facing the lake which was a mere hundred yards from the deck that was my back porch. Couch, cable TV, plenty of closet space, a comfortable wall bed. I didn't need anything more.

During off-season, I could move into more spacious digs if I liked, but I didn't figure I'd bother. Just a short jog across the way was an indoor swimming pool with hot tub and sauna, plus a tennis court; a golf course, shared with Gary's other lodge, was nearby. My duties were constant, but mostly consisted of delegating authority, and the gay chef of our gourmet restaurant made sure I ate well and free, and I'd been banging Nikki, the college girl who had the social director position for the summer, so my staff relations were solid.

I took a shower after my push-ups and got into the usual gray Sylvan lodge T-shirt, black shorts and gray-and-black Reeboks, to take a stroll around the grounds, and check up on the staff. I was sitting on the couch tying my tennies, with a good view of the patch of green and slice of sand below my deck, when I heard an unpleasant, gravelly male voice tearing somebody a new asshole. "Why the fuck *didn't* you rent the boat in advance, Mindy?"

"I'm sorry, Dick."

"Jesus fucking Christ, woman, you think I want to come to a goddamn lake without a goddamn boat?"

His voice carried into my living room with utter clarity, borne by the wind coming across the lake.

I looked up. He was big—not as big as my friend Gary, but big enough. He wore green and red plaid shorts and a lime-green golf shirt and a straw pork-pie hat with a wide leather band; he was as white as the underbelly of a crocodile, except for his face, which was a bloodshot red. Even at this distance I could see the white tufts of eyebrows over narrow-set eyes and a bulbous nose.

He was probably fifty, or maybe more; his wife was an attractive blonde, much younger, possibly thirty-five. She wore a denim shorts outfit that revealed an almost plump but considerably shapely figure, nicely top-heavy. Her hair was too platinum for her age, and too big for her face, a huge hair-sprayed construction with a childishly incongruous pink bow in it.

Her pretty face, even from where I sat on my couch, was tired-looking, puffy. But she'd been beautiful, once. An actress or a dancer or something. And even now, even with the too big, too platinum hair, she made a man's head turn. Except maybe for my chef.

"But I thought you'd use your brother's boat . . ."

"He's in fucking Europe, woman!"

"I know . . . but you said we were going to use Jim's boat . . ."

"Well, that fell through! He loaned his place *and* his boat to some fucker from Duluth he wanted to impress! Putting business before his own goddamn brother . . ."

"But I didn't know that . . ."

He grabbed her arm; hard. "You should've made it your business *to* know! *You* were supposed to make the vacation arrangements; God knows you have little enough to do otherwise. I have a fucking living to make for us. You should've got off your fat ass and . . ."

"Let's talk to Guest Services," his wife said, desperately. "Maybe they can help us rent a boat somewhere in the area."

"Excuse me!" I called from the deck.

Still holding onto the woman's arm, the aptly named Dick scowled my way. "What do you want? Who the hell are you?"

I was leaning over the rail. "I'm the manager here. Jack Keller. Can I be of any help?"

He let go of her arm and the plump, pretty blonde moved toward me, looking up at me with a look that strained to be pleasant. "I called both numbers your brochure lists, and wasn't able to rent a boat . . ."

"It's a busy time," I said. "Let me look into it for you."

"We're only going to be here a week," Dick said. "I hate to waste a goddamn day!"

She touched his arm, gently. "We wanted to golf while we here . . . we did bring the clubs . . . we could do that today . . ."

He brushed her hand away like it was a bug. "Probably have to call ahead for that, too."

"I'll call over for you," I said. "You are . . . ?"

"The Waltons," he said.

"Excuse me?"

"We're the fucking Waltons! Dick and Mindy."

The Waltons. Okay . . .

"Dick, I'll make the call. After lunch, around one-thirty a suitable tee time?"

"Good," Dick said, pacified. "Thanks for your help."

"That's what I'm here for," I said.

"Thank you," Mindy said, and smiled at me, and looped her arm in his, and he allowed her to, as he walked her over to the restaurant.

I called over to the golf course and got the Waltons a tee time, and called Gary over at Gull Lake Lodge to see about a boat.

"They should've called ahead," Gary said. "Why do you want to help these people? Friends of yours?"

"Hardly. The husband's an obnoxious cocksucker who'll browbeat his wife into a nervous breakdown if I don't bail her out."

"Oh. The Waltons."

"Addams Family is more like it. So you know them?"

"They were at Sylvan the last two seasons. Dick Walton is a real pain in the ass, and an ugly drunk."

"Maybe we don't want his business."

"Trouble is, he's as rich as he is obnoxious. He's from Minneapolis—runs used car lots all over the Cities. Big fucking ego—does his own commercials. 'Big Deals with Big Dick' is his motto . . ."

"Catchy."

"It's been popular with Twin Cities school kids for a

couple decades. He's worth several mil. And he brings his sales staff up for conferences in the off-season."

"So we cater to him."

"Yeah. Within reason. If he starts busting up the bar or something, cut him off and toss his ass out. When he starts spoiling things for our other guests, then fuck him."

"I like your attitude, Gary. But what about a boat?"

"He can use mine for the week. It's down at dock nine."

"That's generous."

"Generous my ass. Charge him double the going rate."

The restaurant at Sylvan's is four-star, and it's a real asset for the business, but it's the only thing Gary and I ever really disagreed about. Dinner was by reservation only, and those reservations filled up quick; and the prices were more New York than Midwest.

"The goddamn restaurant's a real calling card for us," Gary would say. "Brings in people staying at other lodges and gives 'em a look at ours."

"But we're not serving our own guests," I'd say. "We're a hotel at heart, Gary, and our clientele shouldn't have to mortgage the farm to buy supper, and they shouldn't get turned away 'cause they don't have reservations."

"I appreciate your dedication to the guests, Jack. But that restaurant brings in about a third of our income, so fuckin' forget it, okay?"

But of course I didn't. We had this same argument at least twice a month.

That particular evening I was having the house specialty—pan-fried walleye—and enjoying the way the moon looked reflected on the silvery lake when I heard the gravel-edged sound of Dick Walton's voice, singing a familiar tune.

"You're a stupid cunt!" he was telling her.

They had a table in the corner, but the long, rather narrow dining room, with its windows on the lake, didn't allow anyone much privacy. Even approaching nine-thirty, the restaurant was full—older couples, families, a honeymooning couple, all turned their eyes to the asshole in the lime sport coat and green-and-white plaid pants who was verbally abusing the blonde woman in the green-and-white floral sundress.

She was crying. Digging a Kleenex into eyes where the mascara was already smeared. When she got up from the table to rush out, she looked like an embarrassed, haunted raccoon.

He shouted something unintelligible at her, and sneered, and returned to his big fat rare steak.

The restaurant manager, a guy in his late twenties who probably figured his business degree would get him a better gig than this, came over to my table and leaned in. He was thin, sandy-haired, pockmarked; he wore a pale yellow sweater over a shirt and tie.

"Mr. Keller," he said, "what should I do about Mr. Walton?"

"Leave him alone, Rick. Without his wife to yell at, I doubt he'll make much more fuss."

"Should I cut him off with the bar?"

"No."

He gave me a doubtful expression, one eyebrow arching. "Personally, I . . ."

"Just leave it alone. If he passes out, he won't bother his wife or anybody, and that would probably be ideal."

Rick sighed—he didn't like me much, knowing that I was lobbying to have his four-star restaurant turned into a cafeteria—but he nodded in acceptance of my ruling, and padded off.

I finished my walleye, touched a napkin to my lips and headed over to Walton's table.

"You got my message about the boat?" I asked.

His grin was tobacco-stained; the tufts of white eyebrow raised so high they might have been trying to crawl off his face. "Yeah! That was white of you, Jack! You're okay. Sit down, I'll buy you one."

I sat, where his wife had been (her own walleye practically untouched on the plate before me), but said, "I had enough for tonight. I know my limit."

"So do I, buddy boy . . ." He pointed a steak knife at me and winked. ". . . it's when the fuckin' *lights* go out."

I laughed. "Say, what was the little woman riding you about? If you don't mind my asking."

His face balled up like a fist. "Bitch. Lousy little cunt. She fucked up royal this afternoon."

"Oh?"

"Yeah, fuck her. We're playing with another couple—the Goldsteins, from Des Moines. He's a dentist. Those docs are loaded, you know. Particularly the Hebrew ones."

"Up the wazoo," I affirmed.

"Anyway, Mindy is a decent little golfer . . . usually. Shoots a nineteen handicap on the country club course back home . . . but this afternoon she didn't shoot for shit. I lost a hundred bucks because of her!"

"Well, hell, Dick—everybody has a bad afternoon once in a while."

His aftershave wafted across the table to tickle my nose—a grotesque parody of the pine scent that nature routinely provided us here.

"I think she did it just to *spite* me. I'd swear she muffed some of those shots just to get my fuckin' goat."

His speech was pretty slurred.

"That sounds like a woman," I said.

He looked me with as steady a gaze as he could muster. "Jack—I like you."

"I like you, Dick. You're a real man's man."

I offered him my water glass for him to clink his tumbler of Scotch on the rocks against.

"I'll have to sneak away from the little woman," he said, winking again, "so we can spend some *quality* time together."

"Let's do that," I said. "You going fishing tomorrow?"

He was lighting up an unfiltered cigarette; it took a lot of effort. "Yeah—me and that kike dentist. Wanna come along?"

"Got to work, Dick. Check in with me later, though. Maybe we can take in one of the casinos."

"One of the ones those injuns run?"

Gambling having been ruled legal on reservation land, casinos run by Native Americans were a big tourist draw in our neck of the woods.

"That's right, Dick. A whole tribe of Tontos looking to fleece the Lone Ranger."

"Hah! How 'bout tomorrow night?"

"We'll see. If you're getting up early tomorrow morning, Dick, to fish, maybe you ought to hit the sack."

He guzzled at his drink. "I ought to hit that fuckin' cunt I'm married to, is what I oughta hit."

"Take it easy. It's a hell of a thing, but a man can get in trouble for hitting a woman, these days."

"Hell of a thing, ain't it, Jack? Hell of a thing."

I walked out with him; he shambled along, slipping an arm around me, cigarette trailing ash.

"You're a hell of a guy," he told me, almost crying. "Hell of a guy."

"So are you, Dick," I said.

Outside the real pines were almost enough to cancel the room-freshener cologne he was wearing.

Almost.

I was sitting in the dark, in my underwear, sipping a Coke in the glow of the portable television, watching a Randolph Scott western from the 1950s. I kept the sound low, because I had the doors to the deck pushed open, to enjoy the lake breeze, and I didn't want my movie-watching to disturb any of the guests who might be strolling along the beach, enjoying the night.

Something about the acoustics of the lake made her crying seem to echo, as if carried on the wind from a great distance, though she was at my feet, really—stumbling across the grass beneath my deck.

Underwear or not, I went out to check on her—because the crying sounded like more than just emotions: there was physical pain in it, too.

"Mrs. Walton," I called, recognizing her. She still wore the flowered sundress, the scoop top of it displaying the swell of her swell bosom. "Are you all right?"

She nodded, stumbling. "Just need a drink . . . need a drink . . ."

"The bar's closed. Why don't you step up here, and I'll get you a beer or something."

"No . . . no . . ." She shook her head and then I saw it: the puffiness of the left side of her face, eye swollen shut, the flesh already blackening.

I ran down the little wooden stairs; if somebody complained to the manager about the man running around in his underwear, well fuck 'em: *I* was the manager. I took her by the arm and walked her up onto the deck and inside, where I deposited her on the couch in front of the TV, where Randolph Scott was shooting Lee Van Cleef.

"Just let me get dressed," I said, and I returned with pants on and a beer in hand, which I held out to her.

"It's all I have, I'm afraid," I said.

She took it and held it in her hands like something precious; sipped it like a child taking first communion.

I got her a washcloth with some ice in it.

"He's hit you before, hasn't he?" I said, sitting beside her.

She nodded; tears trickled from the good eye. Her pink-bowed platinum blonde hair wasn't mussed: too heavily sprayed for that.

"How often?" I asked.

"All . . . all the time."

"Why don't you leave the son of a bitch?"

"He says . . . he says he'll kill me."

"Probably just talk. Turn him in for beating you. They go hard on guys who do that, nowadays, and then it'll be harder for him to do it again."

"No . . . he would kill me. Or have somebody do it. He has . . . the kind of connections where you can get somebody killed, if you want. And it'll just be written off as an accident. I bet you find that hard to believe, don't you?"

"Yeah." I sipped my Coke. "Sounds utterly fantastic."

"Well, it's true."

"Are you sure you're not staying 'cause of the prenup?"

She sighed, nodded slowly, the hand with the ice in the washcloth moving with her head. "There *is* a prenuptial agreement. I wouldn't get a thing. Well, ten thousand, I think."

"But you're not staying 'cause of the money."

"No! I don't care about the money . . . exactly. I got family I take care of. A younger sister who's going to college, mom's got heart trouble and no insurance."

"So it *is* about money."

The good eye winced. "No! No . . . it *was* about money. That's why I married Dick. I was . . . I was trash. A waitress. Topless dancer, for a while. Anything to make a buck . . . but never hooking. Never!"

"Where did you meet Dick?"

"In a titty bar a friend of his used to run. I wasn't dancing, then . . . I was a waitress. Tips in a topless place are always incredible."

"So I hear."

"This was, I don't know . . . over ten years ago."

"You been taking this shit all that time?"

"No. He was sweet, at first. But he didn't drink as much in those days. The more he drank, the worse it got. He calls me stupid. He can't have kids . . . his sperm count is lower than he is. But he calls *me* 'barren' and hits me . . . says I'm fat. Do you think I'm fat?"

I'd been looking down the front of her sundress at the time, and swallowed, and said, "Uh, no. I don't like these skinny girls they're pushing on us, these days."

"Fake tits and boy's butts, all of them." Her lips were trembling; her voice sounded bitter. "He has a girl friend . . . she works in a titty bar, too. A different joint—this is one that he's got money in. She's like that: skinny little thing and a plastic chest and a flat little ass."

"You should leave him. Forget his threats. Forget the money."

"I can't. I . . . I wish he was dead. Just fucking dead."

"Don't talk that way."

Her whole body was trembling; she hugged herself with one arm, as if very, very cold. "I need a miracle. I need a goddamn miracle."

"Well, here's a suggestion."

"Yes?"

"Say your prayers tonight. Maybe God'll straighten it all out."

"With a miracle?"

"Or something," I said.

"Hop in," he said.

He was behind the wheel of a red-bodied, white-topped Cadillac; his bloodshot face was split in a shit-eating grin as he leaned over to open the door on the rider's side. He was wearing a green-and-orange plaid sportcoat—it was like a Scotsman had puked on him—and orange trousers and lots of clunky gold jewelry.

I slipped inside the spacious car. "Didn't have any trouble getting away?"

"Naw! That little bitch doesn't dare give me any lip. I'd just knock some *more* sense in her! Anybody see you go?"

"No. I think we're all right."

I'd had him pick me up at the edge of the road, half a mile from the resort, in darkness; I said I was on call tonight and wasn't supposed to be away.

"You tell your wife where you were going, and who with?"

"Hell no! None of her goddamn business! I tell you, Jack, I should never have married that lowlife cunt. She's got a family like something out of *Deliverance*. Poor white trash, pure and simple. No fuckin' class at all."

"Why don't you dump her, then?"

"I just might! You know what a prenuptial agreement is, don't you, Jack?"

"Got a vague idea."

"Well, my lawyer assures me I don't have to give her jack

shit. She's out in the cold on her flabby ass, soon as I give the say so."

"Why don't you, then?"

"I might. I might . . . but it could be bad for business. I use her in some of my commercials, and she's kinda popular. Or anyway, her big ol' titties are, pardon my French."

"She helps you put up a good front."

"Hah! Yeah, that's a good one, Jack . . . that's a good one . . ."

The drive to the casino was about an hour, winding through tall pines and little bump-in-the-road towns; the night was clear, the moon full again, the world bathed in an unreal, and lovely, silver. I studied the idyllic landscape, pretending to listen to Walton blather on about his accomplishments in the used car game, cracking the window to let some fresh air cancel out his Pine-Sol aftershave and cigarette smoke.

It was midweek, but the casino looked busy—just a sprawling one-story prefabricated building, looking about as exotic as a mobile home, but for the huge LAKEVIEW CASINO neon; the term "Lakeview" was cosmetic, as the nearest lake was a mile away. Some construction, some expansion, was going on, and the front parking lot was a mess.

He pulled around back, as I instructed; a couple of uniformed security guards with guns—Indians, like most of the employees here—were stationed in front. None were in back. A man and a woman, both weaving with drink, were wandering out to their car as Walton found a place to park.

"No limit here, right?" he asked.

"Right. You bring a pretty good roll?"

"Couple grand. I got unlimited cash access on my gold card, too."

The car with the couple in it pulled out, and drove unsurely around the building. Once their car lights were gone, it was as dark as the inside of cow, back here. I got out of the Cad.

"If you need a couple bucks, Jack, just ask."

He had his back to me, as we walked toward the casino. When my arm slipped around him, it startled him, but he didn't have much time to react: the knife had pierced his windpipe by then.

When I withdrew the hunting knife, a scarlet geyser sprayed the night, but away from me. He fell like a pine tree, flopping forward, but the sound was just a little slap against the pavement. The knife made more noise as it clattered against the pavement; I kicked it under a nearby pickup. He gurgled a while but that stopped soon.

Yanking him by the ankles, I dragged him between his Caddy and the Dumpster he'd parked next to; a slime trail of blood glistened in the moonlight, but otherwise he was out of sight. So was I. I bent over him, using the same flesh-colored, rubber-gloved hand that had held the knife, and stripped him of his gaudy gold jewelry and lifted his fat wallet from his hip pocket, the sucker pocket the dips call it. I removed the wad of hundreds and tossed the wallet in the Dumpster.

The jewelry was a bit of a problem: if somebody stopped me to talk to me about the dead man in the parking lot, I could be found with it on me. But a thief wouldn't leave it behind, so I had to take it, stuffing it in my jacket pockets. Tomorrow I would toss it in Sylvan Lake.

Right now, with my couple of thousand bucks, I walked around the front of the casino, said, "Nice night, fellas," to the Indian security guards, who grunted polite responses to the paleface.

Inside, the pinball-machine-like sound of gambling fought with piped-in country western—the redskins seemed to favor cowboy music. I found Nikki where I knew she'd be: at the nickel poker machines. The slender girl had a bright-eyed, pixie face and a cap of brown curls.

"Jack! I'm doing *fantastic* . . . I'm up four dollars!"

"Sounds like you're making a killing."

"How about you?"

"Same."

I had told Nikki I'd meet her here—we usually took separate cars when we went out, since the manager and his social director weren't supposed to fraternize.

She moved up to the quarter poker machines, at my urging, and ended up winning about thirty bucks. Before long, I was up two hundred bucks on blackjack. If somebody found the body while I was there, things could get interesting; I'd have to dump that jewelry somewhere.

But I didn't think anybody would be using that Dumpster tonight, and I knew nobody would use the Caddy. Leaving too soon would be suspicious. So I stayed a couple hours.

"Jeez," I said, as we were heading out finally, her arm in mine, my hand on my head. "I think I drank a little too much."

"That's not like you, Jack."

"I know. But you better drive me home."

"What about your car?"

My car was back at the resort, of course, parked where Nikki wouldn't see it when she went to her own cabin.

"I'll have Gary drive me up for it tomorrow."

"Okay," she said, and she steadied me as we walked back around to the parking lot in the rear.

It was still dark back there, and quiet. Very quiet. I

could barely make out a dried dark streak on the pavement, over by the Caddy, but nothing glistened in the moonlight, now.

First thing the next morning, the police came around to see me; Gary was with them, a pair of uniformed state patrolmen. It seemed, around sun-up, that one of our guests had been found dead in the parking lot at the Lakeview Casino. His wallet, emptied of money, had been found nearby. "Mr. Walton wore a lot of jewelry," I said. "The gold kind?"

"Asking for trouble," said one of the cops, a kid in his mid-twenties.

Gary, wearing a gray jogging suit, wasn't saying anything; he was standing behind them like a mute grizzly, his eyes a little glazed.

"That casino's probably gonna get sued," the other, slightly older cop said. "Bad lighting in the parking lot back behind there. Just asking for it."

"Both Walton *and* that casino," the young one said.

I agreed with them, said sympathetic things, and pointed them to the cabin where they could find—and inform—the new widow.

Gary stayed behind.

"You know," he said quietly, scratching his beard, "I'm glad that bastard didn't get killed on our grounds. We might be the ones getting sued."

"Right. But that's not going to happen around here."

"Oh?"

"Don't worry, Gary." I put a hand on his shoulder; had to reach up to do it. "*We* have adequate lighting."

He looked at me kind of funny, with narrowed eyes. He seemed about to ask me something, but thought better of it, waved limply and wandered off.

I was doing my morning sit-ups when she walked up on my deck, looking dazed, her perfect, bullet-proof platinum hair wearing the girlish pink bow, her voluptuous body tied into a dark pink dressing gown. She stood looking through the cross-hatch of screen door, asking if she could come in.

"Of course," I said, sliding the door open, and took her to the couch where she'd sat two nights before.

"You heard about Dick?" she said, in small voice. She seemed numb.

"Yes. I'm sorry."

"You . . . you won't say anything, will you?"

"About what?"

"Those . . . terrible things I said about him." Her eyes got very wide; she seemed frightened, suddenly, but not of me. Exactly. "You don't think . . . you don't think I . . ."

"No. I don't think you did it, Mrs. Walton."

"Or . . . or hired somebody . . . I mean, I was saying some crazy things the other night."

"Forget it."

"And if the police knew about Dick hitting me . . ."

"Your face looks pretty good today. I don't think they'll pursue that angle."

She swallowed; stared into nothing. "I don't know what to do."

"Why don't you just lean back and wait to inherit Dick's estate? You can do those TV commercials solo, now."

She turned to look at me, and the faintest suspicion seemed etched around her eyes. "You've been . . . very kind, Mr. Keller."

"Make it Jack."

"Is there anything I can do to . . . repay your kindnesses?"

"Well . . . you can keep coming to Sylvan Lodge, despite

the bad memories. We could sure use your business, for those sales conferences and all."

She touched my hand. "I can promise you that. Maybe we could . . . get to know each other better. Under better circumstances."

"That would be nice."

"Could I just . . . sit here for a while? I don't really want to go back to the cabin. It still . . . still smells of Dick. That awful cologne of his."

Here all you could smell was the lake and the pines, real pines; the soothing touch of a breeze rolled over us.

"Stay as long as you like," I said. "Here at Sylvan Lodge, we strive to make our guests' stay as pleasant as possible."